INHERIT THE SHOES

INHERIT THE SHOES

E.J. Copperman

This first world edition published 2020
in Great Britain and 2021 in the USA by
SEVERN HOUSE PUBLISHERS LTD of
Eardley House, 4 Uxbridge Street, London W8 7SY.
Trade paperback edition first published
in Great Britain and the USA 2021 by
SEVERN HOUSE PUBLISHERS LTD.

British Library Cataloguing in Publication Data
A CIP catalogue record for this title is available from the British Library.

ISBN-13: 978-0-7278-9084-9 (cased)
ISBN-13: 978-1-78029-720-0 (trade paper)
ISBN-13: 978-1-4483-0441-7 (e-book)

This is a work of fiction. Names, characters, places and incidents
are either the product of the author's imagination or are used fictitiously.
Except where actual historical events and characters are being described
for the storyline of this novel, all situations in this publication are
fictitious and any resemblance to actual persons, living or dead,
business establishments, events or locales is purely coincidental.

All Severn House titles are printed on acid-free paper.

Severn House Publishers support the Forest Stewardship Council™ [FSC™],
the leading international forest certification organisation.
All our titles that are printed on FSC certified paper carry the FSC logo.

To Jessica Oppenheim, the loveliest ex-prosecutor I know, who married me quite some time ago and says she doesn't regret it.

PART ONE
Tribulations

ONE

'Do you need a handkerchief, Mr Haddonberg?'
The testimony hadn't even begun yet, and already Walter Haddonberg was sweating. The prospect of facing the plaintiff's attorney, Arthur Kirkland, had apparently gotten the glands in Haddonberg's forehead and under his arms working overtime. Kirkland, a handsome, dynamic man, had a reputation in the Portland legal community that had earned him the nickname 'The Barracuda.'

'No, thank you, Your Honor.' Haddonberg pulled a monogrammed handkerchief from his pocket and waved it at the judge, which didn't make him look any more dignified. Kirkland stood, his face betraying nothing but an overwhelming sense of purpose. He passed the defense table, where Haddonberg's attorney, the absurdly attractive Oswalda 'Ozzie' Estrada, didn't even dignify him with a glance. They had their history.

'Mr Haddonberg,' he began in an accent that was now from west of the Rockies but had started out in Brooklyn, 'you are the chief executive officer of the Haddonberg Companies, are you not?'

'I am.' Haddonberg had clearly been coached to keep his answers brief.

'And as such,' Kirkland continued, 'you are responsible for all the employees who work for the companies. Is that true?'

In the gallery, Agnes Haddonberg watched her husband with some concern. Walter looked so worried, she bit her lip in sympathy. Her closest friend, Cynthia De La Hoya, sat next to Agnes and patted her hand.

'In theory, yes,' said Haddonberg, 'but the fact is, I can't be in the minds of over six thousand people at all times.'

'Still, you were aware that the Insulate 4X product being tested had some problems?' Kirkland glanced toward the jury, and so did Haddonberg. Kirkland looked confident, Haddonberg, terrified.

'I had seen previous test results, but there was nothing that would indicate—'

'Are these the test results you had?' Kirkland cut him off, waving a stack of papers that had seemed to magically appear in his hand, but had actually been supplied by Kirkland's improbably gorgeous second chair, Amanda Shaw.

Ozzie stood up. 'Objection, Your Honor,' she said immediately. 'That document has not been entered into evidence.'

'Sustained.' The Honorable Harold T. Stone looked to be in no mood for Kirkland's theatrics this morning. Earlier that day, his wife had left him for a massage therapist named Phyllis.

'I was going to say,' Haddonberg said with some pomposity, 'that I had no indication there was any serious danger involved with the product, and that's why tests were conducted.'

'So, you didn't know that my client would be risking his health by participating in the trials of the insulation material,' Kirkland said.

Raymond Worth, Kirkland's client, sat in the front row of the gallery. At his feet was a German Shepherd, and in his hand was a white cane.

'Of course not,' Haddonberg said, his voice rising. 'The test results I saw were all within normal limits. I didn't know some of the contractors who tested the insulation would go . . .' He hesitated.

'Blind, Mr Haddonberg,' said Kirkland. 'The word is "blind."'

'Objection,' Ozzie said once she got to her feet.

Kirkland walked toward the bench. 'Your Honor, if it please the court, I'd like to submit Plaintiff's Exhibit D,' he said, passing a copy to the judge.

'If there are no objections,' said Stone.

Ozzie, looking over the copy she'd gotten from Amanda, opened and closed her mouth once or twice, then stood. 'Your Honor, I'd like to request a ten-minute recess so I can confer with my client.'

'Objection,' said Kirkland. 'Counsel wants to coach her client before I get a chance to ask him about this document.'

'No recess, Ms Estrada. We'll continue with the testimony.'

Ozzie gritted her teeth but sat back down. Kirkland handed a copy of the document to Haddonberg, who looked like he'd prefer to face Jeff Bezos in a hostile takeover.

'Mr Haddonberg,' the Barracuda began, 'do you recognize the document I just handed you?'

'This is not the original test report,' said Haddonberg.

'No, it's not,' agreed Kirkland. 'It's a copy of a second set of test results, taken from studies made on the insulation material a good two weeks before the human test was conducted with Mr Worth and seven other contractors. Do you recognize it?'

'I don't know,' he began. 'I see so many reports.'

Kirkland swooped in like a vulture, leaning toward Haddonberg and staring into his eyes. 'But those are your initials on the bottom of the page, aren't they? Doesn't that indicate that you read and approved these reports *before* you asked my client to work in an unventilated attic with that product for six hours?'

Haddonberg's eyes widened to approximately the size of silver-dollar pancakes, and he reached out his hand. Kirkland grabbed him by the wrist as Haddonberg stood, shakily.

'I . . . I . . .' Haddonberg fell to the floor and lay still. Kirkland dropped his wrist as the courtroom exploded into action. Agnes Haddonberg leapt up, shouting 'Walter!' and rushed to the witness stand. Ozzie was already on her feet and heading in the same direction.

Kirkland, barely glancing at Haddonberg's supine body, looked up at Stone. 'Your Honor,' he said, 'the witness is being unresponsive.'

'The witness is having a heart attack!' Stone shouted. 'Get out of the way! Mr Kirkland, you are out of order!'

Kirkland smiled a sardonic smile and pointed at himself. '*I'm* out of order?' he said quietly. EMS workers broke through the doors to the courtroom and rushed down the aisle as Agnes reached her husband. She knelt by his side and stroked his head.

'Walter,' she said. 'Walter, please. Please don't die.'

Kirkland stifled a chuckle. 'Die? He's not dying, Mrs Haddonberg,' he said. 'He's faking. I had my hand on his wrist the whole time. His pulse is strong and steady.'

Agnes stood bolt upright and slapped Kirkland in the face, but he barely acknowledged it. 'He's just doing this to avoid answering the question, but if it makes you feel better, you won't be losing much when he goes to jail. He's been having an affair for two years with a Mrs De La Hoya.'

Shocked, Agnes shot a look toward Cynthia, whose guilty

expression told her all she needed to know. But Agnes didn't have time to confront her closest confidante, because her husband leapt to his feet and reached for her hand.

'Aggie!' he blubbered. 'It's not true! It was over *months ago*. I swear!'

The EMS worker heading for Haddonberg stopped dead in his tracks as the other two, setting up a stretcher in the aisle, froze. Agnes stared at her husband, shaking her head. Everything was happening too fast. 'You . . . you were dying . . .'

Walter Haddonberg tried to hold onto his wife's hand, but she pulled it away. 'Oh, Aggie, try to understand,' he said. 'It was the only way I could save the company. I *had* to lie – but the thing with Cyndi was never serious. I don't *care* about her.'

Cynthia De La Hoya burst into tears and ran for the courtroom doors.

'So you were just pretending to be sick so you wouldn't have to admit the company was at fault?' Agnes asked.

Walter nodded. 'That's right, honey. But don't you see, you're all I care about now. You're all that ever mattered.'

Kirkland looked up at Judge Stone. 'Your Honor, I move for a summary judgment. The witness has admitted to his company's liability, and committed perjury in the process.'

Ozzie, a few feet from Kirkland, almost deafened him with her response. 'WHAT?' she cried. 'Your Honor, court was not in session during that exchange. I object!'

Kirkland raised his eyebrows. 'I wasn't aware court had been adjourned, Your Honor. Did you call a recess?'

Ozzie spoke through clenched teeth as Haddonberg, terrified, dropped his wife's hand and stared at his lawyer. '*Your Honor*,' she said. 'This is a cheap trick on Mr Kirkland's part, and should not be condoned. You should rule—'

'Judge Stone,' Kirkland said with considerable gravitas, 'a courtroom is no place for conventional thinking.'

'Don't tell me what I should do in my courtroom, Ms Estrada,' Stone said. 'Objection is overruled. The court reporter was recording everything. The testimony is admissible, and the request for a summary judgment is under consideration. Unless, Ms Estrada, your client wishes to schedule a settlement meeting.'

* * *

'Oh, *come on!*' I looked at the shambles of a courtroom on my TV set and reached for the remote control. It was hard to believe I'd sat through this much. A summary judgment? An exhibit entered before the defendant's attorney could examine it? A lawyer grabbing a witness' wrist and *taking his pulse*? Testimony from a witness supposedly having a heart attack? There was at least one objection that was never ruled upon. *Pul-ease!*

I turned off the TV and surveyed, instead, the shambles of my new apartment. Moving to Los Angeles had seemed like a good idea a month ago; now, not so much. Back then, I'd been thinking about the change in my job – from criminal prosecutor to family attorney, with no more drug dealers, sex offenders, domestic batterers and drug dealers (there were enough of those that I could mention them twice), and more simple divorces, custody settlements and pre-nuptial agreements. The lack of ten-degree winter mornings and 3,000 miles between me and my most recent boyfriend were just perks.

Now, with reality setting in on the permanence of the move and the fact that what I knew about family law was a one-semester class at law school, I found myself yearning for the leaves changing color in fall and the crispness of early winter air. Despite the fact that it was April, and the weather here was just about the same as it was back home in New Jersey, plus or minus some drought. OK, plus.

I had turned on *Legality* to take my mind off the unpacking and the first day at work tomorrow, and as usual with such things, it had ended up aggravating me. Hollywood's idea of the legal system was something that fell between vaudeville and a public execution. In any event, it had nothing to do with the way the law is actually practiced in any country I was aware of.

Let's face it, the only reason I'd turned on the television to begin with was that Angie had told me about this great new show. Angie, my oldest and best friend from back home, watches tons of television and considers herself my unofficial guide to what popular culture exists in America. Without her, Angie often said, my idea of a good time would be sitting alone in a law library looking up precedents.

That, of course, wasn't the least bit true. I like to have a good time, as much as anyone. I love to go see films, especially foreign language films, and enjoy being challenged by a good book or a small dinner with close friends. But sitting in front of the tube like an automaton, watching anything that's offered, no matter how mediocre, was not something I felt was worth my time. Life's too short.

Besides, I had all this unpacking to do. I couldn't believe it had been two weeks since I moved in, and still there were boxes and cartons everywhere I looked. It was depressing – no matter how many enormous containers I unpacked, there seemed to be six new ones that popped up in their place.

I like order in life, even though I know – honestly, I do! – that it can't be perfected. Back home in my apartment in Westfield, I knew where everything was, and I mean *everything*. I'm not obsessive about it – not *really* – but it gives me comfort to know that if I need a paper clip at three in the morning, I can put my fingers on one without turning on the lights. Why I'd need a paper clip in the dark is a question best left unasked.

I hadn't had much time to unpack, in truth, since the van had arrived (two days late) from New Jersey. There had been the introductory meetings at my new law firm, Seaton, Taylor, Evans and Bach, and those had done nothing to ease my anxiety about starting there tomorrow.

Tomorrow!

I should have immediately gone to bed, to ensure that I'd get enough sleep before changing my entire life in the morning, but I was too agitated. Maybe I'd unpack a couple more cartons of books. That was probably a bad idea, as I don't function well on too little sleep, but I *really* don't function well after taking a 'sleep aid,' as they like to say on television, so that didn't seem to be an option.

Of course, it's not like there were any shelves left on which to store the books, either. My apartment, already lined with bookshelves that were full, wasn't going to contain everything I'd brought with me, and that was unsettling, considering it had all fit into my one-bedroom apartment in Westfield.

I opened a carton marked 'Books' in clear block letters and mechanically took them out of the box, without a clue as to where I'd store the volumes on mediation and family law I'd bought since getting this job. Probably should have looked at those, too, before starting tomorrow. Maybe knowing something about the work I'd be doing would have helped.

When my phone rang, in a tone that echoed far too much in this unfamiliar space, I actually gasped. It was late, and I didn't know anyone in Los Angeles.

It took a while to find the phone, but I hadn't turned on voice mail when I'd changed carriers, so it continued to ring long enough for me to trace the sound to the galley kitchen, where the phone was lying under an opened newspaper. I picked it up.

'Did you *see* that?' Angie, three thousand miles and three time zones away, was considerably more alert than I. Angie was, in fact, the poster girl for Alert.

'Angie! It's got to be two in the morning where you are! What are you doing up?' I took the cell phone into the 'living area,' a misnomer, since the only things that could have lived well here were insects that feed off the paper in law books. They probably would have gorged themselves to death.

'I couldn't wait!' Angie breathed. 'Did you see it?'

'See what?' Four books on the psychology of sex offenders. Perfect to display in one's main room. Really livens up first dates. Not that I anticipated a lot of those, but . . .

Angie breathed dramatically. '*Legality*. You can't tell me you didn't see it, after all those times I noodged you about it.'

'Oh, that,' I said. 'Yeah, I saw it.' Damn, these things must weigh thirty pounds each! You'd think with all this lifting, I'd be more buff.

I don't look *bad*, mind you, but in L.A., all the women look like Margot Robbie, and that gets just a little intimidating after . . . about ten minutes.

'Well? What'd you *think*? Wasn't it *great*?'

It was late, and I wasn't in the mood to be diplomatic. Besides, I was carrying about sixty pounds worth of law books to a shelf that had room for ten. 'Oh, come on, Ang! Grabbing a witness' wrist? A lawyer would be held in contempt for seven things this guy did in five minutes!'

A continent away, I could see Angie roll her eyes, and I wasn't even on Skype. 'You always get caught up in the details,' she said. 'Can't you just live the emotion? Besides, that Patrick McNabb – he's not too bad to look at, huh?'

'McNabb? Which one was he?' I tried pushing the books onto the shelf, which luckily was anchored on the other end by a wall, or I'd have moved half the books I'd already placed, and they'd have ended up on the floor. *Damn laws of physics!*

'Oh, stop it. He's the one who plays Arthur Kirkland, and he's definitely your type. All serious and important-looking. You wouldn't kick him out of bed for eating crackers.'

'He couldn't even get *to* the bed – it's surrounded by boxes. Angie, it's late and I . . .'

'How are you doing, really?' she said.

For a second, I wasn't sure whether the question was coming from Angie, or from the inner voice in my brain. But I realized I had to answer. 'I'm fine.'

Angie's voice now took on a formal quality. 'Fine, huh? *Fine* is what people say when their real answer is, "You don't want to know how awful I feel."'

I laughed. Angie could always do that to me, no matter what. It had kept us together through high school and college, and as I went on to law school. Even during the eight years I was an assistant prosecutor for Middlesex County, I'd always been able to count on Angie for a laugh, no matter how much the system made me want to jump out the window.

Now, Angie managed a small chain of Dairy Queen stores in central Jersey, and I'd made an impulsive mistake – highly unlike me – by moving to Los Angeles. 'You were the one who wanted the change,' she reminded me. 'You were tired of criminal law. You didn't want to put people in jail any more . . .'

'I know, I know.' I sat down on the floor again and smoothed back my hair with my palm. Was that a gray hair between my fingers? No. That was my finger. 'It's just that I'm a little nervous, you know? First day tomorrow, and everything.'

'You worried it'll be boring? Doing divorces and stuff like that instead of locking up the bad guys?'

Angie really did think that the law was practiced like it is on TV. I knew Angie was very intelligent, but sometimes she made it hard to believe.

'No, I'm not worried it'll be boring,' I droned. 'I'm worried I'll be bad at it.'

'Oh, please.' Angie's pursed lips could be heard through

satellite feeds. 'You've never been bad at anything, and you know how to be a good lawyer. How bad can you be?'

'I'm about to find out. Listen, Ang, it's late here, and it's *really* late there. I've got to . . .'

'Any guys?'

'Huh?'

'Any guys yet? You go out with anybody?'

I rolled my eyes heavenward, despite the fact that Angie couldn't see the gesture. 'I've been here *two weeks*, Ang.'

'Wouldn't take *me* that long.'

'Maybe I'm more . . . selective than you are.' I could see Angie grinning in my mind's eye.

'You callin' me a slut, Ms Moss?'

'Hey, if the three-inch stiletto heel fits . . .'

Angie ignored that. 'So how come you haven't met any guys yet?'

'You know my recent history,' I said. I didn't want to talk about it.

Unfortunately, Angie did, and Angie generally gets what she wants, because she refuses not to. 'So you went out with your boss and he dumped you for a twenty-two year old refugee from a wet T-shirt contest.'

'She was a court reporter.'

'Uh-huh.' Angie was on a roll. 'That's no reason to move all the way across the country and give up on men forever.'

'Angieeeeee! Let me go to beeeeeeeeed!' I sounded like a whiny six-year-old.

'Alone?' Angie's voice took on a deeper tone. 'Come on, Sandy. How are you *really*?'

'I'm fine. Really.'

'Wow. That sounds so . . . adequate.' Angie never let me off the hook for anything. It was why I loved her, and wanted to wring her neck.

'Oh, come on . . .'

'I'll bet the people out there don't even go down the shore, do they?'

'Angie . . .'

'*Do* they?'

I refrained from sighing. 'No, they go to the beach.'

'Do they drive on Route One?'

'No,' I admitted, 'they get on The Five.'

'Do they go to the diner?'

'Not usually. They take a meeting for breakfast, or for a latte.'

Angie was gaining momentum now. 'Have they ever heard of New Jersey?'

'No,' I allowed, 'they go back East.'

'And they eat guacamole, don't they?' Angie's voice had a defiant, triumphant tone to it.

'Hey, I *like* guacamole!' Angie laughed, and I found myself joining in. 'Angie. I have an idea. They have ice cream out here. You could get a job. Come on out and we'll take over the town together. What do you think?'

'I think you made a choice and now you're second-guessing yourself. You don't need me. You need to be yourself and show those California babes what a Jersey girl can do! You need . . .'

'I withdraw the offer. Ang, it's after eleven, I've been unpacking boxes all day, I have *more* boxes to unpack before I get to bed, and I have to get up and go to a scary new job in the morning. So how about lightening up on me this once?'

Angie took a long pause, thinking about it. 'No.'

We both burst out laughing, and because we both had to get to bed very soon, stayed up talking for another hour.

TWO

'I'm sorry to have to throw you into this on your first day.' Holiday Wentworth (*Holiday! Doesn't anyone out here have a regular name?*), a junior partner in Seaton, Taylor, Evans and Bach, was supposed to be walking with me as we made our way down what must have been the world's longest corridor.

But Holiday's gait was so purposeful and quick that I had a hard time keeping up without actually panting. It didn't help that I'd gotten roughly forty minutes of sleep the night before, and had last gone to the gym the previous September. 'It's just that

Wilson McCavy's daughter fell off her pinto and he had to go to the emergency room, and, well, you know how it is . . .'

'Sure, I know how it is,' I answered, trying not to break into a jog. (*Fell off her* what? *These people have their own horses?*)

'You'll be there just to observe, really,' Holiday continued as I began to despair of my sweat glands. 'Junius Bach' (*Junius?*) 'has been handling this divorce from the beginning, and he knows all the aspects of the case. Your instructions are quite simply to sit there and don't say anything unless you have to.' I was much too busy looking at Holiday's up-to-the-minute suit to listen closely. My own outfit, the fourth I'd tried on that morning (after modeling three others in the mirror the night before) looked in comparison like I'd just walked out of Annie Sez. But it wasn't like I was intimidated or anything.

We'd reached the door, which was both a relief for my legs and lungs and a serious source of concern for my brain and stomach. Holiday looked me over with great care.

'We need two lawyers in there because it's such a high-profile case,' she said. 'After all, Pat and Patsy were *the* couple for a while. Remember?'

'Oh sure, I remember,' I said. *Pat and Patsy who?*

'Well, here's the file.' Holiday handed me a thick accordion file seemingly bursting with documents, and all this was for a preliminary meeting. For a *divorce*? By the time this case reached a judge, they'd need a burro to haul in the paperwork. 'Don't worry. You'll do fine.'

'Easy for you to say,' I blurted. In retrospect, probably not the kind of thing one voices on one's first day of work. There should be a class for the first day of work. Maybe Learning Annex could be alerted.

'I've seen your CV, and I know your work,' Holiday smiled. 'I'm not worried.'

I took the file and tried to look confident, ending up somewhere north of desperate. It was the professional equivalent of a blind date, and that was not one of my strengths. 'Thanks, Holiday.'

Holiday reached for the door as she said, 'You look wonderful. Don't worry.' Then she turned the knob, opened the door, said, 'And by the way, call me Holly,' and literally pushed me into the conference room.

It was, as befit the corridor outside, the largest conference room I'd ever seen, and it was so tastefully (and expensively) decorated, so absolutely up-to-the-minute in its appointments, that I had to wonder if it might just be a movie set, struck and re-designed for each successive meeting. Why not? It was L.A., after all. In the center of the room was a table so long, so highly polished, and so flawless that I thought it should have a gutter on each side and ten wooden pins set in a triangular pattern at the far end.

Instead, there were chairs all around it, but only seven were occupied – as far from the door as possible, of course. There, a Hollywood-perfect beauty, a woman of indeterminate age in this era of cosmetic surgery, sat glumly next to a man of extremely determinate age: he was in his fifties, balding and bulging. This must have been the beauty's attorney, and my opponent (or to be more precise, Bach's). Seated to his left and a little farther off the table was a young woman with a pad and a cassette recorder – the lawyer's secretary (pardon me, *assistant*).

In the last chair, farthest from me, was my own counterpart, the attorney who would not speak, but who was there to show that, hey, they have more than one lawyer in their firm, too. This one, a young man who looked around the room as if pricing it, was probably lining up his next job already, and wouldn't mind if it were here.

'It's about time,' said the cosmetic beauty, whose name must be Patsy Something – unless the *man* was named Patsy; what a horrible thought! 'We've been waiting here ten minutes.'

I headed toward my side (that is, Bach's side) of the table. There, in perfect opposition to the others, sat the Bach team: first up was the soon-to-be-ex-husband (Pat?), a man of such easy and devastating good looks that I wanted to instantly hate him, but couldn't. I hoped he didn't crinkle his eyes when he smiled, because then it would be impossible to remain professional up close.

He stood and held out a hand to me. 'It's not her fault, Patsy,' he said in an upper-class British accent that had surely started out cockney. 'She just got here.' Then he turned to me. 'Hi. I'm Pat.' I took his hand and almost winced – he *did* crinkle his eyes, and I was done for the day.

'My apologies,' I said to the room. 'I hope I didn't hold you all up for long.'

'Yeah, yeah, yeah,' said Patsy, but she didn't elaborate, so I assumed she was quoting the Beatles.

With some reluctance, I let Pat drop my hand, and moved past him. Next in line was Junius Bach himself, a man in his sixties who could surely audition for the role of God and be hired on the strength of his headshot alone. Tall, impeccable, with the air of someone who really *does* own the world, Bach frowned at the way the meeting had begun, and his frown told me to get to my chair quickly. It was a decent bet I wouldn't end up dating my boss in *this* job.

My seat was next to Bach's assistant, a young woman named . . . Mary? Martha? *Marta!* . . . I had met her at one of the orientation meetings, and remembered that she had smiled unnervingly all the time we were speaking, usually looking past my head to see if someone really important was coming.

I sat down, and so did Pat. He stopped crinkling his eyes when he looked at his soon-to-be ex-wife. Patsy wasn't chewing gum, but she should have been. And cracking it loudly.

Seated, I set about trying very hard not to fall asleep. It was too warm in here, and Bach, who spoke first, had a soothing, sonorous voice.

'This meeting,' Bach intoned, 'is to begin the process toward an agreement in your divorce.' He said '*your* divorce' to Patsy as if he were bestowing a gift upon her. 'If we are all willing to be reasonable, we should be able to reach an agreement quickly and without any unpleasantness.'

I scanned through the documents in my file, not looking up as Patsy, between sealed lips, made a noise that sounded like a balloon slowly deflating. 'Reasonable,' Patsy said, drawing out the word like a piece of taffy. 'There's nothing *reasonable* about it. He signed the pre-nup, and he knows he gets squat. What's there to be reasonable *about?*' Patsy's voice had an inflection that would have inspired Gandhi to homicide.

According to the file, Esmerelda Patricia DeNunzio (Patsy, indeed!) and Patrick Allan Dunwoody had wed only sixteen months earlier, in Las Vegas, Nevada (*and they said it wouldn't last*, I thought), then took up residence in Ms DeNunzio's home in Bel Air, California. A pre-nuptial agreement had been signed, which was unusual for a quick Vegas wedding (you had to speculate that Patsy carried the forms with her wherever she went), and it had stipulated that Mr Dunwoody was entitled to only two percent of all property in the marriage should the couple divorce, because his earnings at the time of the wedding were approximately two percent of those of Ms DeNunzio.

The problem was, in the year and four months since then, Dunwoody's income had skyrocketed, while DeNunzio's had, um, not. In fact, her earnings in the past year made up only four percent of the couple's income, according to the tax information in the file. Dunwoody's employment by – I had to check twice – First Amendment, Inc. had included a huge salary, and he had substantial income (in fact, much more substantial than his salary) from various other sources, while DeNunzio's income as (according to her tax return) a 'recording artist and freelance entertainer' had plummeted from the previous year's levels.

Bach ignored Patsy's reaction and plowed on through. 'We believe that the signed pre-nuptial agreement is null and void,' he said. 'During the period of the marriage, the dramatic shift in the incomes involved made the intention of the agreement moot.'

I was trying my best to suppress a yawn, and my eyes started to water just a bit. Pat Dunwoody looked at me with great sympathy, probably wondering what had made this fruitcake burst into tears at a divorce settlement meeting for *someone else*.

Patsy looked at her lawyer, a man who looked like he'd combed his hair for a full half hour that morning. 'What's he mean?' she asked. 'What's this about the pre-nup being mute?'

'Mute is what *you* should be,' Dunwoody said. 'Be quiet.'

'Patrick,' Bach admonished, looking mildly amused, 'keep a civil tongue in your head.'

'Why should I, when she's been putting her tongue down every throat in Hollywood trying to get a gig?' Dunwoody was not a man to restrain his emotions, apparently.

'You want to talk tongues. We'll talk tongues!' Patsy replied, though no one had been speaking to her. 'Let's talk about the tongue on that silicone job you met when we were on our honeymoon, for crissakes!'

I supposed that in another era, Patsy would have been considered 'brassy,' but now she was just obnoxious. She was worth millions, according to the financial statements in the folder, and yet she looked like she aspired to be a Las Vegas showgirl if she could catch the right break. I suppressed the urge to speak, and let Bach handle the situation, in accordance with my instructions.

Dunwoody was not so prudent in his response. He shook his head sadly. 'This is all because your career has gone down the toilet, and mine is flying, so you think you can take ninety-eight percent of *my* money. I'd be happy to do it California style and split everything in half,' he said. 'So you're just being greedy and not seeing how stupid that is. I wouldn't have expected that of you. But of course, if the shoe fits . . .'

Bach gave his client a sharp look, which Dunwoody noticed, but too late. There was something about the word 'shoe' that apparently struck a nerve with Patsy, and she was already rising out of her chair. 'If you think you can sit there and insult me, you limey bastard, you can forget that! I have your signature on a pre-nup that says I get ninety-eight percent of the marital assets, and I'm gonna *get* ninety-eight percent of the marital assets. *Including Jimmy's shoes!*'

Shoes? I rifled through the file again. *What* shoes? And who's Jimmy?

Dunwoody looked positively stricken – his eyes widened (the opposite of crinkling) and, from the outside, I thought his throat looked dry. Surely the choked noise he made led to that conclusion.

'Jimmy's . . . shoes?' he gasped. 'You wouldn't.'

Patsy's smile was positively evil. She wasn't just enjoying the fact that she was controlling the situation. She liked inflicting pain, especially on Dunwoody. The more he struggled to speak, the wider her smile became.

The pure emotion in the room almost made me forget my fatigue. I experienced a moment of complete alertness and total attention, but it faded.

'Sure I would. And I will,' Patsy answered. 'I'll take Jimmy's shoes, Patrick. And then maybe I'll sell them. Or maybe I'll just throw them away in the trash. Or *burn* them.' I couldn't find a reference to shoes, or anyone named James, Jim, Jimmy, Jamie, or Jimbo in my file (not that I looked very hard for Jimbo), and there was no mention of shoes of any kind. Could these be shoes of a tiny child who had died, or . . . no, wait, they'd only been married sixteen months. They couldn't have a child old enough to wear shoes, not if they'd known each other only a short time before the Las Vegas wedding. There were no dependents listed in the file, but . . .

'You bitch!' Dunwoody shot out of his chair and headed for his wife with a fury I couldn't have imagined as little as fifteen seconds ago. 'You can't do that! You never even *cared* about Jimmy's shoes!'

Bach broke his client's resolve with a single 'Patrick!' that spoke volumes about Bach's influence and Dunwoody's respect for him. I was stunned by the power of his simple rebuke, and the silence that followed. Dunwoody walked back to his seat and took it, never breaking his livid stare at Patsy, who was trying to decide whether to continue the petrified look of terror she thought would buy her sympathy, or to go back to her triumphant, smug, horrible grin.

She went with the grin.

'We are not here to argue over individual items,' Bach continued as if nothing had happened. 'We contend that there is no reason to consider, let alone honor, the pre-nuptial agreement, and we believe a judge will find in our favor. So if we are to be' – and here he did indulge in an upper-class smile aimed at Patsy – '*reasonable*, we should begin with discarding the pre-nuptial agreement and move on to a divorce settlement that can be agreeable to both parties.'

'Forget reasonable!' Patsy screamed. 'I don't have to be reasonable! I'm a star!'

'You *were*,' Dunwoody sneered without looking at her. 'Now you're someone who needs to be reasonable.'

Patsy's lawyer put a hand on her arm, and she rewarded him with the kind of look the shark gave Robert Shaw in *Jaws*. He removed his hand, and spoke to her quietly.

'Patsy,' he practically moaned. 'You're not helping your case. Try to sit down and let me negotiate for you. OK?'

'I don't hear you negotiating for me,' Patsy sneered at him, but she sat down anyway. 'You're as quiet as she is – the one we all had to wait for.' And she pointed at me.

Unfortunately, that was the moment I lost my battle with fatigue and was in full-fledged yawn. I at least remembered to put my hand over my mouth, but that was small consolation; you could have fit a Volkswagen in my mouth at the time. Every face in the room turned toward me.

I felt my face burning. The voice in my head echoed Holiday's words, 'sit there and don't say anything unless you have to.' Well, didn't I have to? Especially now, with Patrick Dunwoody's crinkling eyes staring into my face, looking for help and some sense of pride? Didn't I have to prove I'd been listening?

'It seems to me that all this talk about the pre-nuptial agreement is silly,' I said. Bach turned to warn me, but I was using my best professional voice. 'The pre-nup was drafted before Mr Dunwoody began earning *considerably* more than Ms DeNunzio. And from what I can tell, it was executed in a very short period of time before they were married. *And* it was executed without Mr Dunwoody being represented by counsel, which, given the terms, would cause the document to be thrown out of court in a nanosecond. Thus, the pre-nup is absolutely meaningless.'

Dunwoody broke into an appreciative smile that threatened to melt all my undergarments. And Patsy looked like she might actually chew on the water glass from which she was drinking when I spoke. But there was a problem – Patsy's attorney showed a tiny smile of recognition. *He hadn't thought of that, and now he'd be able to defend against it. Uh-oh.* I was afraid – physically afraid – to look at Junius Bach.

When I summoned the courage to do so, I caught an expression of such calm I thought I must have misread the situation. But behind Bach's eyes, when one looked more closely, was a contained rage that would probably rival Mt. St. Helens in its ability to erupt.

Mentally, I began packing my belongings for the long trip back to New Jersey.

Patsy's attorney stood and *he* began packing up – he put his files back into his briefcase. 'I think this conference is unlikely to yield any serious progress,' he said. 'Junius, we will see you in court.'

'I'm sorry you see it that way,' Bach said, standing. 'I think we could work out an equitable solution here and now, if we would all be . . .' He left the word unsaid. The proceedings had gone so far beyond reason that even mentioning it would have seemed comical.

Patsy, taking her attorney's lead for once, stood and started for the door, her legal entourage in tow. As she passed her husband's seat, she said quietly, 'It's supposed to be chilly tonight. Maybe I'll have a nice *fire*.'

Dunwoody's eyes threatened to spring across the room. He began growling, but ended up shouting. 'You touch so much as a shoelace, you cheap whore, and I will personally see to it that it's the last thing you touch. I'll see you dead before I let you have those shoes. You understand, Patsy? I'll kill you!'

'You don't have to let me have Jimmy's shoes, Patrick,' Patsy all but cooed. 'I already *have* them.' Without making eye contact with anyone, she left the room, sweeping her legal team in her wake.

There was an uncomfortable (although, in my case, welcome) silence for a long moment after the conference room door closed. Then, just as Bach was about to stand up and fire me – I could see his fist closing as he stood – Dunwoody leapt out of his chair and turned to me, grinning from ear to ear.

'That was *brilliant*!' he shouted. 'You really saved the day there, Ms Moss! Didn't she, Junius? Didn't she just save the day?'

Bach, stupefied by the glee of his (extremely well-paying) client, opened and closed his mouth once or twice.

I suddenly felt the need to commit professional hara-kiri, so I looked at Dunwoody and said, 'Thank you, but no, I didn't save the day. So, unless I'm reading the situation incorrectly, Mr Dunwoody, you'll be dealing with a different associate in this firm, because Mr Bach is quite justifiably going to fire me.'

I glanced at Bach, who seemed to agree with everything I said, especially the last part. But before he could open his mouth, his client spun on his heels and faced Bach with an expression of utter amazement.

'Fire her? You're not going to do *that*, are you, Junius?' Dunwoody's apparent astonishment took Bach by surprise.

As his eyes did their best not to spin in their sockets, Bach stopped, assessing the situation.

'Ah . . . no! No, of course not, Patrick,' Bach said. 'It's Ms Moss's first day at the firm. She obviously doesn't know all the ins and outs yet.' (*Like just shutting up and listening when you're told to*.) 'I don't see any need to fire her.'

'Great!' Dunwoody shouted. 'Because I want her on my side through every step of this divorce. She's the only one who showed any spark, any juice, any *passion* in here – besides me and Patsy, of course.' He chuckled privately to himself. The eye crinkle was there, but it wasn't as obvious now. He was good, *very* good, I noted. Dangerous.

Bach, however, was seeing a different kind of danger – the kind that happens when you tie yourself to an incompetent and hope to maintain your dignity. 'I'm surely as impressed as you are, Patrick, with Ms Moss,' he said, though he did not mention whether his impression was a favorable one or not. 'But don't you think a more *experienced* divorce attorney . . .'

Dunwoody cut him off at the knees. 'Nonsense, Junius. Ms Moss – may I call you Sandra, Ms Moss?'

'Sandy.' It was someone else's voice. Someone else's brain at work, too. I probably wasn't even here. I was back in central New Jersey, getting ready to prosecute a drug dealer on the grounds that he could have had the eighty-seven bags of marijuana on him *for his own personal use*. Sure, it was possible.

'Sandy. Great!' That was Dunwoody's voice. I recognized it. This was certainly a vivid dream. 'No, Junius, Sandy here is the only one who, in my view, really cares about the case. She'll help, or I'll move to another firm. And I'll recommend they hire her out from under you.'

Junius Bach looked like someone had told him that Dr Pepper really was better than Cristal, and his entire existence was no longer verifiable. But his voice was strong and confident. 'Of course, Patrick. Of course. Ms Moss – *Sandy* – will be with us every step of the way.'

'Good.' Clearly Dunwoody felt the issue was settled. But I shook my head in disbelief. I looked my client – no, *Bach's* client – straight in the face and tried once again to convince him I was a drooling incompetent.

'Mr Dunwoody, please.' Dunwoody tried to interrupt me, but I persisted. 'You have to understand. I've been a criminal attorney for the past eight years. I've never been involved in a family law case, let alone a divorce case. Mr Bach has so much more experience than me that it's amazing I'm allowed in the same room with him. Believe me, you're in the best hands with him. I'd be lucky to sit and listen, which is what I should have done today. Don't let your emotions get the best of your judgment.'

Dunwoody stopped and looked at me thoughtfully. 'Sandy,' he said quietly, as if to a child, 'you are the most loyal, thoughtful employee I have ever seen. Mr Bach is lucky to have you, and he knows it. And I am *glad* you've never been in a divorce court before, because I want someone who's going to have fresh, new ideas. Someone who will think . . .'(*Don't say it!* I thought) 'outside the box.' (*He said it!*) 'But there's just one thing, and you must remember this as long as we are together, all right? It's terribly, terribly important, and could cause us to have an awful falling out. Are you listening?'

I nodded, absolutely transfixed by his calm, patient manner.

'Don't *ever* call me "Dunwoody" again as long as you live!' His eyes crinkled, and I could see he meant for me to be amused. But I had no idea what he was talking about.

'You want me to call you "Pat?"' I asked.

'Well, that's OK, but I don't ever want you to refer to me by the name "Dunwoody." It's Patrick McNabb now and always. All right?'

'Sure. No problem.' I knew better than to ask why, and at the same time, I knew I'd heard that name before. Why was it coming to me in Angie's voice?

'All right, then,' Dunwoody, er, McNabb said. He turned to Bach. 'Junius, don't disappoint me. I want to see that face' – and he pointed at me – 'every time I walk into this office or a court of law. Understand? A courtroom is no place for conventional thinking.'

Bach nodded, but I stood absolutely still. That was where I'd heard of Patrick McNabb. That was why Angie's voice was reminding me.

'You're on that TV show,' I said aloud. '*Legality*. You're Patrick McNabb.'

McNabb looked at me, deciding whether to be offended or amused. The crinkled eyes said he'd decided on amused. 'Yes I am,' he said. 'I'm glad we've determined who I am. And *you*, Sandy Moss. You are now someone else, too.'

'I am?'

'Yes. You're my attorney.'

THREE

Seaton Taylor (as the firm was known to its closer friends) was a large enough concern to have its own cafeteria, despite the fact that there were many lunch places on the same block as the high-rise in which the firm's offices were located. This was a good thing for me, because I could sit by myself, stare at a chicken salad sandwich I had no intention of eating, and wonder why I was such a bad lawyer.

What was passing for rye bread on the sandwich was something I'd normally use to mop up a spill, and the potato chips I might ordinarily get back home were replaced by whole-grain 'snackers,' which appeared to be either a subtle laxative or some form of punishment, or both. I wasn't thinking about the food anyway. My mind couldn't let me off the hook.

Why had I spoken up at the meeting when I knew I shouldn't? Why couldn't I just sit there and be the kind of set decoration Bach had clearly expected me to be? Why couldn't I just once be content to sit by and watch? Why, why, *why*?

I was trying as hard as I could to go back to the moment I'd allowed the impulse to overcome me, and ask for a do-over. Was that too much to expect, really? One little mulligan in the course of a whole life? Why hadn't anyone invented a time travel machine when you really *needed* one?

This self-pity festival might have gone on for hours (I hadn't been assigned any other cases after the McNabb fiasco), but a man, perhaps thirty years old (on his oldest day), with eyes so green they must have been contact lenses, and hair so black it was . . . black, stood across the table from me, tray in hands.

'Is this seat taken?' he asked in a musical voice. Shaken from my stupor by his question, I looked up. Dark, sober-looking, serious, extremely well groomed.

Just my type.

'Yes,' I said. 'I mean, no. I mean, sit down, please.' I gestured at the chair, as if we were in my living room (not my *real* living room, where books and cartons were strewn wall-to-wall, but the living room in my head, where I had furniture and stuff, all where they were supposed to be) and I was the hostess.

'Thanks,' said the man, not smiling in the least. He put down his tray (Caesar salad, dressing on the side, and vitamin water) and sat down. 'I'm Evan D'Arbanville. Are you Sandra Moss?'

I looked up. 'Yes! How'd you know that?'

'Well,' Evan said, 'you'd be the new one here, and besides, everybody heard about the meeting this morning. You're a celebrity around the office.'

I put my forehead down on the table, narrowly missing contact with my sandwich. Luckily, I was wearing my hair back in a bun, or I'd have smelled like mayonnaise the rest of the day. 'Great. I'm here half a day and everybody knows I'm a screw-up. I'm doomed.' I looked at Evan, suddenly, in wonder. 'Why are you sitting near me? Don't you need to be in with the cool kids?'

He smiled a little. 'You *are* the cool kid. All the lawyers here think you're a hero because you got Patrick McNabb to threaten to leave if the Old Man fired you. We who work in the trenches are impressed.'

Evan dug into his salad, which was what I should have ordered. He didn't even need to lose any weight, I noted with both appreciation and envy. He probably just ate salads because he enjoyed them. Typical Californian. *Nobody* enjoyed salads in New Jersey. They ate them as a form of penance.

'You're a lawyer here?' I asked him.

Evan wiped a tiny spot of dressing from the side of his mouth. 'No, I'm a paralegal,' he said. 'But I'm going to law school, and I'm hoping they'll hire me as an associate when I finish.'

'How much longer?' I asked.

'Another year. I'm working full-time and going to school at night. It's a little time-consuming.'

Angie's voice has a habit of talking to me in my head when I'm under stress. Since I'm almost always under stress, this has become pretty typical for me. I mean, I *know* it's just my own mind telling me what Angie would say, but it's become almost reflexive, and I don't much think about it any more. Except when, as now, the imaginary Angie was screaming in my ear: *He's a starving law student. Ask him out! Take him to dinner!* Not only had I never asked a man out in my life, but this didn't seem like my luckiest day so far. And it was only eleven thirty.

'Would you like to go out to dinner?' I'd been rehearsing the line so many times in my head that it took me a moment to realize it was coming from Evan's mouth. I stared at him a moment, and seeing my look, he added, 'You don't have to if you don't want to.'

'No, I'd love to,' I managed to answer. 'But don't you have to go to law school at night and work here during the day? When do you have time to socialize?'

Evan smiled with the left side of his mouth. *My God*, I thought, *I'd probably sleep with this guy on the first date!* 'I get one night off a week,' he said. 'It happens to be tonight. Besides, I have to eat sometime. Would you like to join me? I can't afford much, but I can make you dinner.'

Make me dinner? I might have to sleep with him twice *on the first date!*

'Normally, I wouldn't,' I said when my mind cleared. 'First dates should be in public . . . you know. But I think you're pretty trustworthy.'

Evan's eyes widened a little at the suggestion he might be anything other than a Boy Scout. 'Oh, you don't have to worry about me, Sandra.'

'Sandy.'

'Sandy. I'm completely trustworthy. I won't even make a move on you after a couple of glasses of wine.'

I was disappointed. 'You *won't?*'

Evan never so much as smiled. 'No. I want you to be comfortable with me.'

Damn! I thought. *I'll have to make the move myself!*

But in the end, I didn't. Evan was a perfect gentleman the whole evening, which was infuriating and a little insulting, because I was trying my best to be alluring. *For goodness sake,* my inner Angie said to me, *at least show him you* have *cleavage,* so I wore a T-shirt tight enough to prove I *could* have cleavage if I chose to. *And tight pants, to show off the . . . well, OK, maybe not too tight.* I knew I could lose a little – not a lot – off my tight-jeans area, so I wore pants a little less obvious, but tailored well enough to conceal how less obvious I was being.

Defying Angie's imagined pleas, I didn't choose a skirt to '*show off the gams,*' because I felt the *gams* weren't anything special. Everyone in Los Angeles either was in the movies or looked like they should be, and I wasn't ready to compete. I was, I felt, at best a minor leaguer, and not a very high-level one at that (OK, so maybe I was being a little tough on myself).

Evan opened the door to his apartment, a slightly less luxurious one than mine, in the San Fernando Valley. Clearly not giving much thought to *his* wardrobe, he was dressed in a pair of slightly worn jeans and a USC T-shirt that had seen better days. But he was smiling a warm smile when I entered.

The place smelled wonderful – Evan, it turned out, was making Chicken Diane, and was an excellent cook. If he got any more perfect, I thought, I'd have to drug him and marry him against his will.

Over dinner, we talked about the law. Evan was an especially earnest law student, having already worked in the profession, albeit at a relatively low level. He was fascinated by the way the intent of the law and its wording could sometimes be in conflict, subject to the interpretation of famed (and not so famed) jurists. I had a hard time keeping up with some of the discussion, since my natural inclination in most discussions of criminal cases, based on my prosecutorial experience, was to simply assume the defendant was guilty.

'In eight years as an assistant prosecutor, I ran into maybe three cases where the defendant wasn't at least a little guilty,' I told Evan after dinner. We sat on the slightly worn sofa, in front of a fireplace he said didn't work (which was fine with me, since it was still over seventy degrees outside), drinking red wine. 'If they weren't a hundred percent guilty of the charge, they were at least peripherally involved in the crime, and most often had criminal records that indicated they were intending to be as involved as possible.'

'But you can't make that assumption,' Evan said, sounding almost personally insulted. 'The law assumes innocence, and the idea of guilt through previous crimes is inadmissible in most cases.'

'I'm not talking about theory,' I said, stifling a smile at his naïveté. 'I'm talking about the way it works in real life.'

Stop being the older, more experienced lawyer, and start being a hot babe, the Inner Angie screamed, *or you'll end up in bed alone tonight – again!*

I made a note to tell the voice in my head that I *wasn't* all that much older than Evan, and then noted that the voice should shut up. Sometimes, having a best friend in your head can be a decided nuisance.

Still, I leaned closer to Evan and made what I considered to be a seductive moaning sound quietly in the back of my throat. Of course, the way he reacted, it was clear that what he heard was more like the call of a moose who'd gotten her hoof caught in a bear trap, but you can't have everything.

'Are you OK?' Evan asked, pulling back from me a bit.

'Sure,' I answered in a low tone. 'I'm just getting comfortable.'

'Oh.' A pause. 'Good.' He looked around the room a little desperately, and stood, which almost sent me face down on the couch. I thanked my genes for the ability to balance despite two imbibed glasses of wine. Well, almost two.

Evan blinked a couple of times and said, 'I don't want to be rude, but I have to get up really early tomorrow. I run fifteen miles before work every day, and I have class tomorrow night, so . . .'

'No problem,' I said, standing awkwardly. 'I should really get to bed early myself.' Maybe the word 'bed' would give him an idea.

It did. It evidently gave Evan the idea of walking to the door and opening it for me to leave. *Wrong idea!* the Inner Angie scolded. I walked to the door, determined to win at least a small victory.

The hallway was narrow, but not as narrow as I decided to make it. In walking to the door, which Evan held open, I pressed as close as I could to him and murmured, 'Well, good night.'

Then, intending to make a show of snuggling by him, I pressed
my body into his, except for one little misstep.

I tripped and stumbled into Evan, forcing him to put up his
hands to catch me. They would have caught me in the upper
arms, too, right where Evan had aimed, but, trying to right myself
as I fell, I came in at a different angle, and Evan's hands ended
up right where my implied cleavage was advancing.

He looked absolutely mortified for a moment, then locked eyes
with me and whispered, 'There's only so much a man can take,
you know,' and put his hands behind me, drawing me closer to
him. Evan kissed me luxuriously, longingly, then almost furiously,
and I reveled in every second of it.

When we finally separated, he said, 'Now, get out of here
before I forget I'm trying to be a nice guy,' and opened the door
a little wider.

I grinned and walked out, saying, 'You don't have to be *that*
nice.'

'Yes, I do. Now, scram.'

He closed the door behind me, smiling, and the night air, warm
though it was, sobered me right up. I was alert as could be as I
drove home with what I'm sure was a stupid grin on my face.

Once I got home, my apartment brought me back down from
the near reverie I'd achieved during that evening's one perfect
minute. The place was still full of boxes, they were still vomiting
books all over everything, and I was still a colossal failure at my
new job.

It didn't help that I finally checked my voice mail and found
a message, and that Holiday Wentworth's voice sounded a little
frantic in asking where I might be, and why the office didn't
have a cell phone number for me (I hadn't bothered to get a
California number yet, and had left my New Jersey cell phone
at home tonight). Holly said to call 'whenever you get in, no
matter how late it is.'

So I called, and Holly did indeed sound flustered. 'You've got
to get down to the Beverly Hills police station right away,' she
said. 'We've got a criminal case for you.'

'We're a family law firm,' I said. 'I thought we didn't handle
any criminal cases.'

'We don't, but this client insisted on you, and only you.'

'Let me guess,' I said, my lovely evening entirely gone now. 'What did Pat McNabb do?'

'Well,' Holiday said slowly, 'if you believe the LAPD, he murdered his ex-wife tonight.'

FOUR

B el Air is a Los Angeles suburb so upscale it looks down on Beverly Hills. There is no In-N-Out Burger here. In fact, if there were a fast-food outlet in Bel Air, it would most likely serve Crispy Pheasant Strips and fried caviar sand-wiches. And you would have the ability to supersize your champagne.

It also has no police station, leaving such unsavory details of life to the peons in Beverly Hills, most of whom look down on the rest of the world and wonder what the heck Bel Air's got that's so much better. It drives some into therapy, others into producing reality TV shows.

I drove up to the Beverly Hills station in the 2009 Hyundai I'd driven to Los Angeles from New Jersey. I hadn't been able to have the car washed since arriving, and driving into the ritziest neighborhood on the continent, give or take a few, I felt like I might as well be riding up on a tricycle. The cop cars at the station would probably be Lexuses (Lexi?).

I walked into the station and located the desk sergeant, sitting behind an immaculate barrier in a space more nicely appointed than anything in my apartment. I considered asking if I could move into the police station, but thought about moving all those boxes again and decided against it.

Forty minutes later, after documents were signed and I was searched much too thoroughly for my taste, I sat in an interroga-tion room directly out of *Elle Decor* magazine and faced my client.

'It's horrible here,' McNabb said on arrival. 'We've done prison scenes on the show, and I've got to tell you, they're not nearly realistic enough. When can I get out?'

I looked around at the furnishings in the room and wondered if McNabb was complaining merely because the mauve in the seat cushions didn't match the shade on the wallpaper. But there were more serious issues to settle. 'There will be an arraignment tomorrow morning – I mean, this morning – and in all probability, the judge will set bail. Then . . .'

'I know all that,' my client told me. 'I play a lawyer on television. I just want to know if I'll be able to get out immediately after the arraignment.'

'Patrick,' I began, hoping to muster some semblance of patience at two in the morning, 'if we're going to function here, you need to trust me with the legal decisions. Playing a lawyer on TV is a wonderful thing, but would you trust Hugh Laurie to take out your appendix?'

McNabb looked confused. 'Laurie?' he asked. 'He diagnosed patients; he didn't do an appendix.'

Great. This was going to be easy. 'Let's just agree,' I went on, 'that you're going to do what I tell you, and let me handle all the legal work.'

'Of course.' McNabb seemed almost insulted by the implication. 'That's why I demanded that you handle the case. I trust you implicitly.'

I wanted to ask why. We'd met seventeen hours earlier, spent twenty-five minutes together (during which I made a monumental error), and he trusted me implicitly? But I went on. 'Just tell me what happened.'

'I really don't know,' McNabb said. 'I went over to see Patsy at about ten. I felt badly about the way we'd yelled at each other at the meeting. There was no need for things to be so acrimonious. I did love her once, you know.'

I thought, *probably more than once*, but, once again, I showed admirable restraint. 'So you went over merely to smooth over the meeting at our office this morning, to tell her you were sorry you'd lost your temper?'

McNabb looked away, not wanting to meet my eyes. 'Well . . .' he said. 'There was a little more to it than that.'

'You wanted to talk to her about the shoes.' It was been the only thing that had registered emotionally with McNabb at the meeting.

McNabb's head came to attention, swiveling so fast to meet my eyes that I was afraid he'd hurt himself, or that his head would keep spinning from sheer momentum. 'That's brilliant! How could you have known that?'

'That's not the issue. What I don't understand is . . .'

'No, it's a *huge* issue,' McNabb answered, his face supremely attentive. 'If it's a great lawyer trick, I might be able to use it!'

'Patrick,' I breathed, hoping to get through the static around McNabb's head that prevented simple words to penetrate, 'you can't be thinking about acting right now. You're being accused of an extremely serious crime, and your life is very much on the line.'

McNabb pursed his lips, which I first thought meant he was digesting the information he'd just been given. But a moment later, I realized it was just his way of dismissing what I'd said. 'I have nothing to worry about,' he said. 'I have two enormous advantages. First of all, I didn't kill Patsy.'

'And second?'

'Second, I have *you*. You're brilliant.'

I'm dealing with a raving maniac, Angie. He seems like a nice, handsome, normal man, but in reality, well . . .

'Whether or not I'm brilliant, you have to answer the questions, Patrick, and you have to focus on doing that. So tell me what was so important about these shoes.'

He stared at me as if I'd just suggested he should flap his wings and fly out of the room. McNabb's eyes blinked a few times, and he shook his head. *'Jimmy's shoes?'* he asked. 'You don't know why I care about *Jimmy's shoes*?'

'No. Suppose you tell me. Start with who Jimmy might be.'

McNabb nodded. Oh, *that* was why I wasn't being reverent enough. 'Jimmy was one Mr James Cagney, an actor you might have heard of.' McNabb's accent, in this time of stress, was leaning a little more heavily on its cockney roots. 'The shoes are the very tap shoes he wore while filming the title number in a movie called *Yankee Doodle Dandy*.' He sat there, possibly expecting me to cross myself, but I just looked at him.

'And?'

'*And*, they came into my possession through a series of very favorable circumstances just after I married Patsy. We have them

. . . had them, in a glass case in the bedroom. Used to look at them every night. Even took 'em out every once in a while just to feel them in my hands. His feet were smaller than mine.' McNabb grinned.

'You tried them on.' I wasn't sure why I was asking about the shoes, but I believed deep in my soul that, eventually, the conversation would lead to something relevant.

McNabb looked offended. 'Absolutely not,' he said, his voice an open question as to whether his attorney was the right person for him or not. 'I just . . . held them against my feet, to compare.'

'So you went over to get the shoes? Is that it?' Believing deep in your soul is a lovely thing, but I wanted to still be in my mid-thirties when I understood what I had to defend.

He looked away. 'No, of course not. I really did feel badly about how we'd left it, and so I went over to apologize, more or less.'

'And how did it work out?'

'Well. She and I had agreed to split everything half and half, and I would get Jimmy's shoes. She was going to call her lawyer in the morning.'

Uh-huh. Cruella de Vil had become Shirley Temple in the course of one conversation, and then conveniently ended up dead, so she couldn't confirm or deny his version of the story.

'So you left right after that?' I asked.

'No, I stayed a while, and then she went to the kitchen to get a bottle of wine, to toast our agreement. I heard a noise, then I heard some sounds I couldn't identify. I ran out of the bedroom and found Patsy on the floor in the dining room. She was bleeding rather badly.'

'You were in the bedroom?'

Again, he looked away, which didn't leave him much to look at besides the ceiling and the lovely potted palm in the corner. And the coffee table with a selection of current upscale magazines. And the cappuccino machine. 'That's where the shoes were.' So he was embarrassed about his devotion to the footwear. That was certainly understandable.

'So you went in and found her bleeding. Had she been shot?' I searched his eyes, but found only disappointment – in me.

'They didn't tell you what happened?' McNabb asked.

'No, I won't get the police report until I leave here. They're probably typing it up now.' *On a computer that's cleaner, more expensive, and newer than mine.*

'Well, Patsy wasn't shot, exactly,' McNabb said, biting his lower lip. 'Not with a gun, anyway.'

'What else can you be shot with?' I had to ask. Clearly, I was going from brilliant to imbecile pretty rapidly.

'An arrow,' he said.

FIVE

'**A**n *arrow*?' Angie asked. 'She got shot with an *arrow*? We're supposed to believe that Cochise happened by and decided to have a little target practice at Pat and Patsy's place?'

'Quiet down,' I said in my still-echoing kitchen. 'I'm not supposed to tell you anything about this. And you can't tell *anybody*. It'll be in the papers tomorrow, anyway.'

'Who's going to hear me?' Angie chuckled. 'I'm 3,000 miles away, Sandra. Even *I'm* not that loud.'

'You know what I mean.'

'So did he do it?'

My eyes rolled up into my eyelids. It was five in the morning in Los Angeles. Angie was getting ready to go to work in New Jersey. I hadn't been to bed yet, and Angie had gotten up from a full night's sleep an hour ago. How was this possible?

'He says no. He says that after she went to get a bottle of wine, he heard a noise, so he came out to the dining room and found her bleeding on the extremely expensive Persian rug. With an arrow sticking out of her chest.' Even I was having trouble saying it with a straight face. 'He called nine-one-one, but she was dead before they arrived.'

I could imagine Angie's triangular face shifting into 'thinking' mode, which meant her eyebrows lowered and her lips inverted as she chewed on them. It was amazing people didn't shriek in horror and run screaming from the area whenever this happened, but Angie managed to pull it off with aplomb.

'They must have found the, um, murder weapon, right? I mean, if some guy was running away from a fancy estate like that carrying a bow and a quiver of arrows, he'd be pretty conspicuous.'

'You should have been a cop,' I told my friend. 'But they didn't have to look very far. The bow was Patrick's – part of his collection. Apparently, it was an original from *The Searchers*, with John Wayne.'

'And it's got Patrick's fingerprints all over it, right?'

'Right. But he says that's natural, since it was his. He has all kinds of movie crap all over the house.'

'It's not crap. That's important historical stuff.' Angie was a pop culture fanatic, and believed that a sword used by Russell Crowe would be more valuable than one wielded by Sir Lancelot himself – if there had been a Sir Lancelot. Maybe that's a bad example.

'Nonetheless, that's one of the things the cops will use against him. And, of course, his fingerprints are all over the arrow.'

'Because he pulled it out when he found her on the floor,' Angie volunteered.

'Well, no. He tried to, but it was . . . in a little too deep, he says.' I bit my lower lip.

'Ewwww . . .'

'Exactly.' I looked around and wondered if you could hire someone to come in and unpack for you. I'd moved out here specifically to get away from the criminal justice system, but now I had a murder case on my hands, and I'd have less than the no time to organize my apartment than I had when I woke up . . . yesterday morning. Wasn't that a week ago, at least? If I closed my eyes, I'd be asleep until Wednesday. Unless today was Wednesday. I couldn't remember.

'So what are you going to do?' Angie asked. 'You have to get him out, Sandy. You have to.'

'Take it easy, Ang. The judge probably won't consider him a flight risk. And they're getting sort of used to the whole "celebrity murder" thing out here. It seems like they have one every couple of weeks.'

'You don't understand, Sandy. Patrick McNabb *can't* go to jail. You have a huge responsibility here. Don't take it lightly.'

I was touched that my friend was taking my burden so

seriously. 'I don't know what to say, Ang,' I said. 'I'll do my best.'

'Do better than your best,' Angie answered in a no-nonsense tone. 'He has to be out of jail and back on that soundstage today. Understand? Arthur Kirkland's girlfriend is cheating on him, and if he finds out the wrong way, he might *kill* her!'

I could see this was going to be a very long day. Week. Possibly decade.

'Your concern is touching,' I said. 'I'll do what I can.'

'I can't believe you're on this case!' Angie sounded positively giddy. I sat down on the bar stool and wondered if I could find a low-fat bran muffin with caffeine in it. It seemed unlikely. 'Look, I know you have to keep certain things private, but I just have to ask . . .'

I closed my eyes in grim anticipation.

'What?'

Angie's voice took on a hushed, conspiratorial tone. 'Sandy, was she, you know, *scalped*, too?'

SIX

Patrick McNabb was arraigned in the Clara Shortridge Foltz Criminal Justice Center at ten that morning, amid a media circus surpassed only by all the other media circuses that had taken place in Southern California when a celebrity found him/her/themself in trouble with the law. After all, McNabb was only a television star, not a movie star, and he'd been a leading actor for only a year. It wasn't like somebody really *important* had been arrested for murder.

Still, the tumult surrounding the courthouse was more than enough for my taste. Barely in town for two weeks, I was now on speed dial from every news producer, reporter, and editor in town (and many from New York and London, as well as two from Tokyo). Interview requests were coming into my office at the rate of six per hour. I hadn't bothered to have my home phone number – yeah, I'm an old-fashioned girl and I have a landline, because it just sounds better – unlisted, but because I was new to the area, it wasn't yet in the printed version of the current directory (if anybody still looks at those). Producers, editors, and reporters had to actually call Information and ask for a new listing to get the number. Unsurprisingly, the answering machine's computer chip was full, and the phone was ringing off the hook day and night (which had been a grand total of eight hours so far). I didn't know which particular god had kept my cell number secret, but I resolved to take up their religion as soon as I found out.

The reporters swarmed all over my car when I drove to the (thankfully) underground parking lot at the courthouse, screaming questions: 'Ms Moss! Ms Moss! Did Patrick *mean* to kill her?'

'Was he just showing Patsy his bow?'

'Are you romantically involved with Patrick?'

'Will he plead insanity?'

The question I really wanted answered was, 'How did they find out which car was mine?'

This was not what I'd signed up for, I thought as I got into the elevator at the parking level. I'd told that to Junius Bach himself when he'd called this morning at seven, just at the moment I believed I might catch an hour or two of sleep. And if Bach wasn't peeved at me enough for the screw-up at the meeting yesterday, now he seemed to hold me somehow responsible for Patrick McNabb's arrest, as if Patsy would still be alive if only I'd kept my mouth shut at the conference.

'I'm not a criminal attorney any more,' I told Bach, right after he informed me that he was agreeing to McNabb's wishes and making me the lead attorney on the case. 'And I've never been a defense attorney in my life. You expect me to walk into a courtroom in a state where I've never practiced and defend a famous actor in a murder trial?'

'That is precisely what I expect you to do,' Bach responded. He sounded, at seven in the morning, as if he'd just played a game of squash after a relaxing massage and a very expensive pedicure. It was funny what you could hear in a voice. 'Our client has specifically requested your counsel, and as his law firm, we are going to provide what he requests.'

'But, Mr Bach—'

I didn't get the chance. 'Ms Moss, I'm not any happier about the situation than you are. Perhaps less. But when a client who pays a retainer as large as Mr McNabb requests a service from our firm, and specifies an attorney from our firm to provide that service, we provide it. Are there any questions?'

Beyond 'how did they find out which car is mine?' Yes, I had hundreds of questions, and most of them involved exactly how I'd defend a man I thought probably murdered his wife over a pair of shoes too small for his own feet. As I got off the elevator (and into the swarm of reporters stationed there – did they employ reporters to cover anything else?), I was mostly wondering if I could convince McNabb to hire himself a lawyer who actually knew what they were doing.

After considering very seriously the idea of having 'NO COMMENT' tattooed on my forehead to cut down on having to say it, I wandered around the hall I'd never seen before, looking for Courtroom #4, where the arraignment would take place (evidently, it was the largest of the courtrooms, and could accommodate the press and a few helpful fans, whose 'Free Arthur Kirkland!' T-shirts ignored McNabb's real name). A reporter finally gave me directions to the courtroom, but not before he tried, unsuccessfully, to wrangle an exclusive interview (with McNabb, not me).

I thought I'd find refuge in the courtroom, but it was already filled with press (*what if there's a disaster in Washington today – will anyone be available to report it?*) and sorrowful fans (*Marry Me, Pat! You're Single Again!*). Between my overall fatigue and the delay in finding a. the courthouse and b. the court*room*, I'd barely managed to scramble into my seat at the defense table and open my briefcase when the bailiff opened the door and entered the courtroom, signaling the judge's imminent arrival.

Just as I stood on hearing 'all rise,' my peripheral vision caught Evan sidling up beside me at the second chair. We sat as the judge, the Honorable Henry T. Fleming, said, 'Be seated.'

'What are you doing here?' I hissed to Evan as the bailiff opened the door for McNabb, who looked unshaven and sleep-deprived.

'Bach told me to come and give you whatever help you needed,' he told me. 'I know I'm not an attorney, but I can do the research. I'm at your disposal.'

Smiling as diplomatically as I could, I felt conflicted. It was nice to have a friendly face next to me, but that's all he was – a friendly face. A real lawyer, preferably one with criminal defense experience, would have been far more welcome.

'Great,' I said. 'Welcome aboard.'

McNabb was led to the table, and sat next to me, giving Evan a glance I thought might have been hostile. 'All we have to do is plead, and I get out of here, right?' he asked.

'It's nice to see you, too, Patrick,' I scolded him. 'So long as there are no complications, yes.'

The bailiff called the case number, and the prosecutor and I agreed we were present in the courtroom. The judge asked for the plea, and I tried very hard to look convincing, and convinced, when I said, 'not guilty.'

I added, 'Your Honor, given Mr McNabb's record and his very high public profile, we feel he presents no flight risk, and request his release on bail.'

The elected district attorney, M. Harrison Brady, was so tall he might once have played for the Lakers. At a later date, I was to hear the rumor, supposedly circulating in the L.A. criminal justice system, that the 'M' stood for 'Man, He's Tall.' He rose to his full height, which took a while, and let his deep baritone envelop the room.

'Judge, the state objects to bail,' he said. 'This is a homicide, and we are very close to Mexico – it's easy for someone to leave the country by car in a very short time.'

Already standing, I felt like I should climb onto a chair to argue with Brady, but I fought the impulse. 'Your Honor, a man as recognizable as Mr McNabb would be detained on any attempt to flee, and Your Honor can certainly confiscate his passport to avoid any such possibility.'

Fleming looked me over and was about to speak when Brady cut him off. 'In addition, there is the defendant's prior history of violence. The police went three times to the home of the defendant and the victim in response to domestic disturbance calls, and Mr Dunwoody . . . pardon me, Mr *McNabb*, was arrested on assault charges in London seven years ago.'

I did not spin and stare at my client, who hadn't mentioned any of this, but it wasn't without effort. Through slightly gritted teeth, I said, 'Oh, come on, Your Honor. Seven years ago? In England? And a troubled marriage that required some help from the police? That was all before Mr McNabb became a celebrity, and therefore makes him all the less a candidate for flight at this time. Look at all the reporters in this room. There are twice as many outside the door, and more on the steps outside the building. His face will be on every news show in the country, and many around the world, tomorrow morning. Where would he go? And how would he get there undetected? Your Honor, Mr McNabb will not be going anywhere, because he is anxious to clear his name and see justice done in this courtroom. He has no intention of leaving the city, the county, the state, or the country. He *wants* to be here.'

Fleming took a moment to consider me – it seemed he was considering me, and not what I'd said, anyway, as he looked me up and down like he was deciding whether or not to buy me. 'You haven't been before this court before, have you, Ms' – and he checked the sheet in front of him – 'Moss?'

'No, Your Honor. I moved to Los Angeles earlier this month.'

'From where?'

From where? Now he wants my biography? 'From New Jersey. I was an assistant county prosecutor for eight years.' Maybe he was just checking my credentials. It felt like he'd be examining my fillings in a moment, but that was subjective.

'New Jersey.' Fleming nodded, as if that explained it. 'Well, Ms Moss, I was inclined to comply with the district attorney's request, but you made a strong argument. I hope you're willing to back it up.'

'Back it up? How, Your Honor?' Did he expect me to take McNabb's place in the cell while he walked around free?

'I'll set bail at one million dollars, but I want you to know, Ms Moss, I'm holding you responsible for your client. If he misses so much as one hearing date, I will find you in contempt of this court and throw you in jail. Is that clear?'

'Clear, Your Honor.' *What kind of insane state is this? Do they want me to make sure he eats right and flosses every day, too? I'm his lawyer, not his mother!*

'Very well, then.' A bang of the gavel. 'One million dollars.'

The next few minutes were a carnival of reporters, questions, forms to fill out, questions, and then, just for a change of pace, a few more questions. But I managed to make it back to my car, and somehow, Patrick McNabb was seated next to me as we drove out of the garage and back into what was laughingly referred to out here as 'The Real World.'

The reporters swarmed over the car, but McNabb simply said, 'Don't stop. They'll get out of the way.' That's what happened, and eventually, we made it out to the street and away from the madhouse.

'Well,' Patrick breathed once we were safely ensconced in traffic. 'That was *brilliant*!'

Perhaps I'd taken some of the madhouse with me.

SEVEN

'**A**re you out of your *mind*?'

I didn't think the question was at all inappropriate. We sat in my office, a tiny square in the center of Seaton Taylor's space, a glorified cubicle with no window and an empty pot where a plant must once have stood. My second day on the job, and I had the world's most famous murder defendant sitting across from my metal desk, staring at the blank walls.

'I don't know what you mean,' Patrick told me. 'I thought you did quite well. I mean, he threw something at you that you couldn't possibly have expected . . .'

'That's the *point*!' I was within millimeters of screaming. 'Why didn't you tell me about the police calls, and the arrest in London seven years ago? Were you trying to spare me the unpleasant details of your past?'

Evan appeared in the doorway, having driven from the courthouse in his own car. 'What did I miss?' he asked.

'Nothing,' I said. 'I'll let you know if I need anything, but right now, Mr McNabb and I need to have a private conference, OK?'

Evan looked like a hurt basset hound, but he walked away with a mumbled 'OK.' Patrick smirked after him.

'Best to get rid of him,' he said, looking at the departing Evan. 'He's a devious sort.'

'He's not even a little devious,' I snarled at him. 'I wasn't sure if he was old enough to hear the kind of language I'm going to use with you.'

Patrick McNabb had the nerve to look surprised. 'Me?' he asked. 'What did I do?'

'What did you do? You left me out there to twist in the wind. Mr McNabb . . .'

'Patrick.'

'*Mr McNabb*, if you don't tell me everything you know and everything I need to know, I won't be able to mount an effective defense for you in court, and you'll go to jail for a very, very long time. Is that clear?'

'Look, Sandy. It just never occurred to me that any of that stuff would matter. I got into a shoving match with a guy in a pub a million lifetimes ago. Patsy used to call the cops every time I looked at her funny. I'm not a violent man, and I did not kill my wife.'

I stared at him a moment, trying to think of an adequate response. The man believed that saying something with enough conviction made it true. After all, it always worked on television.

'We're going to go over everything, Patrick – everything you've ever done that might even *appear* to be the slightest bit question-able. Because no matter how innocent it may be, you can take it to the bank that the D.A. will use it in court, and make you look like Jack the Ripper. So let's have it all, now. Everything I need to know. Tell me truthfully why you went to Patsy's house last night, and what happened after you got there.'

'I told you. I felt bad about the argument, and—'

'Come on, Patrick. You and I both know you didn't feel at all badly about that. After Patsy left the conference room, you practic-ally did the chicken dance, you were so charged up. So let's have the real story, or I promise you, I'll quit this case.'

Patrick McNabb closed his eyes and bowed his head. I thought for a moment he was going to start snoring any second. *Honest to goodness, Angie, the man is a raving maniac. I don't know what you saw in him to begin with.*

Yes, you do. Look at those eyes. That hair. That cleft chin. You know exactly what I see in him, and you see it, too. Besides, he's a wounded soul and you're supposed to help him.

Stop it. You're my imaginary version of my best friend. You're not supposed to win arguments.

Patrick snapped me out of my reverie by opening his eyes and looking up, directly into my face.

'All right. I went to the house to get Jimmy's shoes. But I did let Patsy think I felt bad about the argument. The problem was, she'd been drinking a little, and we had another argument. A bigger one. I guess there wasn't anyone to break us up this time, so we kept yelling things at each other. Is that what you want to hear?'

'Only if it's the truth.'

'Then I'm going back to my original story. That *was* the truth.'

I could see where this was going. 'OK. So things got out of hand. But I don't see how that leads to the bow and arrow.'

Patrick looked astonished. 'You think I did it?' he whispered.

'Well, wasn't that what you were saying?' OK, so maybe I *couldn't* see where this was going.

Patrick stood up and turned his back to me. I thought his shoulders might be shaking a bit, and there was definitely a catch in his voice. 'I thought you believed in me, Sandy. I thought you knew what kind of person I am. If you don't . . .' As his voice trailed off, the shoulder movement became more pronounced.

My hand went to my mouth. This kind of display was the last thing I'd expected. 'Patrick, you have to understand. The way you were talking, the words you chose . . . I thought you were confessing to me. Please forgive me if I misconstrued.'

Patrick wheeled and faced me, beaming. 'Right,' he chirped. 'I understand. Now, let's get to work.'

My mouth opened and closed once or twice, but emitted remarkably little sound. When I finally found my voice, I heard it say, 'But . . . but you . . . weren't you . . .?'

'It's called acting, my love,' he said. 'Remember, I do that for a living.'

I shook my head, slowly, three times, but my brain was just as addled as before. 'Then I can never believe anything you say.'

'Of course you can,' he answered. 'I always mean it at the moment I say it.'

'That doesn't help at all.'

Patrick sat down again, and looked at me with an expression of absolute admiration. 'What must we do next?' he asked, ignoring my remark entirely. 'Can you check with your sources at the police to see what they have on me?'

'I don't *have* sources at the police, Patrick. I've only been in Los Angeles for two weeks! Besides, this is not a television show. Lawyers don't do that stuff themselves. They have investigators who look into and gather the evidence. I do the law, the police and the investigators do the detection. OK?'

'But surely the prosecutor's office will share their discovery with you? I mean, they have to tell you what the evidence is against me, don't they?'

'No, Patrick, they're not going to just hand me all their evidence and tell me where the holes are. They're going to give me a list of their witnesses and physical evidence, and maybe a little more than that, but they'll be tickled to death if I don't know things they know, and they'll be even more tickled to exploit the difference in our information base if it'll help put you behind bars. They really believe you killed Patsy, so they're not terribly interested in finding evidence that doesn't prove your commission of the crime. That's *our* job.'

Patrick nodded. 'I see. This is very useful. I'll have to mention it to our writing staff.'

My God, he still thinks he's a lawyer on television!

'Your first concern shouldn't be your show,' I suggested slowly. 'Your first concern has to be this trial. For the next six months or so . . .'

'*Six months!* This is going to take six months?'

'At least. It's not the movies, Patrick. The court system is backed up beyond belief, and we want as much time as we can get to do discovery and plan a defense. So more time is better for us.'

'But I have another two episodes to shoot this year, and we'll be back at work in August for the next season,' he said, seemingly thinking out loud. 'I don't see how I can be on the set and out finding the real killer at the same time.'

My jaws were now pressed together so hard I was afraid a tooth might actually shoot up into my nose. 'You're *not finding the real killer*!' I shouted. 'You have to let the investigators do their work. You have to answer my questions and do what I say! Do you understand?'

His smile only broadened. 'That's *brilliant*!' he said. 'Can I use it?'

I put my hands over my eyes and hoped that when I took them away, I'd be back in New Jersey prosecuting a B&E artist for breaking in through someone's back door and stealing a $75 Blu-ray player. I tried picturing myself alone on a beach, but in my mind's eye, Patrick kept washing out of the surf and asking if he could watch the way I sat on my blanket to research his character. I breathed in very hard and coughed. When I took my hands off my eyes Patrick was handing me a bottle of water.

'Thank you,' I said. I took a large sip and composed myself. I spoke very slowly. 'Patrick. Please. Try and block out all the other voices in your head and listen only to me. I'm going to explain to you how this will work one . . . more . . . time. You can't go back to work on television while you're accused of murder. You can't use anything I do for your character. You can't go out and search for the real killer. All you can do is answer my questions and follow my instructions. And you must not expect that huge pieces of evidence are going to find their way here from the D.A., or that a surprise witness will appear at the end of trial and exonerate you by breaking down and confessing on the stand. That doesn't happen in real life. Things that happen on television won't happen here. There won't be any car chases, our lives won't be threatened, and I'm never going to sleep with my client. I can also guarantee you that phone will *never* ring with a sympathetic policeman on the other end calling to offer some help because he thinks the wrong man is being accused. OK? Never!'

The phone rang.

I stared at it, but he didn't even blink. 'I'm sorry, Patrick. I told them to hold all my calls,' I said. 'It must be awfully important.'

'Not at all. Go ahead.'

I picked up the phone as if it might explode. 'Hello?'

'Ms Moss?'

'Yes.'

'I work in the medical examiner's office. I have some information you might need.'

This doesn't happen, I thought. *This doesn't ever happen.*

'Can we meet?' I asked. 'What's your name?'

'No. They'll find out I called you. It's against policy. Look, they just did the autopsy on Patsy . . .'

'I know.'

'The M.E. found traces of semen in her. Fresh. Like she'd had sex right before she died. There won't be DNA for weeks, but the blood type matches your client's.'

I closed my eyes again. 'My client?'

'Yeah. That's why I'm calling. Tell Patrick I'm a big fan.'

And then he hung up.

EIGHT

'**O**f *course* I had sex with her,' Patrick said. 'We always had sex after a big argument – it was always our best sex. I don't see what the big fuss is about.'

Riding in my car, Patrick wore a baseball cap pulled down over his eyes and a pair of dark sunglasses to ward off reporters and enthusiastic fans. He insisted on opening the car window despite the admittedly ineffective air conditioner, and seemed disappointed that people weren't noticing him and asking for autographs.

'That's what worries me, Patrick,' I told him. 'You don't seem to understand why any of this is a big deal. Your wife is dead. Someone shot her with an arrow, and left enough evidence to convict you seven times over, and you don't see why it's relevant that you had sex with her right before she died.'

We'd decided that, with media requests coming in by the minute and reporters camped outside the door, a conference in the office was going to be impossible. Patrick's house was decidedly out of the question, so we headed for my apartment, hoping that because I was not yet listed in any local law records, the media might not have uncovered my address yet.

'I don't have to worry about it,' Patrick said with great cheer. 'I have you. You're . . .'

'*Please* don't say "brilliant" again,' I pleaded. 'I'm *not* brilliant. I'm not even sure I'm any good. You can't simply rely on me to get you out of trouble. You have to work with me.'

'All right, all right, I won't say "brilliant" any more,' he said, although his downturned lower lip betrayed his disappointment. 'So *you* tell *me*: how are we going to find out who killed Patsy?'

The one thing I'd decided I liked about Los Angeles was the city's decision to display large signs indicating which street you were approaching. That way, you knew well in advance if this was the street where you needed to turn. Of course, given the traffic, you had plenty of time to study the signage, because it was impossible to drive an entire block in less than fifteen minutes. But one had to find the positive wherever one could. Fixating on the signs was also a good way to avoid strangling Patrick, as I'd already answered his question at least three times previously.

'We're *not* going to find out who killed Patsy,' I finally managed. 'That's not our job. We're going to let the investigator Mr Bach assigns to the case look into it and see if he can find evidence that you *didn't* kill her. If he finds evidence that someone else did, he'll pass it on to the police so *they* can determine if the evidence is compelling enough to drop the charges against you. Do you understand all that?'

'Oh yeah, that's what I meant.'

Sure it was. 'Tell me about Patsy's career,' I tried. 'Why did her income drop so quickly in the past year?'

Patrick took off his sunglasses and stared at me. 'You don't know?' he asked.

'No, I don't. And put those glasses back on.'

Amazingly, he did. 'Don't you ever turn on a TV? A computer? *Entertainment Tonight*? *E!*? Even *TMZ*?'

'Sorry. I like books.'

Patrick shook his head in astonishment. 'Books. Really. Well, all right then. Patsy had a big hit with a record when she was only sixteen. Huge. The next Lady Gaga before there *was* a Lady Gaga.' He paused. 'You know who Lady Gaga is?'

'I'm pretty sure. She's from New Jersey.'

'OK. So Patsy was on top of everything – movie deals, concert tours, more record contracts, the whole works. And for almost a decade, she did very, very well. But starting about five years ago, when she was almost thirty, the record sales started to slip. Lady Gaga became the next Patsy. And she did it better. So Patsy started trying to be a serious singer, you know, like Celine Dion.'

'Serious?' I said.

'Right. But that didn't work. So she tried rap, and had a rap album all ready to go. The record company took a listen, heard this Italian woman in her thirties trying to sound like Jay-Z, and cancelled the contract. Just like that.' Patrick looked at the floor in what appeared to be honest sympathy. 'Poor kid couldn't pull herself together after that.'

'You met her when?'

'Right when she was recording the rap album. I knew it was lousy, and told her so, but she wouldn't listen. I told her to try Vegas, sing the old hits – come back like Rod Stewart and sing standards. She really did have a lovely voice, you know, but Patsy didn't think I understood show business until *Legality* came along. I came in during the sixth season of the show when everybody thought it was going to be cancelled. And for some reason people latched onto Arthur Kirkland and I became this big thing. My manager renegotiated my contract and I was making a *lot* of money. And then, all she knew was that I was doing much better than she was financially, and she resented it.'

'That's what broke up your marriage?' I asked as I looked for a left turn lane. *In Jersey, we have traffic circles, which everyone but Jerseyans pretend they don't understand. They make a hell of a lot more sense than these crazy turning lanes.*

'That, and the fact she slept with everyone who passed by the front door,' Patrick said.

'Can you think of anyone who might . . . *DUCK*!' I shouted. The barrel of a shotgun was sticking out the back window of the car to our right, and it was aimed directly at my car.

'Anyone who might duck?'

I swerved severely into the left turn lane, the only place where there was room for another vehicle, and made the left turn without looking, but with plenty of gas. I felt like my shoe had been nailed through the gas pedal to the floor. I couldn't move it, and the car was speeding up violently.

The car with the shotgun, a black Cadillac Escalade, barreled across two lanes of traffic to follow us. Patrick, startled by the sudden turn of events, turned in his seat to see who was after us.

'Get down, now!' I shouted.

Then I realized I was driving the wrong way on a one-way street, and suddenly, that required most of my attention. I took the first right turn I could after dodging sixteen angry horn-blowing Angelinos, and the Escalade followed doggedly, the shotgun still extended a few inches out the rear driver's-side window.

'Where are we?' I screamed..

He'd ducked his head under the dashboard. 'How the hell would I know?' he asked.

A shot rang out, and the passenger's side mirror flew off my Hyundai. My eyes narrowed. You can threaten a Jersey girl's life and chase her through the streets, but you damage her ride at your own risk.

'Son of a bitch!' I yelled out the back of the car. 'Who the hell do you think you're dealing with?'

'Is this the right time to be calling them names?' Patrick asked from somewhere below me. 'I mean, mightn't that get them a tad peeved?'

We reached . . . a major boulevard (I was traveling too fast to read the sign, no matter how conveniently located it might be), and I turned left onto it. Luckily, the rest of Los Angeles appeared to have taken another route, because there was just normal traffic here.

Another shot rang out, and the rear window of my car shattered. I screamed, mostly with rage, and noted that the speed-ometer had me driving at over eighty miles an hour. That was an interesting statistic, I thought. Really should take the time to analyze it someday soon.

'Raise your head long enough to look at that car and tell me if you recognize it,' I said to Patrick. He seemed liberated by the idea, and sat up eagerly.

'It's an Escalade,' he said. 'Every fifth person in Southern California has one. The other four have Teslas.'

'Swell. Which way are we going?'

'The wrong way. We'll hit the ocean soon, and then we'll be cornered.'

There was no left turn lane, and the gun was still poised outside the Escalade window. The way I saw it, there was only one way out.

I had to drive like a Jerseyan.

Pulling to the far right lane, I noticed the gigantic vehicle pulling up on our left. It was almost close enough for a shot, but on the wrong side. I surveyed the traffic and determined it was just about time to make my move.

The rear window on the passenger side of the Escalade slid down enough for the barrel of the shotgun to fit, and it was pointed directly at my head.

I slammed on the brakes, and the Escalade, taken by surprise, passed my Hyundai. As soon as it cleared, I hit the gas and went right, directly onto the sidewalk, barely avoiding a fire hydrant and two miniature dachshunds walked by a six-foot tall woman in a skin-tight exercise outfit. People screamed, but the dog woman kept right on walking and talking on her iPhone.

I swung a hard left, imagining the traffic circle in my mind, and rolled the car into the far lane, going in the other direction, across five lanes of traffic, before the Escalade could slam on its brakes. It crashed into a palm tree, which did not have very much yield, and stopped.

My Hyundai, still traveling at top speed, made up a lot of ground in a very big hurry as Patrick, staring out the now non-existent back window, beamed.

Finally finding a freeway entrance, I pulled onto a northbound lane and exhaled. *Never attack a Jersey girl's car*, I thought.

Patrick, still smiling, sat forward in his seat and regarded me with something approaching adoration.

'Well,' he said. 'We've had the phone call from the cop, our lives have been threatened and there's been a car chase. What was the last item you mentioned?'

NINE

'What kind of city is this?' I wailed at Junius Bach. It was bad enough I'd had to tell my boss about the events of the past hour, but now he was standing in my devastated living area, surveying the scene with the air of a man whose servants would have had this mess cleaned up weeks ago. 'People were shooting at us! In New Jersey, people don't shoot at you. Not strangers, anyway.'

Bach looked around the room again, with a slight degree of desperation on his usually placid face. 'Is there . . . something on which to sit in this room?' he asked.

'Oh, sure.' I moved some cartons off the sofa and gestured for Bach to sit down. He managed to do so without actually taking the handkerchief from his pocket and covering the cushion. But it was obvious he'd considered it.

'Now then, Ms Moss, you called me here because you're upset, and that is certainly understandable,' Bach said in tones that belonged on a public radio station. 'But we need to attack this problem rationally. Now, do you know for certain that the car behind you was actually shooting at you?'

Patrick was staring out the window in the vain hope that someone on the sidewalk many stories below would recognize him. 'The shattered back window and the side mirror flying off would seem to indicate that, Junius,' Patrick said.

'That's right,' I told him. 'Someone obviously doesn't want Patrick or me alive to upset the apple cart of the police investigation into Patsy's death. If we're dead, the case is closed and the details never heard in public.'

'That's hardly obvious,' said Bach. 'This is Los Angeles. This is the world capital of drive-by shootings. There are any number of reasons it might have happened.'

Oh my God, I thought, *he's in on it!* I *knew* it was right not to call the cops first! It was a conspiracy! Just because you're paranoid doesn't mean they're not after you. Besides, the judge had threatened *me* with prison if anything untoward happened involving Patrick. That was to be avoided.

'Don't be ridiculous, Junius,' said Patrick, coming to my rescue. He walked from the window to the center of the room, dodging boxes along the way. 'Sandy doesn't know anyone in this city, and nobody would have expected me to be driving in a car like that. It must be connected to Patsy, all right. It's the real killers trying to cover their tracks.'

'Of course you're right,' Bach said, immediately capitulating. 'I hadn't thought it through.'

I marveled again at how an imperious godhead like Bach could be reduced to sycophant by the presence of a television actor who happened to pay his firm a lot of money on a monthly basis. But in this case, it was working to my favor, so I didn't let it bother me.

'Mr Bach,' I began carefully, 'this case is not going to be simple, and it's not fair to Mr McNabb that only one attorney in the firm be dedicated to it. He needs a team, a group of the best criminal defense minds in the city, to . . .'

'Are you saying you can't handle it?' Bach immediately looked for weakness he could exploit later, and I was happy to provide him with some.

Have I ever said anything else? 'Not alone, by any means,' I answered. 'There must be others in the firm with experience in criminal law.'

'Not really, no,' Bach answered. 'At least, none who could handle a case of this type. We'd have to bring in someone to act in an of counsel capacity.'

'Other lawyers?' Patrick's eyebrows were so low they threatened to meet on his chin. 'I told you, Junius, I want Sandy on this, and no one else.'

Oh my God, he was going to blow it for me! 'Mr McNabb,' I said, pivoting on my left foot because my right ankle was still angry with me for all the pushing on the gas pedal, 'no single lawyer can handle a case of this magnitude all by herself. I'll still be your first chair at the trial, if we get that far.'

'Why can't one lawyer handle it?' Patrick wanted to know. 'Didn't Gregory Peck handle the case all by himself in *To Kill A Mockingbird*? I have a pair of glasses he wore in that movie.'

'That's the point, Patrick. It's a *movie*,' I said with a little too much force, prompting Bach to give me a poisonous look and turn his attention to his client.

'Patrick, if you want Ms Moss to handle this on her own, that is what she'll do,' he said. 'But every lawyer requires some support. For example, there will have to be at least one investigator assigned to the case, and it sometimes helps to have a second opinion from a lawyer when you need to make a decision.'

'The investigators are bad enough,' Patrick said, sticking out his adorable chin. 'And we already have the weasel . . .'

Bach looked at me. 'The weasel?'

'He means Evan.'

Bach turned back toward Patrick, raising his eyebrows. 'You don't like Evan?'

I walked toward Patrick before he could answer, demanding his attention and making threats with my eyes. 'He likes Evan,' I told Bach without looking at him. '*You like Evan*,' I said to Patrick.

He stared at me for a moment, then said to Bach, 'I like Evan.'

'All right then,' Bach said, choosing to ignore the dynamic that had evolved. 'We have a course of action. You, Ms Moss, will handle the legal end . . .'

'And I'm sure I can count on you for support when I need it, Mr Bach,' I added.

Bach's mouth tightened, but he said, 'Of course. We'll get an investigator working on the case immediately, and you can have the full use of Mr D'Arbanville whenever it's necessary. I think that concludes our business here today.' And with that, he stood and headed for the door with the speed of a man used to living in a palace who'd been dropped into a sewer.

'Just one thing, Mr Bach,' I said in lieu of bringing him down in a flying tackle (which, to be honest, was what I would have preferred). 'Who's going to take care of my car?'

TEN

The preliminary police report on the killing of Esmerelda 'Patsy' DeNunzio didn't offer much in the way of information: the victim was found on the floor in her dining room, an arrow through the chest. The victim's husband, one Patrick Dunwoody (aka McNabb), found the body and called EMS. His bloody fingerprints were found on the arrow and the bow nearby. The suspect did not confess under questioning, but admitted he and the victim had quarreled that day at a conference designed to settle their divorce before proceedings began in earnest. The argument had been over the disposition of their property.

That wasn't much, I thought, sitting in my office that evening – Patrick had 'had a car brought round' to drive me back to my office. Before making an arrest, the police usually had either a confession or some physical evidence that clearly proved the suspect committed the crime. In this case, all they had was a bizarre murder weapon, a prop from some long-ago movie that had been part of Patrick McNabb's pop culture collection, and fingerprints on both the bow and the arrow, which could be easily explained without his having done any violence at all to his wife. There must have been *something* else the police had that compelled them to act so quickly.

If I really had the sources in the police department Patrick believed I had, I could have called and made a few discreet inquiries, but the only people I knew in Los Angeles were the suspect, the head of the law firm representing him (who hated me), and a cute paralegal who looked like a kicked puppy if I didn't include him in everything I did on the case.

I hoped our investigator knew what he was doing, because I had remarkably little to work with.

Then again, maybe the situation wasn't that bad. My pessimistic outlook might well have been due to my recent lack of sleep or food. I needed to get some rest, and attack all this with fresh eyes tomorrow morning. I also needed to shave my legs before people started to mistake me for a very well-dressed gibbon.

Just as I was thinking of leaving the office and thanking my good fortune no one else would possibly be here this late, Evan appeared in my doorway. Naturally, I thought, the only guy who's kissed me in how many months, and he shows up when I bear a striking resemblance to Ernest Borgnine. *Sorry, Angie, I'm never going to date anyone ever again. God doesn't want me to.*

'You going to eat tonight?' Evan asked, a pleasant, if serious, smile fixed to his face.

'What are you doing here?' I asked in response. 'Don't you have class tonight?'

Evan walked in, which I thought would be an olfactory miscalculation on his part, given my recent lack of a shower, but he didn't flinch as he sat in the chair facing my desk. 'I decided to cut class tonight,' he said. 'I want to hear about what's going on with our case.'

Our *case? When did this become* our *case?*

'What's going on is that I'm going home to bed so I can think straight about *our* case tomorrow,' I told him. 'I haven't slept since sometime during the Obama Administration, and I haven't eaten since a very nice man fed me Chicken Diane and kissed me at the door.'

He grinned. 'Come on. We can catch a hamburger and I'll drive you home. I heard about your car. Are you OK?'

'Yeah, I'm all right. It's my car that took the shots. I gotta tell you, though, being shot at is not my idea of a fun afternoon. I was shaking like a leaf for two hours afterward.'

'What do the cops think it was?' He was so cute and wide-eyed.

'The cops.'

'Yes, what did they say when you reported it?'

'Evan, I, er, I didn't report it.'

His eyes were the size of pancakes, and not the silver dollar kind. 'You didn't?'

I felt like I was telling him there was no Santa Claus, and I was pretty sure there wasn't. 'The cops would have thought we planned the attacks, or simulated then, to make the newspapers and gain sympathy for Patrick. The judge might very well have revoked his bail, and Patrick doesn't respond well to jail.' Even one that has potpourri in its rest rooms.

'But you were shot at!'

'Yes.'

'It must have been terrifying,' Evan said. He stood and walked around the desk. 'They should have one of the investigators with you at all times from now on. Bach really doesn't seem to be taking this threat to you too seriously.'

He leaned against the wall a few feet from me. 'I don't think it was a threat to *me* at all,' I said. 'I think they were after McNabb, and I just happened to be sitting in the driver's seat at the wrong time. He's the one who needs protection. Mostly from himself – the man's crazy.'

'I don't care about him. I care about you,' Evan said. 'So come on, let me get some food into you and drive you home. What do you say?'

I smiled and rolled my head on my neck. 'I don't know. I might skip dinner and go straight to bed.'

He slipped behind me and started massaging my neck. Damn, that felt good. The sneaky little . . . 'Hey, watch it,' I murmured. 'You don't want to get too close. I stink to high heaven.'

'Oh, you do not.' His fingers were really untying all the knots in my neck muscles, and if I didn't keep a level head, it might not be my bed I ended up in. But I did need sleep, above all else. 'Come on. Quick bite, drive home. No funny business.'

'None?'

Evan chuckled a very controlled chuckle. 'No. I never take advantage of a woman who isn't awake.'

'Do you take advantage of the awake ones?' My voice sounded like I was eight years old. I'd better give in before he started massaging something other than my neck. 'OK, you win. Let's go eat and then you can take me home. To my home. To bed. You know what I mean.'

I stood up, and he slid his arms around me and kissed me again, a little more insistently than last time. I couldn't actually process all that had happened in the past thirty-six hours, and wasn't sure I wanted to, right at this moment. I kissed back, with all my mouth.

And, of course, the phone rang.

I shouldn't pick it up. I *knew* I shouldn't pick it up, and yet, there went my hand to the headset, and there went Evan's lips, back to his side of the room, where they believed themselves to belong. Life ain't fair.

'This is Nate Garrigan,' the voice said after I admitted to being Sandy. 'I'm the investigator working the McNabb case for you.'

'Oh hi, Nate. Nice to meet you. But it's a little late, so why don't we do this in the . . .'

'You don't understand. I'm calling with a situation. I was out doing some preliminary interviews with a few people who knew the victim. I think you need to talk to your client.'

'McNabb? I just left him a few hours ago. What's the problem?'

'Well,' Garrigan said with a perplexed, if not annoyed, air, 'so far I've visited four of the victim's friends and her sister. And every one of them says your client has been here ahead of me. He told them he's investigating the case himself.'

I don't have to work on his defense any more, I told myself. *I have to work on my own, because I'm going to kill him!*

ELEVEN

Nate Garrigan turned out to be a large man in his fifties, who must have been an ex-cop – he would have been perfect as a station house extra in a tough police movie. With a face that had obviously come into contact with a large, hard object at some point in his life, Garrigan was also not one for levity, and standing in the driveway of Patrick McNabb's 'house,' Garrigan looked especially unamused.

'The man's stopping me from doing my job,' he said as I gawked at the huge Tudor mansion and wondering if this was where all Hollywood bachelors came after their marriages broke up. 'All the witnesses are talked out, and they think I'm just mopping up for the big TV star who's *really* going to solve the crime. It's no way to work.'

I nodded with great sympathy, and Evan, who'd insisted on

driving me ('you're so tired you'd wrap yourself around a telephone pole, and besides, you have no car'), looked dour, as if
he was deciding whether to hang McNabb by his toes or some-
place more sensitive.

'Believe me, Mr Garrigan, I feel your pain,' I said. 'He's been
doing this to me for three days now, and I'll be with him all the
way to the end of his trial.'

'God be with you,' said Garrigan.

'Now, here's what we'll do,' I continued. 'We'll go in there,
and we'll explain to him why he has to stop doing these interviews.
He'll agree, and he'll be convincing, but he'll be lying. So we'll
explain it again. And he'll be annoyed that we're telling him what
we've already told him, and he'll insist that he gets the message.
This, too, will not be true. So, we'll be forced to tie him to a chair
and hire someone to feed him and take him to the bathroom for
the next six months. How does that sound?'

'Sounds like a plan to me,' Garrigan said, nodding.

'Yeah, that works,' Evan agreed.

'Let's go.'

The lights were on in the windows, and Patrick's vintage Aston
Martin was parked at the main entrance to the cozy little twenty-
three-room cottage. I rang the doorbell, and we stood in the
entrance for some time. Receiving no response, I rang again.

Nothing.

My mind, against its will, began to worry about Patrick.
Suppose he's so distraught he's trying to kill himself, I
thought. *Suppose he hears the bell but won't come to the
door out of pride, or simple inertia at the events of the past
few days. Suppose . . .*

The door opened and standing before us was a butler so dapper
he could have been a tuxedo model, with the kind of complete
contempt for visitors only a truly cultivated servant can have.

'May I help you?'

'We're here to see Mr McNabb,' I told him, trying to see past
the man. 'Would you tell him his attorney is here?'

'Mr McNabb is not in,' the butler said. He was standing so
straight and tall, I had to sneak a peek to make sure he didn't
actually have an ironing board stuffed up the back of his coat.
He didn't.

Wait a minute. What does he mean, he's not in?

'Are you sure?' I asked, realizing what a stupid question that was. 'Isn't that his car in the driveway?' I pointed to the vintage British sports car.

'That is *one* of his automobiles,' Ironing Board said. 'It is part of his collection. From a James Bond film, I believe.'

'*Goldfinger*,' Garrigan said admiringly. 'That's the car from *Goldfinger*.' He sounded like he might actually be having a spontaneous sexual experience just standing in the entranceway.

'A replica,' the butler noted with a disapproving tone.

'So, he's out in one of his other automobiles?' Evan asked, clearly trying to break Garrigan of his reverie, but the ex-cop's eyes could barely stand to leave the car. 'We do need to speak to him.'

'He said he would be back . . . nine-ish,' Ironing Board said, his tongue slumming over the word. 'That isn't long from now. Perhaps you could come back later.'

Garrigan's eyes never left the Aston Martin, but his eyebrows rose and his voice became louder and more insistent. '*Perhaps*,' he said, 'we can come in and wait. *Perhaps* you can call him and tell him that the people who're trying to keep him out of *jail* are here and need to speak to him immediately. *Perhaps*.'

The butler, who probably wouldn't have been rattled if someone had set his pants on fire, moved into what seemed a more comfortable mode, which was condescension. 'Oh, very well,' he said. 'If you must. I will try Mr McNabb's mobile phone.' He moved aside.

The entrance hall was huge and marble. But it looked like a well-preserved museum rather than a home. There were glass cases, lit expertly, at various places throughout the room, on either side of the immense marble columns holding up the ceiling. I felt like I was entering the Great Shrine of Movies.

The cases held such artifacts as a space pistol of some sort from a science fiction movie (I wasn't much for all the space sagas – fiery explosions in oxygen-free space? Come on!), a large pointy tooth, a man's shoe (rather large), a false mustache, and a bottle of ketchup.

It was like entering the Louvre and seeing, in place of the *Mona Lisa*, a Chuck Jones animation cel. Still nice, but not exactly what I'd call high art.

Garrigan, who apparently was a movie fan of a very enthusiastic sort, was absolutely enthralled by what he saw, and could identify every artifact, despite the lack of any identifying plaques.

'That's from *Forbidden Planet!*' he said when he passed the space blaster. 'And look! That tooth is from *Jaws!* I'll bet it's the one they took out of the side of the boat! And the ketchup bottle.' He looked at the butler. '*Rebel Without A Cause?*'

The butler could barely contain his contempt. '*American Graffiti,*' he said, as if it should have been obvious.

'This place is *amazing,*' Garrigan gushed. The tying-McNabb-to-the-chair plan was fast losing one proponent.

Evan looked merely disapproving – except when he looked at me. Then he always managed a warm smile. It was a little scary.

'When do you expect Mr McNabb to be back?' I asked Ironing Board.

'I would be surprised if he were not here in a very few moments,' the Starched One said with great weight, as if he'd foreseen the future.

Apparently he had, because Patrick McNabb then opened the huge oak door, walked in, and stopped in his tracks when he saw the three visitors in his entrance hall. He was carrying a small shopping bag marked 'Bergdorf Goodman.'

'Sandy!' he shouted, all beer and skittles (*or something British like that,* I thought). 'How lovely to see you!'

'Patrick, we need to talk,' I said. 'Where can we sit?'

'Meadows, have you kept them waiting?' Patrick admonished the butler. 'This is my attorney, and she's . . .' He stopped himself, and turned impishly to me. 'Sorry. I was going to say the "b" word.'

Evan's eyes widened, but I shook my head. Not *that* 'b' word.

'And this is the young man who follows her around,' Patrick continued, looking at the hooded-faced Evan. 'What is your name again, lad?'

'Evan D'Arbanville, Mr McNabb.'

'Of course. And this fellow I don't really know, do I?'

Garrigan turned and pointed at one of the cases. 'Nate Garrigan, Mr McNabb. I'm the firm investigator assigned to your case. May I ask you – this shoe?'

Patrick's head turned quickly. '*What* shoe?'

'The one in this case, sir. What movie is that from?'

Patrick approached the case with reverence. 'Ah, that one,' he said. 'That's from *North By Northwest*. Mr Cary Grant himself wore that shoe in the famous crop dusting scene.'

Garrigan looked like he might genuflect. 'My goodness,' is all he could manage.

'Indeed,' Patrick agreed. He put down the shopping bag and gestured to us. 'Please. Follow me.'

We walked into a large library, where the shelves that would normally be lined with books were instead crowded with movie memorabilia, ranging from scripts to Academy Award statuettes (none of which had been awarded to Patrick). After the requisite gushing by Garrigan, I managed to shift the conversation to McNabb's case, and his insistent meddling in it.

Patrick, of course, dropped his jaw and stared at me. 'I didn't ask you to investigate,' he said. 'I was doing it myself.'

'Which is *exactly* what I asked you *not* to do,' I responded immediately.

'You mean you want to do it yourself?'

I gave Garrigan a desperate look, and the investigator finally seemed to remember why he was there. 'Mr McNabb,' he said in the best gargled-with-glass-slivers voice I'd ever heard. 'The accused doesn't do the investigating. The lawyer doesn't do the investigating. The *investigator* does the investigating. That's me.' He pointed to himself, just to make the point a little clearer.

'So, you want me to come with you? Is that it?'

Evan stepped forward, practically wringing his hands with pent-up frustration. 'Mr McNabb, I believe you're deliberately trying to misunderstand us, so when you do what you intend to do anyway, you can pretend we didn't ask you specifically not to. Well, I'm going to tell you to your face – *you don't get to do any investigating*. This is not a TV show. Your life is on the line. So stop trying to twist our words – we don't want you anywhere *near* witnesses who might help or hurt our case. Is that clear?'

I'm going to have to talk to him about that 'our case' stuff, I thought.

'Look, sonny, I'm only keeping you on this case because Sandy asked for you. Otherwise, I'd have told Junius Bach I want you to go back to . . . whatever it is you do and leave me alone. So don't ever talk to me like that again, you understand?' Patrick turned his body away from Evan's direct onslaught and faced me. 'I'll do whatever Sandy tells me to do. Sandy?'

And, naturally, my cell phone rang. Startled, I checked the number, which was local. Nobody in town had this number.

'Hello?'

'Ms Moss, this is Detective Lieutenant K.C. Trench of the Los Angeles Police Department.'

'Lieutenant Trench,' I said, trying to get Patrick's attention as the other two men snapped their heads in my direction. 'How did you get this number?'

'We're the police department, Ms Moss. We're allowed to do things like that. Do you have any idea where your client, Mr McNabb, might be?'

Questions like this are never good.

'Yes, I'm here with him in his home, Lieutenant. How can we help you?'

'Well, Ms Moss, it seems that a piece of evidence from the crime scene is missing, and one of our uniforms said he saw Mr McNabb at the house not more than an hour or two ago.'

I looked at Patrick and gave him a very hard stare, to indicate he should pay attention. 'Something is missing from the scene, *Lieutenant*?'

Patrick looked away.

'That's right.' Trench clearly knew I was signaling Patrick and stalling for time. 'And we know he was there not long ago.'

'You say they saw Mr McNabb at the house an hour ago?'

Patrick stared at his feet.

'Yes, Ms Moss,' Trench exhaled, not pleased. 'Is there anything else you want to tell your client, or should I talk to him directly?'

'My client has no information on this matter, Lieutenant. May I ask what's missing?'

'A pair of tap shoes that once belonged to James Cagney. I understand your client was fighting over them with his wife at their divorce settlement conference, and the shoes were the point of contention. In fact, I'm told that's when he threatened to kill her.'

TWELVE

'Someone is leaking information to the police,' I told Evan in the car on the way home. My eyes were closed, partially because I hadn't slept in more than forty hours, and partly because Evan was the slowest, most meticulous driver I'd ever seen, and it was impossible to watch him go about his business so deliberately without actually crying out in anguish.

'Because they knew about the shoes?' he answered. 'Anyone could have told them that.'

'Yeah, but Lieutenant Trench knew about the argument at the divorce conference, right down to the part about Patrick threatening Patsy, or at least using those words. I don't think he meant them literally.' I sat back as far as I could in the seat, but in a four-year-old Toyota, that wasn't very far. Not that my late, lamented Hyundai would have been any better. How was I going to afford a new car? Once Bach fired me I wouldn't even be able to afford my apartment.

'You just don't want to think that. She ended up dead the night after he threatened to kill her. That's some coincidence,' Evan said, staring at the road with the concentration of a diamond cutter. (I had opened my eyes for a moment, then closed them again.)

'Don't color this because you don't like him,' I scolded, though I had to admit I couldn't actually counter his argument. 'Besides, you're going off on a tangent. The point was, somebody is talking to the cops.'

'Anybody could have told Trench about that comment.'

'No, anybody couldn't. It had to be someone at the conference, because we were the only ones who heard it.' I didn't open my eyes, and now the motion of the car was making me even sleepier. 'I know it wasn't me, I doubt it was Patrick, and we can eliminate Patsy.'

'It was probably McNabb.'

I ignored that. 'That leaves Patsy's lawyers, the two assistants, and Junius Bach.'

Evan sniffed. 'Why would Bach do that?'

'He probably wouldn't. I'm just saying he was there, and he *could* have done it if he wanted to.' My own voice was starting to sound very far away.

'Who were Patsy's lawyers? I wasn't at the conference, you'll remember.'

'I don't think anyone said their names.' There was a long pause. 'I'll have to look in the file.'

And then I fell asleep.

When I regained some semblance of consciousness, Evan had pulled the car up to the curb in front of my building, and appeared to be trying to determine if the space was a legal one. I blinked an indeterminate number of times, and reached into my purse for the access card to the underground garage. 'Here,' I said. 'You can park in the garage. Or you can just drop me off.'

'I think I'll park and come up,' Evan said with the hint of a grin. 'Just to make sure you don't fall asleep in the elevator.'

He parked the car in the lamentably empty space normally reserved for my car, and we took the elevator to my floor. I noticed that Evan was back in his 'good boyfriend' mode, keeping his distance but waiting for me to be ready. *So what's not to be ready?* my Inner Angie was asking. *Look at him! You should be ready!*

I am ready, I answered her. *But right now, I'm mostly tired. I'll be ready tomorrow. I swear.*

Yeah, sure.

Leave it to me to have a sarcastic best friend in my head.

As we walked silently to the apartment door, I got my keys out. When we stopped at the door and I unlocked it, I looked up at Evan.

'Um, I'm not asking you in, but it's only because I'm so tired, OK?' I said. 'I don't want you to think . . .'

'I'm not thinking,' he said. 'I don't want to take advantage of a woman who hasn't slept since the Obama Administration. Besides, you haven't had a shower, and you smell bad.' He was kidding, but I could have lived without the reminder.

'I'm glad you understand,' I said, opening the door.

Then I gasped.

'Someone's been inside here,' I managed to say, just a decibel or two above a whisper.

Evan looked in, and then stared at me, bewildered. 'How can you tell?'

'You don't understand.'

The apartment was immaculate. Everything was in its place. The books were on their shelves, the paintings were hung, the clothes were nowhere to be seen. There was a fresh bouquet of roses on the coffee table, and in the kitchen, where every speck of food was put away, the smell of a slow-roasted turkey filled the air.

'No,' Evan said. 'Clearly, I don't. But if you were expecting someone else to be here, you should've just told me.'

'I'm not expecting someone else. I don't *know* anyone else on this coast. Evan, when I left for work, all my moving stuff was still in cartons. I'd barely made a dent in the pile, and this place looked like the Salvation Army had thrown up all over it. Somebody broke in and neatened things up for me.'

Evan walked a little farther into the apartment, and examined the vase of flowers. 'Someone sure did.' He picked up a card lying next to the flowers, and handed it to me. 'Here. It's for you.'

From the envelope, which said simply, 'Sandy,' I removed a printed note:

Perhaps this will make up for all the trouble I've caused you. Please enjoy the dinner. – Patrick.

'Well, that was sweet,' I said aloud.

'Yeah, wasn't it?' said Evan, a definite edge to his voice.

My mouth twisted in one direction. 'Now, what's *that* supposed to mean?'

'It means he's trying to buy your trust, and it means he knew the place was a mess, which in turn means he got to see your apartment before . . . anyone else did.'

'He had special circumstances. He was in the car when we were being shot at.' I couldn't believe Evan would choose this moment to become jealous. Figures. *You should've slept with him when you had the chance.* I told my Inner Angie to shut up.

'Right. Well, everything's right where it should be, so I'll be going,' Evan said. 'Enjoy your dinner . . . with whomever happens to come by.' Even in a huff, I noted, he used proper grammar.

'Oh, don't be ridiculous. I'm going straight to bed.' But Evan was already walking to the door.

'I'll bet you are,' he said, and walked out. Probably wondering what that meant.

Just to show Evan, I ate a healthy portion of the turkey and the accompanying mashed potatoes before I went to bed. I skipped the Brussels sprouts. Let that be a lesson to him, and to Brussels.

I didn't wake up the next morning until eleven, and immediately began worrying that I'd lost my job for being late, and my best boyfriend prospect for being tired. Then I realized the office would have called if they were concerned about me, and with such a high-profile case on my hands, it was unlikely they'd be asking me to leave anytime soon. No doubt Bach would fire me the second Patrick was convicted.

As for the boyfriend . . . well, one out of two isn't all that bad.

The first thing to do (after a turkey sandwich for breakfast and a long, hot shower) was to call my client. There had been a lot of unanswered questions when I'd left Patrick's house the night before, and besides, I hadn't thanked him for getting all my stuff put away. Besides, I didn't know where anything was in my apartment now, and I wanted the name of the service he'd used.

Meadows answered the phone with a voice you could spread on a cracker without creating so much as a crumb. 'McNabb residence,' he intoned.

'Hi, Meadows old boy. It's Sandy Moss. Is Patrick there?' Fueled by sleep and food, I was feeling extremely chipper – until he answered me.

'No, Ms Moss, I'm afraid he's out. He'll be addressing the graduating class at UCLA Law School this noon.'

Of course he will. The rest of the world is normal, and I'm losing my mind. It all makes sense now.

'He's doing what?'

'Do you wish me to repeat it?'

I did not.

I found Patrick McNabb standing in front of two hundred smiling, black-gowned graduates, himself in a mortarboard and gown, at a podium overlooking the class. My Uber let me off near the grounds, where I could hear him before I could see him.

'. . . so the intent of the law and the actual rule of the law are not always going to be the same thing,' Patrick was saying in his Arthur Kirkland voice. 'Justice is not always exactly what is written in the books, and legality – if you'll pardon the plug' – the crowd chuckled – 'is not always what we feel is right in our hearts. A good attorney must balance that knowledge of the law, the respect for the word on the page, with compassion, with interpretation, and above all, with humanity. Without that, the law serves no one, and every attorney is merely a slave to it. Go out today – well, maybe not *today* – and temper your judgment with emotion, but always, *always*, do what you think is right, even if it requires a leap of faith. Then, and only then, will you have lived up to the promise that you have made today. Thank you.'

Patrick walked back to his seat among distinguished-looking men and women, all of whom were standing and applauding, as the crowd of young law graduates leapt to its feet and began roaring approval. I walked to the side of the podium, and caught Patrick's eye. He smiled broadly, and as the next speaker began with, 'Well, I don't know how I can top *that*,' Patrick walked to where I was standing.

'Did you hear?' he asked. 'Did you catch my speech?'

'I heard the end of it,' I answered. 'Patrick . . .'

'Wasn't it *great*? All those lawyers listening to me explain my philosophy of the law. It was the most gratifying experience of my career.' From behind the podium, Patrick led me out of the sun, where there was a cooler holding cans of soda. He took one, and handed another to me.

'First of all, those weren't lawyers. They were law school graduates,' I pointed out. 'They still have to pass the bar to practice law. And someone probably wrote that speech for you. You don't *have* a philosophy of the law – you're an actor, not a lawyer, Patrick! Are you out of your mind?'

'You didn't like it?'

'That's not the point! Stop missing the point! Patrick, you've been accused of murder, you're a defendant in a homicide, and you're an actor. How could you address the graduating class of a law school?'

He stuck out his lower lip like a six-year-old. 'They asked me,' he said.

'From now on, you don't appear in public without talking to me first. Understand? You don't talk to a reporter without clearing it through me first. Jesus Christ, I'm amazed they're not swarming all over you right now.' I'd noticed the diminished press presence as I approached, and wondered how the law school had managed that.

'I think they're satisfied. I spoke to them before the graduation ceremonies began.'

I felt the blood drain from my face. 'You did what?'

'Gave a little press conference. They asked their questions and I gave my answers. My publicist said she thought it would be best to face the issues head-on, so I decided I'd do that, and maybe public opinion would . . .'

'I don't care about public opinion! I care about the jury pool and the impression that you're living the high life after killing your wife! Patrick, you absolutely have to do what I tell you to do, and ask about anything else before you do it. Do you understand?'

'But I *didn't* kill my wife.'

I thought first about finding a dentist in Los Angeles, because, at this pace, I was certain I'd grind my teeth to a fine powder within two days. 'Maybe you didn't, Patrick,' I managed to squeeze out, 'but if you don't start following my instructions, *I'm* going to kill you!'

The sound came from high above, from one of the buildings on one side of the quad. It didn't sound like a gunshot, but like a balloon popping. I barely gave it a thought until I saw the expression on Patrick's face, and the blood on his robe.

'Sandy,' he said. 'I think I've been shot.' And with that, he fell to his knees.

THIRTEEN

I t took the ambulance sixteen hours to arrive. At least, that's how it felt. My screaming stopped the graduation cold, brought a huge crowd to my side, and produced in excess of sixty cell phones, all dialing 911 at the same moment. Newspaper reports would later claim the line was overloaded at that moment, and that three burglaries, a sexual assault, and a convenience store robbery were put on hold, but that wasn't true. It was only one burglary.

In fact, the ambulance (the first one) arrived in seven minutes, and a second arrived shortly thereafter, only to be told it wasn't necessary. The TV star was big, but not so big as to require two separate transports to the hospital.

Regulations required that only an immediate family member could ride with the patient, but my insistence that I was Mr McNabb's cousin, his attorney, and his oldest and dearest friend, coupled with my tearful yelps, as well as the star's fading but still powerful smile, managed to get me on the ride with Patrick, and as he was examined, I sat nearby and wept piteously. It was something of an embarrassment.

'I'm fine,' Patrick managed, but he wasn't a good enough actor to hide his panic and pain. 'Please, Sandy, don't make a fuss.'

I couldn't manage coherent words. What came out of my mouth was more in the category of squeaks and mumbles, punctuated by long, deep breaths.

'Check his BP,' one MTS technician told the other, but a cuff was already being fixed to Patrick's arm and his robe was being cut away to assess the damage done by the bullet.

I couldn't quite wrap my mind around the event. One minute, I'd been livid with rage at my client, and the next, he was struck down from far away, bleeding and moaning on the ground at my feet. It was too fast, too illogical, too improbable, for me to grasp all at once. I'd need a day or two. Or maybe a year.

All I could think was, *Please don't die, Patrick. Just don't die and I'll forgive you for being crazy. Don't die, don't die, don't die, don't . . .*

'Patrick,' I managed as the MTS technician blocked my view of my client, 'I never thanked you for having my apartment unpacked. I mean, it was such a sweet gesture, and all I wanted to do was yell at you. I'm such a jerk.'

'Stop it,' Patrick countered with surprising strength. 'You're a friend and you needed help. That's what a friend does. Especially one with money that came too fast and too easily.'

'I'm sorry for everything I ever said to you,' I blubbered on. 'I'm sorry I kept yelling at you, but you wouldn't act like a real client, and . . .'

'Ma'am, if you could please move back a little,' said the second MTS worker. 'We're going to need a little room here.'

I slid down the seat to the farthest point in the ambulance, essentially leaning against the door, which I hoped was locked. The second MTS worker, an African-American woman in her twenties, watched with interest for a moment, then turned in my direction.

'You two been dating long?' she said, cocking her head in Patrick's direction.

'Dating?' I wondered how this woman might have known about Evan, and why she was choosing now to ask me about him. 'Not really. Just . . .'

'Don't worry, I think he'll live,' she answered, a confusing glint of humor in her eye. 'I understand your concern, but . . .'

'*Him?* You think I'm dating Patrick McNabb?' It had finally dawned on me what the technician meant. 'Oh, you don't understand.'

'Sure I do,' the woman answered. 'I can always tell. The ones who force their way onto the ambulance are always the ones who care the most. I'll bet you guys last a long, long time.'

'I'm not . . . we don't . . . no, no, no.' Suddenly, there was a sharp intake of breath and a moan from Patrick's direction, and, startled by the sound, I stopped protesting. And all the while, my brain kept shouting, *Don't die, don't die, don't die, don't die . . .*

'He's such a drama queen,' I said, sprawled on the couch in my newly neatened apartment, and talking into my wireless phone. 'A little scratch on the arm, and you'd think he was dying. All that carrying on. It was barely visible. They let him out of the hospital with six stitches and some cream to put on it. Honestly.' So I'm a hypocrite.

Angie's voice on the other end was far less casual. 'I can't *believe* he got shot right next to you, Sand! I mean, you probably saved his life!'

'Oh, give me a break. It barely bled . . . I was scared for a minute before I knew where he'd been hit, but . . .'

'For crissakes, Sandy, somebody was *shooting* at him. That's the second time in two days, and you were with him! What does that say to you?'

I thought hard and long, and my voice was much less forceful when I said, 'It says maybe they were shooting at *me*.'

FOURTEEN

The news of the shooting was a media event that eclipsed the news of the murder, which had eclipsed the news of a public official's dalliance with an office worker, which had eclipsed . . . well, you get the idea.

After only two weeks in Los Angeles, I had to have my landline changed to an unlisted number. It was the price of fame, which I reminded myself I'd never sought. It had come barreling after me like a locomotive.

Patrick, who'd driven himself home from the hospital (after having 'a car sent round'), seemed to enjoy the attention, and was actually back on the set of *Legality* later that afternoon. He did hire himself a security team to follow him around, including a very large, very intimidating bodyguard named Rex, who snarled at anyone who came close to Patrick, and who probably bared his teeth if that didn't work. Rex, surprisingly, was not a Doberman Pinscher, but a human. Sort of.

Lt Trench did not arrive personally, but sent one of his detectives, Sergeant Roberts, to question Patrick and me at the hospital. We told him what we knew, and he looked skeptical and left.

The *Legality* producers, apparently, did not much mind having an accused murderer in their midst, so long as he did the proper publicity and ratings spiked to see how his character would get through the travails plotted for him by the same producers, almost all of whom were on the writing staff.

They did, however, plan a special announcement to run before the Sunday night episode, and had to cut forty-five seconds from the show in order to accommodate it. An extra, who had one line of dialogue (and therefore would have received her Screen Actors Guild card until the cut was made), was not amused. Patrick promised to specially request her the very next time an extra would get a speaking line. I'm sure he crinkled his eyes at her, too, and she left smiling.

I went to my office, where the usual throng of reporters was gathering, and did my best to read over the paperwork in Patrick's case again, trying to determine exactly how I could disprove the guilt of a man who had sex with a woman and, then, less than an hour later, was found standing over her body, trying desperately to pull an arrow from her chest.

Still, what ate at me was the swiftness of the police department's assumption that Patrick was the killer. Circumstantial evidence was persuasive, but it wasn't such a slam-dunk that the investigation should have been concluded within three hours of the murder.

They had to have something else, something I didn't know about.

I hadn't been considering the matter long when the phone rang and Garrigan was on the other end. At the home of Patsy DeNunzio's sister, he had 'a question for the defense attorney.' That, I reminded myself, was me.

'Can a witness be given immunity by the defense?' Garrigan wanted to know. Clearly, he was putting on a show for the sister, because any ex-cop would know the answer to this one and wouldn't bother calling the attorney for clarification.

'No, we can't offer anything,' I explained patiently. 'Only the prosecution can offer immunity for testimony.'

'That's what I thought,' Garrigan said. He paused, obviously turning to Patsy's sister. 'Yeah, if your information's good, we can strike a deal,' he told her.

'WHAT?' I shouted.

I could hear Garrigan put his hand over the phone. After a moment, his voice returned, this time much quieter. 'I think you'd better get over here,' he said. 'She's willing to talk, but she wants assurances.'

'Assurances?' I said. 'I can't *give* assurances.'

'Sure you can. I'll see you soon.' And he gave me an address in Long Beach.

Calculating the cost of a taxi ride to Long Beach (and assuming it would set me back about a month's rent), I started for the elevator when Holiday Wentworth stopped me in the hallway.

'Sandy, I'm glad I caught you. One of the secretaries said there was a delivery for you at the front desk.' Holiday dashed off so quickly I couldn't thank her for the information.

At the desk, I asked for any messages. The secretary, a woman named Felicity (honestly!), whose paper-thinness indicated she had indeed stepped off the pages of a fashion magazine, said nothing, but handed me an envelope. I opened it, and found a set of car keys attached to a remote device. I looked back at Felicity and asked, 'Who left this for me?'

'A very big guy who's been working out a lot came by and said Patrick McNabb wanted you to have it,' Felicity said in the least interested voice I'd ever heard. 'Something about making up for your car. I don't know.'

'How am I supposed to figure out which car it's for?'

'Go down to the parking level, push the button, and see what happens.' Felicity went back to looking gorgeous, her full-time job.

In the elevator on the way down, it occurred to me that there had been two attempts on my life in the past two days. Inasmuch as I considered this a bad thing, I decided to take steps to make sure a third attack did not take place. I pulled out my cell phone and called the number Patrick had given me.

I got Rex. 'Did Mr McNabb leave something for me at my office?' I asked.

'Wait. I'll get him.'

'You could just answer the . . .' But Rex was gone.

Patrick picked up a few moments later. 'Sandy! I told Rex he should get me if you called. I hope you're all right after what happened yesterday.'

He hoped *I* was all right? He was the one who got shot! 'I'm fine, Patrick,' I said. 'I'm just checking. There was an envelope waiting for me at the office.'

'Yes. It contains a set of car keys. I had a car sent round for you.'

'Why?'

'Because you didn't have one,' he said, with a tone that made it clear I must be insane. 'I felt responsible, what with the bullet holes and all.'

'You're not responsible. The people with the guns are responsible.' The elevator doors opened, and I walked out into the parking level. 'Anyway, I just wanted to be sure. You know, with all that's been happening, I wanted to be certain the keys came from you.'

'Were you afraid the car would blow up?'

'Something like that.' I knew I sounded foolish.

'Well, it won't. It's a red . . .'

But I had already pushed the button and seen the headlights flash. '. . . A red Ferrari,' I said with wonder. 'A new one.'

'Yes.' *Sure. Happens every day.*

'Patrick, that's a two hundred thousand dollar car.'

'Have you priced one? Actually, to be accurate, the two hundred thousand would be for one without any of the extras. With the moon-roof and the custom audio system, it's . . .'

'Don't tell me.' I started walking toward the car, which, luckily, had not blown up. 'I don't want to know. Patrick, why didn't you just send me a Honda or something?'

'Don't you like Ferraris?' he asked.

'I wouldn't know. I've never even seen one up close before. We don't have a great many Ferraris driving around in New Jersey.'

I reached the car and opened the door. Even the remote entry key was a novelty for me. My lamented Hyundai had the old fuddy-duddy keys you had to actually insert into the door locks.

'Well, you'll love it,' he said.

'It'll scare me. This car probably costs more than any house I've ever lived in.' *But the leather seats were soft, weren't they?*

'Don't worry about it. You deserve it.' Patrick sounded so chipper. I figured it must be the painkillers.

'Well, it's only for a few days until my car is back.' I started the Ferrari, wincing that it might explode on ignition, but it started so quietly I wondered if it was even running.

'Oh, no. That's for you to keep, Sandy. For your trouble.'

He's kidding. Surely he's kidding. TELL me he's kidding!

'You're kidding.'

'I'm not. And that settles it. The car is yours. By the way, where are you going?'

Oops. 'Going? Where am I going?'

'Yes,' he said. 'I was just wondering if you'd have a drive on the freeway to test out the car.'

OK. Don't tell him. If you don't tell him, you can't get in trouble.

So of course, I told him. 'I'm meeting Garrigan to talk to a witness. He asked me to come and offer legal advice.' After all, Patrick was on the set of his show; he couldn't just up and leave whenever he wanted to.

'I'll come meet you!' he said.

It was then that I began to feel disappointed that the car had, indeed, not blown up.

FIFTEEN

'I helped Patrick steal the shoes,' said Melanie DeNunzio, a short, slim, slightly mousy version of her late younger sister. 'I talked to one of the cops while Patrick went inside and took out the shoes.'

The house was a small clapboard Cape Cod near the beach. With five rooms, it seemed comfortable, but hardly luxurious. A six-year-old blue Acura sat in the driveway. Not what you'd expect from someone so closely related to a woman who'd been making millions for more than a decade.

'Why?' Garrigan asked. Patrick hadn't arrived at the house yet, so Garrigan and I were trying to get as much done as possible before he could walk in and . . . be Patrick. And yes, Garrigan had almost caused me physical pain with the look he had given me when I mentioned Patrick was on his way. And frankly, I wasn't sure why I'd told Patrick where I'd be – no doubt some misplaced sympathy for the shooting victim, and maybe a little guilty appreciation for the guy who had given – *lent!* – me a Ferrari.

Melanie looked at the floor, with its relatively cheap wall-to-wall carpet, and blushed a little. 'I'd do pretty much anything for Patrick,' she said. 'I'm . . .'

'You're in love with him,' I said, and Melanie nodded, a little embarrassed.

'Not *really*,' she said. 'You know, not like I want to marry him or something. But you have to admit, he's awful cute, you know, and well, having him around all the time when they were married, I just got . . . attracted to him. You know.'

No, I don't know! I'm not attracted to Patrick McNabb! I'm not!

'So he asked you to distract the cop while he went in to get Cagney's shoes? Is that it?' Garrigan didn't seem to care who was attracted to whom. He just wanted some answers before the doorbell rang.

Melanie shook her head. 'He didn't *ask*,' she said. 'He just . . . he said he was going over to check some things out, to see if they'd found anything that would make it clear he didn't kill Patsy. But I knew he wanted Jimmy's shoes. That was the only thing in the whole house he really cared about, and he'd mentioned them at least six times that day.'

'You distracted the cop at the door.'

'Yeah. You know, sometimes I can look nice. And if I put some effort into it, guys can notice me. Not like Patsy, but they do. You know.' Melanie clearly thought everybody knew everything, except her.

She never looked anyone in the face. She spent most of her time looking at the carpet, as if the answers were scribbled there. But I guessed Melanie was a woman who'd been overshadowed all her life, and wasn't comfortable with people who looked *at* her rather than *past* her.

Unlike me, Garrigan wasn't worried about the pathos on display. Apparently, he merely wanted a trail to follow. 'What was so important about those shoes?' he asked. It was an interesting question from a man who had practically fainted at the sight of Cary Grant's Oxford.

But we didn't have time to hear an answer, because Patrick McNabb let himself in through the front door, which Melanie had left unlocked. 'Hello, all!' he shouted as Garrigan gave me the kind of look strychnine would give you if it had eyes.

'What have I missed?' Patrick's tone was so happy, it seemed to me he might be taking some kind of prescription drugs that 'doctors' let celebrities have for 'exhaustion.'

Garrigan turned to him. 'Melanie was telling us how she helped you steal Cagney's shoes out of Patsy's house.' The investigator clearly preferred the full frontal assault, trying to catch Patrick off guard.

But I was learning that off guard was not a position Patrick knew well. 'No she didn't,' he said. 'I went in to get some shirts I brought with me that night. I'd stopped at Bergdorf's on the way, and forgot to take them with me when I left.' He gave Garrigan a pointed look. 'I didn't think they qualified as *evidence*,' he said.

'Shirts,' Garrigan said.

'Yes. A blue and a white. Would you like to see them?'

'Patrick,' I said, hoping the two men might not mark their territory in the house. 'How do you explain the fact that the shoes disappeared from the house at just about the same time you were there?'

'I can't,' he said. 'I checked on them, and they were in their case when I went to pick up the shirts. I didn't touch them.'

Garrigan looked at Melanie. 'Did you see the package when he brought it out?'

She looked at Patrick, then at Garrigan, as if deciding. 'He had a bag that said "Bergdorf Goodman" on it,' she said. 'I thought Jimmy's shoes were in the bag. They were all he ever talked about.'

'Sorry, darling,' Patrick said to her in a soft voice. 'I never did take those shoes out of the house. If they're missing now, someone else has them.'

Melanie looked at him with the most pitiable expression I'd ever seen, one that spoke of absolute trust, admiration, and devotion for a man who'd forget she existed the minute he walked out the door. And the sad part was that Melanie knew it, and still felt that way.

'I'm sorry, Patrick,' she said. 'I didn't mean to place any more suspicion on you.'

'Not to worry, my dear,' he replied. 'You did what you thought was right.'

What I thought would be right at this moment was to throw up, but I managed not to do it. I couldn't possibly have had more contempt for Patrick McNabb than I felt right now – the man was clearly stringing along a poor damaged woman for reasons that fed only his ego. Could you withdraw as counsel because your client continually pissed you off?

Patrick turned to me, a wide grin on his face. 'So,' he said to the gathered group, 'who shall we go visit now?'

There was little else to do. Melanie clearly wouldn't say anything Patrick didn't want to hear while he was in the room, and even if she did, he'd be able to twist it into any pretzel he wanted as effortlessly as the rest of us respirate. So we bade Melanie a good day and walked out into the unrelenting sunshine to head for our cars.

'I've just been dropped off,' Patrick said to me, a glint of mischief in his eyes. 'Do you mind giving me a lift back?'

I'd rather give you a kick in the . . .

'Not at all,' I said, amazed anything was audible through my clenched teeth. 'It's your car.'

'No, the car's all yours. Your name is on the title.'

I just didn't have the energy to argue. To test the range of the car's 'unlock' button, I pushed it while standing at the front door of Melanie's house.

This time, the car blew up.

SIXTEEN

Lieutenant K.C. Trench of the Los Angeles Police Department was a very dapper, distinguished-looking man in his mid-fifties, silver hair very nicely cut and combed, suit well pressed, shoes shiny. But he didn't give the impression of someone who fussed over each detail – it was more as if the clothes he wore and the body on which he wore them were too intimidated to even consider defying his will.

Sitting across a desk from Trench in his office, I briefly considered defying his will, but that was as far as I got. Actually refusing to answer Trench would require more courage than I could muster.

'Explain to me why you were driving a two hundred thousand dollar Ferrari in the first place,' Trench said with a hint of superiority in his voice. He knew the answer, his tone was saying. He just needed me to say it out loud for the record. I thought I should observe his technique closely and take notes for when I had to cross-examine witnesses at trial.

Through the window in Trench's office, I glanced at Patrick, sitting across the hall, being questioned by another detective. Patrick was smiling and appeared to be having a fine time. I felt like I was being placed in an enormous pasta-making machine. Some people have the capacity to relax in any situation, and then there are the other ninety-nine percent of us.

'It was a . . . loaner,' I answered.

'A loaner.' Trench raised one eyebrow, and it had as much effect as if another man had hit me across the jaw with a closed fist. If he raised both eyebrows, I'd probably confess to the Kennedy assassination. Both of them. And I wasn't even born then.

'Yes. My car is in the shop, so I got this one to borrow until it was fixed.'

Trench sat down behind his immaculate desk, which looked as if it were not only neatened but vacuumed, polished, and refinished on a daily basis. He sat back in his chair, his hands joined behind his head, and still looked as if he might pounce out of his chair and attack me if I said the wrong thing.

'Interesting,' he said. 'That fails to explain why the car was registered in your name yesterday. It does not explain why *another* car, also registered in your name, is currently undergoing body work at Bob's Auto Body Shop in the City of Industry, to repair damage caused by gunfire. As a criminal attorney you should know body shops are required to report bullet holes in cars they repair. It also fails to explain where you suddenly came up with two hundred thousand dollars to pay for a car, since it seems to have been bought with cash. Now, can you shed some light on these questions?'

The man's fingernails glistened. He must have had regular manicures. I shuddered to think about his toenails.

'It's very simple. Well, OK, it's not *very* simple. It's just . . . here's what happened. My car, which is the 2009 Hyundai in the body shop, was involved in an incident two days ago during which guns fired at it. Obviously, it required some repair, so . . .'

'*Guns* were fired at it?' Trench leaned forward and put his hands on his desk. 'Guns – more than one gun – were fired at your car two days ago, and this is the first the police are hearing about it?'

'Well,' I said, 'I don't know if it was more than one gun. It might have been one gun firing a number of bullets. I was driving, so I couldn't see . . .'

'Why didn't you report the shooting?' Trench pronounced every consonant. The man's middle name was probably 'Impeccable.' Except that doesn't start with a 'C.'

'This is L.A.,' I said. 'I figured everybody was involved in a drive-by shooting sooner or later. Besides, no one was hurt.'

Trench's surprisingly thin lips were pulled back in a rather controlled smile, one that resembled a straight horizontal line. 'Ms Moss, it is *not* a Southern California social custom to welcome a newcomer by blowing out the back window of her car and seriously threatening her life. We don't like you well enough to do something like that. I also know that a black Escalade, with stolen license plates, was found wrapped around a telephone pole, and a shotgun, all fingerprints and identification numbers removed, was found in its back seat on the day in question. So spare me the cute little evasions and tell me how you came into possession of an extremely expensive automobile that exploded within four hours of being in your possession.' He gave me utterly no wiggle room.

'It was a gift from a client. I intended to give it back as soon as my car was repaired.'

'You only have one client so far,' Trench noted.

'Do the math,' I said.

'So the man accused of murdering his wife, a man who was shot by a sniper yesterday on the campus of UCLA Law School, who I would bet my mortgage was in the car with you when *guns* were fired at it – that man gave you a brand-new Ferrari as a gift after having known you for . . .'

'Three days.'

Trench nodded once or twice, but it seemed more an exercise to loosen his neck muscles. 'Three . . . days. He gave you a Ferrari after three days. You must be some . . .'

'Watch yourself, Trench.'

'. . . lawyer, Ms Moss.' His eyes showed appreciation for my anger – the bully is always respectful of one who stands up to him.

'I am. And in about six to eight months, I'd estimate, you'll be able to see exactly how good a lawyer I am. I imagine you'll be at Mr McNabb's trial.'

'Wouldn't miss it. But I think the six-to-eight months is a little optimistic on your part.' Trench knew something I didn't, and I wasn't happy about it.

'You don't think it'll come to trial that fast?'

'On the contrary. I've been served notice that Judge Fleming has accelerated the court date and you'll be showing me just how good a lawyer you are in about six weeks.'

Six weeks? SIX WEEKS?

'That's not possible, Lieutenant,' I said. 'No court system in the country could . . .'

'We're getting tired of celebrity trials out here, Ms Moss,' Trench said. 'We don't like the spotlight that much, especially on those rare occasions when we lose one.'

'Rare?'

Trench's eyes flashed. 'And so we're trying to expedite this matter as swiftly as possible. The judge has moved this up to the front burner.'

The word *continuance* began playing a continuous loop in my head, and would continue to do so until I could file a motion.

'Now that we've established your need for speed, Ms Moss,' Trench was saying, 'suppose you help your own case along by telling me about the car that shot at you, and then we can talk about the car that blew up a few scant yards from you. You don't seem to have very good luck with vehicles, do you?'

'I was doing fine until I moved here. I think it's you guys, personally.' (This might be the moment to mention that I was doing my best to keep a brave face with the cops, who let's face it were on the prosecution side of the ledger, while my intestines were liquefying over the fact that I could have been in as many pieces as that Ferrari if I'd waited to unlock the car until Patrick and I were standing next to it.)

'That's very amusing,' Trench said, although his face did not look at all amused. 'I must remember it for Skit Night at the next departmental retreat. Very well then, Ms Moss, let's cut to the chase and ask you, who do you think is trying to kill you?'

'I honestly don't have the faintest idea, Lieutenant,' I said. 'I wish I did. If I did, I'd tell you. I swear.'

'Like you told us about the shooting?'

I looked into the hallway. Patrick had been joined by Evan, and the two of them were sitting, one plastic folding chair between their own, but they might as well have been in separate states. Careful not to look at each other, they sat in polar body postures, one sure to change immediately if the other's arms crossed or legs stretched in anything resembling the same position. Four-year-olds would have envied their childishness.

'Is there anything else I can help you with, Lieutenant?' I asked. 'There are two men waiting for me in your hallway.'

Trench had never so much as glanced in their direction. 'Are they waiting for you, Ms Moss, or are they just trying their damnedest not to notice each other?'

'A good question. But if you're really trying to cut down on the violence in this city, perhaps you'd better let me go out there and claim one of them.'

'Oh, all right. But which one are you going to claim?' Trench made it sound dirty.

I didn't know why, but I liked Lieutenant Trench, and I wanted him to like me. 'Cards on the table, Lieutenant? Just between us? Off the record?'

'My lord, aren't there any other clichés you can brandish? Go on.'

'I don't get how Patrick McNabb was arrested so quickly. All the evidence against him is circumstantial, and while I understand he merits suspicion, it's not nearly enough for arrest and arraignment. What have you guys got that's not in the police report?'

Trench's eyes narrowed, and it wasn't with the sarcasm I expected. Something on his face was showing either surprise at my question, or amazement that I'd graduated from high school, let alone passed the bar.

'That depends. Did you get the preliminary police report, or the complete one, with the medical examiner's findings?' OK, so there *was* something Trench knew that he clearly believed I'd known, and it wasn't good.

'I wasn't aware you had issued anything more than one report,' I said.

'You must have picked yours up the night of the arrest. No?' said Trench.

I nodded.

'Your office should have someone here every day for such things, Ms Moss. I'll have the sergeant hand you one of the final reports on your way out. Now, if there's nothing else you care to lie about at the moment, I have other cases on my desk.'

I reached for the door and turned back to face him. Trench's head was already down, and he was reading a file in front of him.

'Thank you, Lieutenant.'

He waved his arm wearily at me as I closed the door.

Both men in the hallway stood as I walked out, and they walked in the same direction toward me, but without appearing to walk together. It was truly something to admire.

But when I reached them, Evan, in a fit of possessiveness, engulfed me in an embrace and held me tight to his chest. Head pushed to the side, I could see Trench through his office window, and he was grinning, or the Trench version of grinning, which was a slight twitch of the upper lip.

I pushed away. 'Evan!'

'Sandy, I'm so sorry. When I heard about the car . . .' He hugged me again, and this time my head was pointed toward Patrick, who merely looked sour.

'Really,' Patrick said in his most British of accents, 'we weren't anywhere *near* the car when it blew up.'

Evan let go quickly and spun on his heel to face McNabb. 'I blame you!' he shouted. Heads turned all the way down the hallway. 'If it weren't for you, she wouldn't be in danger!'

I felt my face flush with embarrassment, like it was radiating heat beams people could use to follow in a power emergency. 'Gentlemen,' I hissed, 'can we please get off the set of *Days of Our Lives* and discuss this calmly outside?'

To my amazement, they agreed, and walked outside like two repentant boys, eyes fixed on their shoes. Evan even had a fore-lock dangling in his eyes that made him look about twelve years old. It annoyed me that I found this adorable.

After retrieving the revised incident report on Patsy's murder from Sgt Roberts, I stood them out on the sun-drenched pavement like the two naughty schoolboys they were, and read them the Riot Act, v. 9.0, on How Not to Treat a Professional (or any other) Woman in Public.

'Honestly, the two of you act like I'm the pretty red ball you both want to play with. I'm a woman, and I'm your lawyer.' I pointed at Patrick. 'And if you want to get technical, I'm your boss,' I said to Evan, 'so from now on, you're both going to do what *I* want. Is that clear?'

They mumbled something resembling 'yes, ma'am,' and looked at their feet some more.

'It's been a long day,' I continued. 'I'm going home. Evan, can you give me a ride?'

Patrick looked up, his face bright. 'No need!' he said. 'I've had a car . . .'

'Don't tell me,' I said. 'I don't want to know.'

SEVENTEEN

'I acted like an idiot,' Evan said. 'I acted like an obsessive, jealous, possessive, vindictive . . .'

'You could have stopped at "obsessive,"' I told him from the passenger seat, wondering if he'd ever go even one mile over the speed limit, or perhaps move sometime out of the right lane.

'The point is,' he continued, 'I'm sorry. I shouldn't have stormed out of your apartment like that, but it caught me off-guard that he'd had your place cleaned and bought you dinner, and all that.' *You should have been around for the Ferrari*, I thought.

'It's OK,' I said. 'I can see how Patrick can be . . . overwhelming, but there's nothing between us. Nothing at all. Sometimes, I don't even like the guy.'

'Sometimes?'

My lip curled. 'You don't go through an intense period like this – getting shot at, him getting shot, almost blown up – without developing a little affection for the person who's been with you through it all. Either that, or I'll shoot him myself, and you'll be trying to keep *me* out of jail.'

'It's an option,' Evan scowled. He drove in silence for a few minutes, which took us all of a city block, and there wasn't even that much traffic.

When he finally turned, it took me a moment to realize we were going the wrong way. 'This isn't the way to my building, is it?' I asked. 'I mean, you don't know some L.A. shortcut I'm not familiar with, do you?'

'I'm taking you to my place,' Evan said.

I closed my eyes and shook my head. The last thing I felt at this moment was romantic, but I couldn't tell Evan that without wounding his rather obvious ego. 'Evan, as much as I'd like to . . .'

'No good sentence starts that way,' he said grimly.

'I don't have a toothbrush or anything, and I look lousy . . .'

'You don't. You look . . .'

'You know, just because a girl doesn't want to spend the night at your apartment after her car blows up, doesn't mean she doesn't like you.' We chuckled. 'There's a sentence you don't hear every day.'

'Around you I do.'

'Tomorrow night. Can we make it tomorrow night? I promise I won't have anything blow up near me tomorrow, and I'll be in a much better mood. Really. I might not even be scared to death, like I am now.'

'You hide it well.'

'Better mood. I promise.'

I saw Evan sneak a glance at me from the corner of his eye, a wild maneuver for a man who kept both hands on the steering wheel, at ten and two o'clock, the whole time he drove. 'How much better?'

I grinned. 'Much.'

'OK.' Evan turned the car at the next corner, and headed for my apartment.

Once there, Evan parked in the underground lot again. 'You want to come up for a snack?' I asked. 'I've got a ton of turkey left over.'

Evan pulled me close and kissed me with more passion than

you'd expect from a guy who always obeyed the speed limit. 'Tomorrow,' he said. 'I'll see you tomorrow. And you'll be in a much better mood. *Much.*'

'I swear, I will.' I kissed him this time, and it was even better. I considered re-thinking this whole 'tired' thing.

But Evan got out and actually opened my car door. I had no choice but to respond to such a chivalrous gesture. I hugged him, then watched as he got back into the car and drove away.

In the elevator on the way up, I watched a young couple practically inhale each other's faces, and wondered if I'd looked that way with Evan. I preferred not to think so, but hey, love isn't always pretty.

Love?

Attraction! Attraction isn't always pretty! That's what I meant to say! When I reached my floor, I managed to wedge myself around the groping couple, who were all but naked, other than their body piercings and tattoos. I got out of the elevator, and heard them groan behind me as the door closed. I worked very hard at not thinking about what was going on in the elevator as I walked to my apartment door. I'd have to use that elevator again sometime.

I gasped when I reached the door, and this time, it wasn't because everything inside was neat and clean. In fact, I didn't even manage to get the door open.

Nailed to the door of my apartment was a Barbie doll, with something approximating blood – probably Karo syrup and food coloring – dripping from the nail wound. The head was turned around, and the legs and arms were bent in grotesque positions. The doll was naked, and behind it was a piece of paper, on which, in the same substance as the 'blood,' was written in block letters, 'DIE, BITCH!' On the doll's abdomen, such as it was, had been scratched the word 'PIOUS.' What could THAT mean? Now I was involved in a religious controversy? But even that, I'll admit, wasn't my first thought.

A Barbie doll? I go to law school for three years, the Middlesex County Prosecutor's Office for eight, and then a trip out to L.A. to work in a civil law practice, and they think of me as a Barbie doll?

Who could have done such a thing, and why would they want

to? I didn't know anyone in Los Angeles long enough to inspire this kind of anger. And after shooting at me, wounding my client, and blowing up 'my' two hundred thousand dollar car, they thought a mutilated Barbie doll would send me over the emotional top? What did they expect, that I'd cry tears of horror, rush inside, quit the law firm, and book a flight back to Newark? Was that what they thought of me?

One thing was certain – this whole case was really beginning to piss me off.

EIGHTEEN

Angie was not pleased about the exploding Ferrari, but the Barbie doll nailed to my front door was enough to have her practically jumping through the phone. It was at times like these that I felt Angie most resembled my own mother (whom I had assiduously avoided telling anything but the bare bones of the McNabb case), and her insistence on 'being careful' was just short of quaint. How exactly could I have been vigilant enough to prevent someone from nailing a plastic symbol of sexism to my door?

So I found myself calming Angie down when it should have been the other way around. And then I went to bed. Luckily, Angie never slept – in fact, considered it a waste of time ('I'll sleep for a really long time when I'm dead') – so I could call at virtually any hour and find my best friend awake.

I dreamed, but didn't remember anything when I woke up – only a general sense of anxiety. A swell way to start the day. Followed by a bus ride to the office, something no self-respecting Southern Californian would ever even consider. Luckily, I was neither.

The work day began with a meeting in Bach's office, during which he managed to point out every flaw in what had been done so far, but refused to supplement my efforts with more attorneys ('we are not a criminal firm, Ms Moss – except for you'), and smiled vaguely at how badly everything was going. It was really going to satisfy him when he got to fire me after the trial was over and Patrick was in jail.

After that, I met Garrigan and Evan at the office of Lucien DuPrez, Patsy's business manager, who'd been on Patrick's list when he'd been interviewing people independently. Patrick had insisted on meeting DuPrez, then further insisted on having me present, and by now, we all realized there was virtually no point in mentioning what a complete and total waste of our time this would be.

Patrick was there already, of course, leaving me to wonder when he got time to step before the cameras for *Legality*. He said it was lucky there was only one episode left to film this season, because it was distracting his attention from the investigation of Patsy's death. I kept my observations on the subject of 'luck' to myself.

DuPrez was a man in his mid-forties who obviously couldn't decide between being a successful business executive and keepin' it real in the world of rap, yo. He'd chosen to straddle the fence, and wore a suit jacket and black T-shirt, with baggy leather pants and enough gold around his neck to keep every dentist in the world in fillings for the next fifty years.

'To tell the truth,' he was saying in his high-backed leather chair, behind a dark oak desk the size of my office, 'Patsy's death is a loss, but if I'm going to be completely honest, not a great loss. I mean, I don't like to speak ill of the dead, but the woman's career was gone and buried long before her.'

Patrick's cheeks were bulging and relaxing, bulging and relaxing, as if he were doing his best to keep from throttling DuPrez by exercising his jaw.

Garrigan asked, 'She was still making a large amount of money, though, wasn't she, Mr DuPrez?'

DuPrez raised one eyebrow and tilted his head, as if to say, 'Large? What's large?' Then he said, 'Large? What's large? She made a couple of million a year, but she really had to work at it – making personal appearances at every car show and mall opening in the country. She made enough to get by, but nothing like what she was doing two, three years ago.'

'A couple million a year,' Garrigan says. 'Sounds awful. And you only getting, what, fifteen percent?'

'Twenty,' DuPrez corrected. 'I was her personal manager as well as her business manager.'

'So if she made two million, you got four hundred thousand a year. Is that right?'

'Yes, that's right,' DuPrez agreed. 'Like I said, barely worth the trouble.'

'Plenty for doing nothing,' Patrick muttered.

'*Nothing?*' DuPrez's tender sensibilities were clearly injured. 'I worked my ass off for that girl.'

'Funny,' McNabb said, 'from where I'm sitting, it's still there, and quite formidable.'

I couldn't initially understand why Garrigan wasn't intervening in this, er, discussion, but I realized after a moment that he wanted to observe the interaction and see if, in the heat of anger, one man or the other would say something he might not think through beforehand.

'You might not have been privy to her finances, Patrick, but that girl would have been on the breadline but for the way I handled her money.'

'I'll bet you handled it quite thoroughly,' said McNabb, 'and stop calling her "that girl." She had a name.'

'Forgive me for being inconsiderate,' said DuPrez, sarcasm dripping from his voice, 'but at least when I was calling her "that girl," I wasn't firing an arrow at her.'

Patrick's eyes flared, and I could see he was considering lunging at DuPrez, but when he saw no one was going to stop him, he restrained his urge. He stayed still, and his voice was preternaturally calm.

'Neither was I,' was all he said.

A remarkably uncomfortable silence followed, after which Garrigan cleared his throat. 'So, Mr DuPrez, what were Patsy's plans? Did she have bookings that she cannot fulfill now? Any recording sessions in the works? What did she leave behind?'

DuPrez, still staring at Patrick, sniffed. 'Behind? She left nothing behind. A stupid rap album that sounded like Eliza Doolittle Goes Hip-Hop. Couldn't sell that to Paris Hilton on a shopping binge. Lohan wouldn't even shoplift it. That's what that . . . *Patsy* left behind.'

'I don't see any point to staying here, then,' Patrick said, standing. 'The smell is starting to get to me.' He headed for the door and seemed surprised when no one rose to follow him, but he left anyway.

When the door closed, DuPrez seemed to exhale for the first time. 'I'm sorry for my behavior,' he told the remaining group, 'but that man has always brought out the worst in me. Can we start again?'

'Sure,' said Garrigan. 'Why don't you start by telling us why you have such resentment against Patrick McNabb.'

'Even when Patsy was alive, he hated me,' DuPrez began. 'Always hinting I was cheating her, always intimating that his manager could do better for her. He said I didn't believe in her talent. Can you believe that? I found the girl when she was *nothing* – a little string bean with an OK voice singing at county fairs – and I turned her into someone who didn't even need a last name! *I paid for her breast implants, OK?* And here's this guy, this actor, this *TV* star, telling her she should dump me because I was crooked! Then he goes and kills her, and comes in here like it's my fault. Can you imagine?'

'I *can* imagine,' Garrigan said, but DuPrez didn't add to his story.

'You seem awfully upset,' I said. 'Were you close to Patsy?'

'If you mean was I sleeping with her, the answer's no,' said DuPrez, his voice quivering a bit. 'But we had a lot of years together, and I do miss her. Look, I know you're the defense people and all, but could you . . . is it possible for you to make sure McNabb goes to jail? Maybe do your jobs badly or something? I'd hate to see him get off on a technicality.'

'First of all, Mr DuPrez, people don't really get off on a technicality,' I said. 'That's a TV thing. And besides, how can you be sure Patrick McNabb was the person who killed his wife?'

'I saw them together,' he said. 'I know how much they fought. If it wasn't McNabb, then who loved her enough to kill her?'

I hadn't thought of it that way before, but it was worth pursuing. 'That's a good question, Mr DuPrez,' I said. 'But I'm sorry. We're obligated to do our jobs to the best of our ability and provide our client with the best possible defense. You know, he's innocent until proven guilty.'

'Well, if I can help you prove it, you let me know,' DuPrez

told her. 'The guy who killed my little Patsy should spend the rest of his life in prison.'

I didn't expect to see Patrick again that day, but he was standing outside the building when I left with Garrigan and Evan. He had reverted to bubbly Patrick.

'So,' he said, 'whom shall we see next?'

'It's "who," actually,' I said, although I wasn't the least bit sure. 'And we're not going to see anyone. I'm going back to read through the files and start preparing a list of witnesses we want to testify, and you're going back to acting on a TV show. Nate here will go about investigating, and he'll report back to us on anything he finds. Right, Nate?'

'Absolutely,' Garrigan said, grinning.

'Well, if that's the way it's going to be, I think Mr Garrigan should pay a call on Silvio Cadenza,' Patrick said, a dare in his eye.

I was an eyelash from asking who this person might be when Garrigan said, 'Patsy's latest boyfriend. The building contractor who came to your house while you were still married with the idea of putting on an addition, and instead stole your wife. That's the guy, right?'

An addition? I thought. *They have a house that an entire country could live in, and they needed an addition?*

'Yes,' was all Patrick said, apparently accepting the fact that Garrigan could interview Cadenza alone.

Before Patrick could make a Lamborghini appear, Evan and I bid a hasty retreat to Evan's car. I considered asking if I could drive, but that would spoil his mood (which I wanted to keep at a high level of anticipation), and besides, he really did know the streets here better than I did. So did most people who had lived here longer than a day.

'You haven't changed your mind about tonight,' Evan said as he crawled the car through relatively clear streets (for L.A.).

'No, of course not,' I told him. 'I'm looking forward to it.' *My God, Moss, you sound like he's invited you to his cousin's eighth grade science fair! You're talking about sex!*

'Good,' Evan said. Because his tone wasn't exactly inspiring wild erotic fantasies, I started to wonder if we were talking about the same thing. But before I got a chance to think of a tactful way to ask if I would see him naked later that night, Evan added, 'You know, I've been doing some thinking about the case.'

'Really.' Wow. A true romantic.

'If you don't mind my saying.' I'd accosted him so much about taking the lead in the case that Evan was being tentative. Great. I'd scared him off professionally, and we were discussing sex as if it were a real estate closing. *Nice work, Sandy, you've done it again.*

'No, go ahead.'

'I think the defense should be built on the lack of physical evidence. All they have is the arrow, which he could have touched trying to remove it from her chest, or at any other time since he bought it. They don't know that he fired it at Patsy, or if he was trying to kill her. A bow and arrow isn't exactly the weapon of choice in the twenty-first century.'

'No,' I said, shaking my head. 'The defense has to be built on the law. All the evidence against Patrick is circumstantial. It's another way of saying what you said, but the fact is, if they can't prove, with a witness or a piece of physical evidence, that Patrick was the only one who could have killed Patsy, then the jury can't convict.'

'Don't you think the jury needs to be led emotionally?' Evan moved into a turn with the agility of a panther, carrying a grand piano on its back. 'They're going to react to Patrick and the other witnesses with some degree of emotion, and that's going to influence their votes.'

'You can't think that way,' I told him with a slight edge of condescension in my voice. *Listen up, kid, and I'll tell you how the legal system really works.* 'If they get the proper instructions from the judge, they'll know they have to base their decisions on the evidence, not who makes them feel more nurturing.' I thought a moment. *Still, it won't hurt to get a lot of women on the jury. Those crinkling eyes . . .*

Evan raised his eyebrows. 'Wow. You really know your stuff. I wouldn't have thought of that.'

'I've had a lot of practice,' I answered. *Yes. I'd like a jury with at least five women. A few gay men would be good, too.*

We drove in silence as I tried to decide how to get the topic back to sex. It occurred to me that if he did that as slowly as he drove, Evan could be a true find.

But I didn't have time to maneuver the conversation in that direction. 'You didn't tell me about the Barbie doll,' Evan said quietly.

My head practically swiveled all the way around. 'How'd you find out about *that*?' I asked.

'Holly Wentworth told me,' Evan said. 'Apparently, it's the talk of the office.' *Swell. Religious Barbie fanatics are creating a reputation for me at my place of work.*

'I was going to tell you,' I said. 'It just happened last night.'

'What do you think it means?' Evan asked as he pulled into the office building's underground lot.

'I think it's plain enough,' I said. 'Somebody thinks I'm a bitch and wants me to die.'

'Who would want that?'

'Well, it's got something to do with the case, obviously.' We got out of the car and headed for the elevator. 'But I can't figure out whether it's people who think I'm defending Patsy's killer, or people who don't think I'm doing a good enough job for Patrick. Either way, the letters scratched on the doll's belly . . .'

Evan stopped and stared. 'There were letters scratched on the doll's belly?'

I didn't know why, but that made me feel good. 'You mean Holly didn't know that? Yeah, it spelled out the word "pious." Any idea what *that* might mean?'

The elevator doors opened and we got on as Evan's face got even more serious than usual, which was really saying something. 'I can't think of anything,' he said as we started to rise. 'If a person is pious, why do they want someone else to die?'

Try not to be too emotionally distraught, I thought. *They're talking about me, you know.* Maybe I was doing too good a job hiding my abject terror.

We were silent the rest of the ride, and went our separate ways when the elevator reached the 32nd floor. Grateful to be acting like a lawyer and not a gumshoe again, I immersed myself in the McNabb file.

During the next hour, I completely forgot about the amended police report Trench had given me, and I couldn't help but say 'idiot' out loud as I went through my briefcase to find it. It was not terribly thick, but I started in on it as if it held some well-hidden key to my life, and resolved to find every nuance I could.

That diligence wasn't necessary, however. I found what I needed in the medical examiner's report, and it was so obvious, it might just as well have been written in neon.

Patsy DeNunzio had been two months pregnant at the time of her death, and based on the blood type, the baby was not Patrick McNabb's.

NINETEEN

'This goes right to motive,' I said. Evan, comfortably deposited on my sofa, was drinking a glass of the red wine he'd brought, and looking like this month's centerfold in *Better Homes and Gardens*. In a jacket but no tie, blue pants but not jeans, casual shoes but not sneakers, he was the epitome of playing it safe. Exactly my type.

'I don't see how,' he said, watching me with a puppy-dog devotion both touching and a little creepy. 'She was having another man's baby. McNabb admits he knew she was having affairs.'

I opened the oven and took out a perfectly prepared roast duck (I'd had enough turkey to last me three more Thanksgivings). Forget the fact that I'd bought it at Trader Joe's – it's the thought that counts. 'It doesn't matter that he knew about the affairs. The shock of hearing about the pregnancy could have gotten him emotional, out of control. That's how the prosecution will play it.'

Evan's eyebrows crinkled, which wasn't quite the same as Patrick's eyes crinkling, but did indicate thought. 'So he immediately ran into the next room, picked up his bow and arrow, and did an impression of Robin Hood?' He shook his head. 'No. This doesn't play as a crime of passion. You can counter it.'

'Come eat,' I said, and put the duck on a platter, and the platter on the table. Evan walked to the table and smiled at the way I'd set it.

'This is really nice,' he said. 'You shouldn't have gone to all this trouble.'

'You're a poor law student,' I said jokingly. 'You probably haven't had a good meal since . . .'

'Lunch?' We both laughed. I held out the carving knife and offered it to Evan.

'Carve?'

'Oh, no thanks. I'd just hash it up, and you went to all this trouble. You go ahead.'

Great. I had no idea how to carve a duck, or even if you *should* carve a duck. Maybe you just cut pieces off and eat it with your fingers. For all I knew, I should have put out wooden sticks and made Duckcicles.

'I'm not the best at this,' I admitted, but soldiered on. It was surprisingly easy, once I got the hang of it, and we were both eating in a minute. Trader Joe had done a fine job.

'Was there anything else in the new police report?' Evan asked after the requisite compliments about the food, which I deflected, knowing I'd disposed of all evidence it was store-bought.

'I thought we weren't going to talk shop.'

'Sorry. We don't have to. I'm curious.'

I'd never had duck before, and though not exactly like chicken, it wasn't bad. I chewed for a while, drank some wine, and said, 'It's OK. Only one other detail wasn't in the first report – that the arrow went directly into Patsy's heart. Considering everything, a terrific shot.'

Evan put down his fork. Maybe he didn't like the duck. What did I care – I didn't cook it. But still . . . 'If Patrick wasn't terribly proficient with a bow . . .'

'I asked him,' I said. 'He had training for a Western he made in Australia ten years ago. He was playing a Comanche; can you imagine it? Patrick? But he keeps up with target practice twice a week at a place in Encino. He's supposedly very good.'

Evan stuck out his lips in disappointment. They were nice lips, and I could think of other things they should do.

It was the wine talking; honestly. I *never* sounded like this. I mean, it had been a while since . . . you know . . . but I'm just not the aggressive type in this sort of situation. But I am, lamentably, a very cheap drunk. And after two glasses of wine, I was hearing thoughts in my head that weren't mine, or Angie's. They were from Wanton Woman, the sexual superheroine.

'That's a problem,' Evan said, unaware of the carnal presence in the room. 'How will you counter that when the prosecution brings it up?'

'It depends on who their witness will be, but the best argument is that they don't have anyone who saw Patrick with the bow in his hand, and they can't prove he'd ever fired a shot at a living person. That dining room, no matter how big, isn't the best place to shoot off an arrow with any accuracy.'

'Maybe get an archery expert,' Evan suggested through a bite of potato.

'Yes, I'm planning on that.' OK, so I'm planning on it *now*. 'Very good.'

He grinned, the apt pupil complimented by his encouraging mentor. 'Thanks.'

Time to change the subject. 'So, how come, for a guy getting his law degree in the evening, you have all these nights free?' I asked.

Evan actually blushed, which was so adorable I almost leapt over the table at him. 'I've been cutting class,' he said. 'I wanted to be with you.'

What does that mean? He wants to be with me, or he wants to be with me on the case? Who cares! He wants to be with me!

'Maybe,' I said softly, 'we should have dessert later.'

He grinned again, and I no longer cared about motive. Evan stood, walked to my chair, and pulled it out for me to get up, a gesture I would've lambasted if done by anyone else, but one I found charming coming from him.

We walked to the couch, with Evan leading the way (I'd have gone directly to the bedroom, but I didn't want to appear over eager – perhaps the Victoria's Secret special I wore under my clothes would send enough of a signal later on – it had taken me forty-five minutes to work up the courage to put it on, before the wine).

Not a word was exchanged as we faced each other and Evan took my face in his hands. He leaned in, and the kissing began, slowly, tenderly, almost too politely. But after a few minutes of this, I felt my patience start to wane, and I sent my tongue to deliver a message, which was obviously received and appreciated. Wanton Woman was in da house.

It took another few minutes before I decided that what had worked for a tongue could also work for hands, and I took his and guided them to my torso, just under my breasts, giving a hint I didn't think could be missed. But it appeared for a while that it could be, as Evan merely moaned a little and put his hands around my back, rubbing and caressing.

Just when I was debating the idea of reaching for his belt and ending the suspense, Evan's libido appeared to come back from its siesta, and he began very carefully, deliberately, unbuttoning my silk shirt. He started at the top, and went three buttons down, seeming to wonder why I wasn't stopping him, as if we were in the back seat of his father's Impala in our junior year of high school. I moaned my approval, and pulled him closer.

Finally, he got the idea, and responded lustily (there's no other word for it). I was just about to discover what kind of lover he might turn out to be. I reached for his belt buckle and undid it.

And that, of course, is when the apartment door was unexpectedly opened by Angie, a huge suitcase at her feet.

On first spotting us on the couch, she closed the door and said. 'OK, who's trying to kill my . . .'

Then, things began to properly register with her. 'Oops,' she giggled.

TWENTY

'You could've told me she was coming,' Evan hissed at me. We'd retreated to the bedroom to compose ourselves, leaving Angie an inch away from a laughing fit in the living room. The introductions had been awkward, to say the least.

'I didn't *know* she was coming,' I hissed right back. 'She didn't say anything about it. I thought we'd have the whole night to ourselves. And for all I knew, the rest of the month as well.'

'The least you could've done was lock the apartment door,'

he said, still annoyed and looking for some solid ground to stand on. 'People are threatening you, shooting at you, trying to blow you up, and you leave your apartment unlocked?'

I smiled a little, and my hand went to my mouth. Then I felt my face redden. 'What?' Evan said.

'Angie has a key,' I explained. 'It's an old tradition that goes back to high school. We were going away for a vacation and Angie was watching my dog, so I gave her a key, and she never gave it back. Since then, whenever I get a new address, she gets a new key. She even had a key to my college dorm room. It never occurred to me she'd *use* this one. Until two minutes ago, I thought she was three thousand miles away.'

Angie called through the door. 'You weren't *that* undressed. If you're talking about me, come out and do it to my face.' She giggled again. 'You know what I mean.'

I tucked my silk shirt into my pants and smoothed my hair down. I gave Evan, who was completely composed again, a glance, and said, 'Let's go.'

'This should be fun,' he said with an odd tone.

The strange part was that for me, it *was* fun. I knew Angie was the human equivalent of comfort food – that she was there strictly as support, and not to assume or demand anything. She was the unlimited, always reliable backup everyone should have.

I could tell, though, that Evan was having a lousy time, and I couldn't really blame him. After being promised sex, sitting through a reunion of the New Jersey Girls Club had to be something of a letdown. He wasn't showing much, smiling at the right times and asking questions about me when he could get a word in edgewise, but it wasn't long before he noted the hour and his need to study for class tomorrow night. Evan left with a kiss and an unspoken promise.

'Well, *that* was a guy to find with his pants open!' Angie began as soon as I returned from the apartment door. 'How'd you get him on the couch so fast, Ms I-Gotta-Be-Friends-With-the-Guy-First?'

'He *is* a friend,' I said, realizing how stupid that sounded. 'But he has a nice body, too.'

'Amen.'

I sat and gave Angie my most searching stare. 'So what are you doing here?'

'It was the Barbie doll that did it,' Angie said, swirling the wine in her glass. 'I mean, shootings and car explosions are bad enough, but killing you in tiny effigy was too much for me. I had to come out and see for myself.'

'How long are you here for?'

She shrugged with a failed effort at casual indifference. 'I dunno,' Angie said. 'Until things blow over.'

I narrowed my eyes. 'What about the Dairy Queens?'

'What, you think they can't peddle soft serve without me for a little while? Don't worry. My job'll be there when I get back.'

'You're a maniac. What are you going to do? Follow me around with a blackjack in your pocket? You're an ice cream manager, not a bodyguard.'

'I'm a Jersey girl. I can do both. So tell me about the guy with almost no pants.'

I looked at the kitchen and tried to estimate the clean-up time with Angie factored in. 'He's a nice guy,' I said. 'He's working with me on the McNabb case, and . . . I've spent too much time listening to you.'

Angie raised an eyebrow. 'Meaning?'

'Meaning I wanted to get laid. Is that so awful?' Angie practically spit wine across the room, and we laughed ourselves into a helpless heap on the couch and easy chair.

Finally, I managed, 'Thank God the couch pulls out. It's a one-bedroom, you know.'

'So you'll be sleeping out here, then?' Angie had a glint in her eye, and I sighed.

'Sure.'

'I'm kidding. You stay in your bedroom. Guests are supposed to sleep on the couch.'

'You don't really have to stay,' I told her. 'I'll be OK, really. And it'll only be a few months until the trial is over.'

Angie looked up, suddenly reminding herself of something. 'Oh my God, I forgot to tell you. The phone rang while you and your . . . *friend* were putting your clothes back on in there.' I made a mental note to take my phone *everywhere* I went, then looked at the answering machine.

'There's no voice mail.'

'I picked up,' Angie said. 'A woman from your office named Holiday – can you believe it? Holiday?'

'I can believe it. What did she say?'

'I'm so sorry I forgot to tell you right away, but the whole pants thing threw me for a loop. She said the court had called, and the judge set a trial date for three weeks from today.'

Three weeks? 'That can't be right,' I said.

'She said it over and over,' Angie told her. 'I'm sure that's what she said.'

'I'm going to be trying a homicide case before the whole world, with no evidence in my favor, in three weeks, and Patrick McNabb's life will be on the line if I screw up?'

'I believe that was the message,' Angie told me.

'Three weeks?'

I sat for a while and let my mind reel. All I could hear was Gene Wilder's voice from *The Producers* chanting in my head: *'No way out . . . no way out . . . no way out . . .'*

Finally, Angie's voice broke through. 'Hey, Sand?'

I snapped to attention, and looked to my friend, whose sympathetic eyes were clearly trying to ease my pain.

'What?'

'Can I meet Patrick McNabb?'

PART TWO
The Things That Aren't Tribulations

TWENTY-ONE

The courtroom was packed, as was expected. The case had been in the newspapers, on television, and all over the internet for weeks, with theories flying about as to motive, opportunity, and of course, method. But the verdict seemed to be a foregone conclusion: everyone agreed he was guilty.

Famous people don't live like anyone else when times are good, and there was no reason for that to change when times were . . . like now. Even in the back of the courtroom, ardent fans were wearing 'Free Arthur Kirkland!' T-shirts, as if that was going to be any help. He couldn't help but notice, and he made a point, from the defendant's table, to give them a warm smile – the one he considered his best – but this one didn't have its usual juice. He was tired, weary and wary, and more than anything else, afraid.

The judge entered the room looking grim, but then, why should he be any different than everyone else (except the prosecution team, whose members were trying unsuccessfully to hide their giddiness)? He sat, and instructed everyone else to do the same.

'Ms Foreperson, I understand you have reached a verdict?'

Slim, attractive, but somewhat unassertive (just what a prosecutor wants in a foreperson), she nodded. 'Yes, Your Honor.'

'Would you hand it to the bailiff, please?' She nodded again, and gave a small slip of paper to the burly bailiff, who'd been lifting weights for an hour and a half downstairs in the bowels of the courthouse when the news of the verdict had been received. At this point, he was lucky he could lift the paper.

He managed to bring it to the judge, who took the paper and opened it. The judge always did his best not to move a facial muscle when a verdict was presented to him. He would not betray any emotion that might lead onlookers to believe he'd been prejudiced in either direction, even on those occasions when he had.

But this time, he couldn't help but smile just a bit and stare in the direction of the defendant's table. He saw the defendant look at his lawyer, but she was staring into the judge's eyes, and that stopped his smile. The look he saw, one of utter and complete outrage, was enough to make any man's blood run cold. He cleared his throat.

'The defendant will rise.'

He did, and his lawyer did the same. She reached over and patted his hand, then put her own on his and left it there.

'Arthur Kirkland, you have been found . . . guilty of murder in the first degree . . .' The gasp that went up in the courtroom drowned out the rest of the verdict.

'Oh, my God!' Angie wailed. 'They found him guilty!'

I'd been coerced into watching *Legality* again because, as Angie put it, 'I'm your guest and you have to be nice to me.' I shook my head back and forth, mouth agape, absolutely and totally stunned.

'They put him on trial for murder . . . on his own *show*?' I said when speech once again became possible.

'Sure, didn't you know about that?' Angie couldn't believe that everyone didn't have the same popular culture priorities she had. 'This has been going on for weeks. Remember, I told you his girlfriend was cheating on him, and when he found out . . .'

'He killed her? On television? Just when he was being charged in a real courtroom for killing his wife? What are these people *thinking*?'

'No, no,' Angie said, trying to calm me down. 'He didn't kill her. He went to confront her, and found her body on the floor already. Or at least, that's what he told Ozzie.'

'*Ozzie?*' *Ozzie Nelson? Ossie Davis? Ozzy Osbourne? The Wizard of Ozzie?* 'Who's Ozzie?'

'The one who was defending him in court. He told Ozzie . . .'

'I don't *care* what he told Ozzie! They had the nerve to write a storyline where Patrick McNabb's character is put on trial for murder, and, with this on half the DVRs in America, I have to defend him in a *real* murder trial?' I stood up and turned off the TV. 'How am I going to find a jury who didn't just see *that*, or at least hear about it?'

'You're not,' Angie said. 'Does that mean you should get a change of virtue?'

'*Venue*, and there's no advantage to a change of venue in this case. Besides, where are we going to move it to where they don't have American television? Bangladesh?'

I couldn't stop shaking my head in wonder. 'I'm gonna *kill* him,' I said. 'The least he could have done was tell me.' I went to the kitchen to pick up the phone. 'What time is it?' I asked Angie.

'Just after eleven.'

I hesitated. 'Do you think it's too late to call?'

Angie stood up and pulled the phone out of my hand. 'Oh, for Pete's sake,' she said. 'He's an actor. They're constantly out at clubs and stuff until four in the morning. He might not even be home.'

I chewed my lower lip. 'That's true,' I said. 'I guess it can wait until tomorrow.'

'You won't be this mad tomorrow,' Angie said. She picked up a worn denim jacket from the sofa. 'Come on.'

'Where are we going?'

'Patrick McNabb's house. You're going to introduce me, and then ream him out.'

It wasn't until we got to Angie's rental car that I stopped and looked at her. 'If he's not home, how does going to his house make more sense than calling?'

Angie got in on the driver's side and unlocked the doors. 'If he's there, he's more likely to see you than he is to pick up the phone. If he's not there, it gives us that much more time while we drive over for him to get there. Besides, I'm hungry and we're out of . . . everything.'

I sat in the passenger's seat as Angie started the car. 'This is just so you get to meet Patrick, isn't it?'

'Not *just*.'

I supplied directions. Otherwise, we drove in silence until we reached Patrick's 'bachelor pad.' Angie's mouth was open in an oval as we approached the gate.

'Wow.'

'Huh,' I scoffed. 'This is just a temporary house. Wait until he gets his *permanent* place.'

'Am I dressed all right?'

'For a midnight ream-out? Yeah, you look fine,' I smiled.

'You're ragging on me, Ms Moss,' Angie said with a hint of the original Angie voice.

'You're acting like a TV groupie, *Angela*.'

'I'm not acting.'

Angie pushed the button on the intercom, and Meadows answered almost immediately. From the passenger's seat, I shouted, 'Hey, Meadows, old chum! It's his lawyer! Let us in!'

There was no reply, but the gate opened, and Angie, breathing a little more heavily than usual, drove the car up the winding driveway.

'Just keep in mind that nothing about him is real,' I advised Angie. 'His name is really Dunwoody.'

'Actors change their names. They're supposed to. You, on the other hand, know that, a few generations back, your family name was Moskowitz, so let's not have too much superiority, OK, Sand?'

'It was at Ellis Island! I didn't do it myself!' I wanted Angie on my side in any dealings with Patrick, and was worried that Hollywood glitter might get stuck in her eyes.

'Yeah, yeah.'

At my insistence, we parked near the door ('don't they have, like, a parking lot or something?') and walked to it, Angie adjusting her cleavage once or twice for maximum effect. Angie's cleavage could achieve maximum effect on its own, thank you, and here she was helping it. It was a good thing we weren't competing. Right?

She was a little disappointed when Meadows, and not Patrick, opened the door, but managed to overcome her discouragement when she heard him say, 'Mr McNabb is at home,' and 'will of course see you immediately.'

As we were ushered into the hall, where the best memorabilia was kept, Angie's eyes grew so wide and round that I thought she looked just a little like Little Orphan Annie, but for the irises and pupils (which Angie had, and Annie, not so much). But it was an empty display case that caught *my* eye.

It was the one set up much like that for the Cary Grant shoes Garrigan had found so fascinating. It was in a much more prominent place, an area that couldn't be missed, practically right in front of the main entrance. But the shoes weren't there – only a small engraved plaque. I couldn't get close enough, but I was relatively sure I could guess what was carved into the flawless silver.

The case was meant to house James Cagney's tap shoes. That meant Patrick already had them, or expected to have them very soon.

TWENTY-TWO

It wasn't just the opulent room that caused Angie's sudden inability to speak. It wasn't the fact that her current TV idol was sitting in front of her, perhaps six feet away. It wasn't even the fact that said idol was in an honest-to-God silk dressing gown.

It was the fact that this was his bedroom.

Angie, her mouth squeezed shut for fear she'd actually say what she was thinking, couldn't take her eyes off Patrick McNabb. He, to his credit, was giving her just as much eye contact as she wanted, which might have been a testament to her cleavage, but also might have been at least partially due to the fact that he didn't want to look me in the eye as I mercilessly berated him.

'Do you know how this *looks*?' I wailed. 'How long has this storyline been playing out? Practically the day after you appeared on the front page of every newspaper in America arrested for murder, you were being arrested for murder on your TV show, right in front of every juror?'

'How was I supposed to know?' Patrick retaliated. 'You know, love, we don't exactly make this thing up as we go along. They wrote those scripts weeks before Patsy died. We shot the beginning of the arc more than a month before that night. Besides, it'll drum up some sympathy for me, don't you think?'

I bit so hard on both my lips that I was sure I'd draw blood. 'Don't you see,' I said with great effort, 'that they've already seen you convicted of murder on television, and the *real* trial doesn't start for twenty-one days, assuming I can't get the continuance I'm requesting?'

'A continuance? Why do we want a continuance? Let's get in there and get this done!' Patrick was smiling. That, more than anything else, convinced me he was completely insane.

'We want a continuance because we don't have a single shred of evidence that even *suggests* you didn't kill Patsy!' I barked at him. 'We want a continuance because there's never been a trial this high-profile in history that went off this fast! We want a continuance because *I don't know how to save you!*'

That last part just slipped out.

Patrick only smiled more broadly. 'You'll think of something,' he said. 'You're . . .'

'No, I'm not!'

Angie's brow furrowed and she stopped gawking at Patrick for a moment, despite his insistence on seeing us while lounging on his silk-sheeted bed. I thought Angie was going to come to my rescue, but instead, she turned her disapproving gaze on me.

'You don't have to yell,' she said.

I heard noises coming out of my own mouth. I was sure I was trying to say something, but instead, sounds that one usually associates with fictional characters were emitting from within me. Characters like Frankenstein's monster and Rocky Balboa. And Elmer Fudd.

'Didn't you . . . don't you . . . did you hear . . .?'

'Mr McNabb has such heartwarming confidence in you, Sand, and all you want to do is tear him down,' Angie continued as I opened and closed my lips to no effect. 'Try to focus on the facts, not on your emotions.'

The whole world has gone insane. There's nothing left for a rational person like me to do. Maybe I should move, like to Saturn or something.

'Call me Patrick,' McNabb said to Angie, who looked back at him with an expression of adoration usually associated with Renaissance paintings of religious figures.

'Patrick,' she said. I couldn't recognize the woman sitting on the chair next to where I was pacing. It *looked* like my longtime friend, but it didn't act like her at all. I began to wonder if an evil genius had created a robot Angie and was using it to destroy my tenuous hold on reality. I realized I hadn't actually *called* Angie on the phone since this thing had arrived at my door, and couldn't be completely sure she wasn't home. But then, wouldn't the evil genius have found a way to forward Angie's calls to her cell?

'I'm so sorry we woke you,' the Angie Thing continued. 'We didn't think you'd be in this time of night.'

'Oh, television is a very demanding mistress,' Patrick twinkled. 'We're still shooting, you know, and I have a six a.m. call tomorrow. Later today, really.'

Angie – if she *was* Angie – practically launched herself out of her chair. 'Then we shouldn't be keeping you up.'

'Not to worry,' Patrick told her. 'I'm only in two scenes tomorrow. Perhaps you'd like to come by and watch.'

Perhaps? Angie would miss her mother's funeral to watch them film Legality.

'I'd love to,' she/it said, all but melting into the carpet.

It was time to seize back control of the conversation. 'Patrick. Your defense. We're going to get the discovery from the prosecution tomorrow. That's everything they have to use against you that they have to show us. After you finish filming . . .'

'Then there will be a wrap party,' Patrick said, still looking at the imposter in the room. 'I hope you'll both attend.'

Perhaps this was Angie, after all, because she reacted just as I would have predicted. 'Of *course* we will!' she said.

'Maybe *you* will,' I interjected, 'but I'll be going over the evidence. Patrick, please . . .'

'The day after tomorrow, I promise, Sandy. I'll be all yours then, all right? But I have to attend the wrap party. The crew counts on our showing up.'

I felt like the mother of an especially precocious five-year-old child. *Oh, all right, but brush your teeth afterward, and no crossing the streets by yourself!*

'OK, Patrick. But it's got to be the next day.' I decided it was no longer possible to do anything that would help my case. I'd simply go to trial, lose, and hope that the world ended before the inevitable appeal also failed. I turned and headed for the door, Angie reluctantly behind me. Then I stopped, and regarded him for a moment. 'Patrick. The shoes. Where are they?'

'How should I know?' Forget butter; light margarine wouldn't melt in his mouth.

'You should know – you went with Patsy's sister to get them. You should know because I saw you had a Bergdorf's bag when you got back and it did *not* have shirts in it. You should know because you've already got the pedestal set up to display them in your entranceway, with an engraved plaque sitting right there. So don't bullshit me, Patrick. Where are Cagney's shoes?'

Worried that Angie would actually resort to violence in her hero's defense, I didn't dare look at my best friend's face. But Patrick, switching from debonair to defeated, sighed and hung his head.

'I admit it,' he said. 'I did go there that night with every intention of removing Jimmy's shoes from the bedroom in Patsy's house.' Then he raised his head so his eyes were looking directly into mine. 'But I swear to you, Sandy, when I got there, they had already been taken. They were gone.'

'Oh, come on.'

'No, truly,' he said. 'I had the bag, and a shoebox inside, all ready to carry them away, carefully, and hide them here until the trial was over. But the case had been opened, the shoes were taken, and I couldn't report the theft to the police, or they'd think *I'd* taken them.'

'That's *awful*!' said Angie, from just to my right. 'Who would do such a thing?'

'I haven't the slightest,' Patrick said, playing to a more sympathetic audience. 'But it's been killing me since then. Sandy, do you think Mr Garrigan might be able to investigate?'

'Mr Garrigan is paid to investigate how we might keep you out of the gas chamber,' I said, trying to jar Patrick into something approaching candor. California actually uses lethal injection, on those rare occasions it doesn't kill by being too sunny all the time. 'Not to track down nostalgic footwear. How do the shoes fit into all this? Why all this drama over some old movie props?'

Patrick McNabb was a good actor, so his sputtering and shock almost seemed convincing. 'Old movie props!' he erupted. 'Do you have any idea how rare, how important to the history of the cinema, how . . .'

'How *much*?'

'How much *what*?' Patrick seemed genuinely confused.

'How much can someone get for them? I did some looking

on eBay, and I've got to tell you, Patrick, no matter how beloved and rarefied those shoes are, as far as I can tell, they're not likely to pull in much more than thirty or forty thousand dollars. Not really worth all this fuss to a guy like you, is it?'

'Sandy!' Angie couldn't restrain herself any longer. 'Do you really think that poor Patrick here is concerning himself with the value of . . .'

'Two-point-five million dollars,' Patrick said. We stared at him for a moment. 'I don't know why, but I was contacted about a month ago by an anonymous buyer who offered two-point-five million for Jimmy's shoes. Naturally, I didn't want to give them up, but . . .'

'But since you'd found that big a sucker, you were going to forego sentiment,' I said, nodding. 'That was right when you and Patsy were really hitting the skids, and just a couple of weeks before she was killed. Do you think it was for the shoes?'

Angie was aghast at her hero's alleged avarice, and unable to do much more than exercise her jaw soundlessly for a few moments. Patrick looked at me, and shook his head.

'I don't know,' he said. 'Patsy needed the money, but would someone have killed her for the shoes?'

'Was that reason enough to kill her?' I asked.

'It wouldn't have been necessary,' Patrick said. 'There were more than enough reasons to kill her.'

TWENTY-THREE

Ten hours later, I was on my second extremely caffeinated cup of coffee of the day, sitting at my desk, and reading over the file of discovery materials sent over by the McNabb prosecutor, Bertram Cates. So far, I hadn't garnered much in the way of new information. Included in the packet were the M.E.'s report that showed Patsy was pregnant, the police report describing the 911 call, as well as a recording of the call itself (Patrick sounded far too calm to be sympathetic, and the prosecution would use that). The police report also detailed the scene as the officers entered the house, McNabb kneeling over the body with the bloody arrow in his hand.

I was glad I hadn't ordered a cinnamon bun to go with the coffee. The evidence against my client was making me nauseous.

Still, there remained a huge file of documents yet to be examined, and I could be hopeful. Maybe the smoking gun (or in this case, the flying arrow) could still be ferreted out.

Angie was at my apartment, trying to decide what to wear to *Legality*'s wrap party, a mere ten hours hence. I knew she'd be deciding until the last minute, and then would go with something guaranteed to draw gasps, although not necessarily the appreciative kind.

Evan appeared in the doorway, carrying two cups of coffee, and looked disappointed when he saw I already had one. It seemed I was programmed to disappoint Evan at every turn, despite my ever-stronger desire to do anything but. I smiled and waved him in.

'Oh good, you got coffee,' I said, throwing my almost-full cup into the wastebasket. 'I was out.'

Once again useful, he grinned and handed me a cup from the Starbucks not far from the office. At least the coffee would be better than the stuff I'd gotten from the newsstand downstairs.

'You look like you've been up all night,' Evan said, sinking into the chair in front of my desk.

'Thanks a lot.'

'I mean, you seem a little tired.' He gestured toward the papers in front of me. 'Is that the discovery?'

I nodded. 'I haven't found anything yet. But there's plenty more, and I need to look over their list of witnesses, and add the few we can call. We need an expert on archery, an expert in movie memorabilia, character references for Patrick . . .'

'Do we really need those?' Evan asked, looking over the autopsy report. 'Everyone's heard of Patrick McNabb.'

'Yeah, but everyone doesn't know what kind of person he really is,' I answered.

Evan puckered up his lips in an expression of dislike. 'I don't see how it'll help if they know *that*,' he said.

I rolled my eyes and shook my head. 'You have to stop acting like a fifth grader who's got a crush,' I said. 'Patrick's not a bad guy. He's very warm hearted and considerate, even if he is kind of nuts. He's not the gigantic ego attached to a person that most actors are.'

Evan exhaled heavily and looked at me. 'You've dealt with actors before?'

'I dated one from New York when I was in college,' I told him, adding, 'It's not an experience I'd care to repeat.'

'What can I do to help?' Evan said. I was undeniably grateful he'd decided to change gears and get with the program.

'OK. First, I've got a request for a continuance. Three weeks to prepare for this trial is outrageous. I should have filed it a week ago. So I need you to go down to the courthouse today and file it.'

He sighed. 'Can't that be done electronically?

'I want to be certain it gets into the judge's hands. That's your job.'

He reached for the file I had in my hand. 'Right.'

But I didn't let go. 'It's got to be *today*, Evan. If the judge doesn't approve the request for a continuance, given how little we have left, we have no chance. OK?'

'Of course, OK. No problem.' He looked hurt that I'd even suggest such a thing, so I let the document pass into his hand and smiled.

'Second,' I continued, 'Nate Garrigan has had no luck finding Silvio Cadenza, Patsy's boyfriend and probably the father of her child. See if you can help him out with that. Also, you mentioned knowing something about archery . . .'

'Yes. A little. From high school.' My high school had been lucky to have a basketball and his had an archery program.

'Find me a bona fide expert on the subject who can testify that Patrick McNabb couldn't possibly have fired that arrow, and I'll be really grateful.'

'*How* grateful?' Evan asked playfully, his grin as wide as I could've hoped.

After Evan left to file the motion for a continuance, I chugged the coffee he'd brought and went back to looking through the D.A.'s case against Patrick McNabb. It was tiring work, reading through the police report over and over (it failed to yield anything I hadn't seen before), the medical examiner's report (*see previous parenthetical statement*), and financial records from Patrick and Patsy, before and during their marriage. I felt like I was trying to understand a person's life by reading his electric bill: usage was up this month, so he must have been depressed.

From the new information, such as it was, I extracted the list of witnesses the prosecution intended to call. The M.E. who had performed the autopsy on Patsy was no surprise. Neither was the appearance of Lucien DuPrez, Patsy's business manager. No doubt the coroner would testify that Patsy had been killed by an arrow through her chest – big news – and DuPrez would attest to her decline in popularity and profitability. That meant the D.A. was going to use the money Patrick would have lost in the divorce as his main motive for murder. Normally in California the property would be divided neatly in half, but Patrick and Patsy were married in Las Vegas. The ninety-eight-vs.-two-percent argument they'd been having, which had been the key to the inflammatory meeting I'd messed up, might well have gone with Patrick getting the two. In a normal person that would be a motive. And the prosecutor, bless him, thought Patrick was a normal person.

Patsy's sister, Melanie DeNunzio, was also on the D.A.'s witness list and I figured she'd testify about Patsy's state of mind and the animosity between Patsy and Patrick leading up to the settlement conference, where things truly got dicey. Would the D.A. bring up the issue of Cagney's shoes? I didn't think it likely, because they seemed to have nothing to do with Patsy's murder, and were only a side issue. Perhaps, though, I should be ready to question sister Melanie about the day Patrick went to steal the shoes, to show how valuable they were to him, and to counter any notion the tap shoes were Patrick's motive for killing Patsy.

I had to stop and think about that theory of the case – a grown man killing his wife over a pair of eighty-year-old tap shoes. Life was indeed an odd journey.

Still, the fact that someone was willing to pay two-and-a-half million dollars for the shoes – if true – threw a wrinkle into the case. It was at least possible the anonymous buyer was inflating the price of Jimmy's shoes (even I'd begun calling them that) as a way of increasing Patsy's worth once the divorce became final, even if California law and not the pre-nuptial agreement or Nevada law were enforced (any of which might have been a possibility if the divorce had reached the court). Someone wanted Patsy to get half the value of the shoes, and wanted that value to be substantial. It was a possibility, but there was no evidence to support it.

Eating lunch four hours after starting on the discovery file, I noted that the prosecutor's witness list included a number of financial experts, producers from *Legality,* record producers Patsy had worked with, one expert on show business memorabilia (so they *were* going to talk about the shoes!), Henderson T. Meadows – it took me a moment to realize that was Patrick's butler – a host of psychologists, one of whom had actually spoken to Patrick for fifteen minutes on the night he was arrested, and a few names I didn't recognize. I'd ask Patrick about them later.

It surprised me that no prosecution expert would be called on the subject of archery, but I supposed that, because no claim had been made that someone else had fired the arrow (with the exception of Patrick's saying he hadn't done it), there was no need for expert testimony. Everyone knows how a bow and arrow works.

There was one last name, however, that I did recognize, and its inclusion on the list was, to say the least, surprising – Junius K. Bach.

TWENTY-FOUR

'How should *I* know why my name is on their list?' Bach asked as I stood in front of his desk holding the document in my hand. 'I haven't been served with a subpoena yet.'

'You will be, and soon,' I said.

Bach smiled a thin smile. 'I had suspicions, of course,' he said with almost no inflection. 'But I had no confirmation until you walked in here just now.'

He knew! He knew he was going to be called, and he didn't say anything to me! What kind of a lawyer deliberately holds back information on a case handled by a firm with his name in it? Was he trying to . . . yes! That must be it!

'You're trying to lose this case,' I said, unaware I was speaking out loud to my boss and quite likely stringing up my own noose. 'You're doing your best to make sure your own client is found guilty. Why would you do such a thing?'

Bach did his best to look shocked, but his best wasn't very good – the most he could manage was slightly miffed, which is a long way from the devastation he was aiming at. 'I'm going to pretend you didn't even suggest such a thing to me,' he sniffed.

'Then I'll suggest it again,' I persisted, anger driving my voice this time. This time, it wasn't the wine speaking – it was the coffee. I didn't care any more that this guy could make or break my future with the firm. I wasn't about to let him interfere with my case. 'You're sabotaging this case, and I'm at a loss to understand why.'

Bach raised one eyebrow. 'Are you?'

I stared at him for a long moment, confusion turning to disbelief. 'You can't be serious. All this is because I messed up at the first task I was ever assigned for your firm? Because I was thrown into a situation with no warning whatsoever on my first day of practicing a new kind of law and I let my emotions get the best of me for ten seconds? For that, you're breaching all sorts of ethics and shooting torpedoes at your own firm's biggest case? You must be kidding!'

Bach sniffed again, this time in contempt. 'I'm doing no such thing, Ms Moss, and there is no way you could possibly make such an accusation stand up in court, before a legal grievance review board, or anywhere else. I'm merely complying with the letter of the law, and responding to requests from the district attorney that I cooperate with a case. To do anything less would be criminal.'

I wanted to stand there and look shocked, but I decided it would be much more effective to drop my eyebrows into a deep 'V,' curl my lip into a sneer, and head for the door as if I knew exactly what I was doing. I stopped there, mustering as much Barbara Stanwyck as I could, and said, 'Thank you for making it clear that I can't trust you in the least. I'm now completely justified in not reporting to you on this case.'

'On the contrary,' Bach responded in a voice that could freeze molten lava. 'You will report absolutely every development in this case, every piece of strategy, every scrap of information you get and intend to use, to me immediately. Or else . . .'

'What? You'll fire me?' I was defiant. 'If you could do that, you'd have done it already. No, Mr Bach, you'll get no information at all from me. Why don't you ask your pal, the district attorney, and then report back to me on what he says?' This time, I didn't give him a chance to respond, but flung open the door to his office, and left with a great Joan Crawford swoosh, picturing Bach weeping quietly into his hands. All right, so he probably didn't react at all, but a girl can dream, can't she?

Back in my own office, I ignored the ringing phone and buzzing intercom and gathered my file on Patrick McNabb. From now on, I'd have to keep it all on the cart I'd use for court, and work out of my apartment, to be sure Bach couldn't send in any of his emissaries to confiscate it. This was war.

It wasn't until I piled it all into the taxi that I had a chance to stop my shaking hands and think. If Bach was indeed helping the district attorney, in any way, it meant the prosecution had some concerns about the case. And that presented a possibility I hadn't considered that was so startling, and so revolutionary, that it stopped me dead in my tracks – as stopped dead as I could be in a moving cab – for a solid minute.

It was possible – not definite, not even probable, but possible – that Patrick McNabb actually hadn't killed his wife.

TWENTY-FIVE

I f you're not a veteran of the film industry, the first thing you notice about soundstages is how large they are. The ceilings are so high it's like being outdoors, but for the lack of natural light. The soundstages have no windows, because the lighting must be tightly controlled, and if no sets are built, there's a staggering amount of space sitting there doing nothing.

I thought the sight of a soundstage perfectly encompassed the Hollywood experience – it was tremendous, and totally empty.

For a cinema aficionado like me, the illusion was more important, indeed, more desirable, than the reality of the process. I didn't want to know how things were done – that would ruin the experience of watching the serious films I favored. If something looked on the screen like a park at sunset, I wanted to believe it was a park at sunset. Seeing the colored cellophane 'gels' over the lights that hung so high overhead, and the fake grass underfoot, was hardly awe-inspiring to me.

Here, on the set of *Legality*, only one scene was left to shoot – naturally, because it was out of continuity or context, it made no sense to me. But Angie not only hung on every word as if it held her own fate, but somehow managed to overlook all the artifice of craft and work, and see *only* the illusion. Angie was magically transported to the Portland, Oregon that existed only in the minds of the show's creators, who had once spent a weekend there doing 'research' during ski season. To her, this was Arthur Kirkland's world, and the extra equipment needed to make it come to life might as well have been invisible.

The scene being filmed involved Patrick, as Arthur, being visited in his jail cell by his attorney, Amanda Shaw. But on the set immediately to the right of the tiny jail mock-up was what clearly passed for Arthur's office, and it was that area that Angie's eyes never wavered from – at least until the assistant director began to yell for quiet and a loud bell rang over our heads. This was the signal that the scene was about to begin, and for Angie, that was when reality would once again reign.

'Action,' the director, a slightly portly but sharply dressed (business casual) man in his fifties, said in a conversational tone. A moment went by.

'I can't believe it,' Patrick/Arthur said to his former associate. 'I thought surely the link to Haddonberg would have cemented the motive.'

'The judge didn't see it that way,' the actress playing Amanda answered, letting just a hint of wistful desire flash across her eyes before regaining her professional demeanor. 'He said you were convicted, and there was no reason to reopen the case based on innuendo.'

'Innuendo?!' Patrick/Arthur did his best to appear distraught and outraged at the same time, but to me it came across as petulant. 'It's clear that Haddonberg wanted revenge, and he saw a way to get it. How could—'

'It doesn't matter,' Amanda said. 'We're not getting a new trial this way.'

The camera, on a device that looked a lot like railroad tracks, pulled in for a tight close-up of Patrick looking determined/frustrated (which registered again as petulant), while Amanda stepped out of the shot and rolled her neck a bit.

'OK,' the director said in a tone that implied a slightly agitated lunch order at the deli. 'Let's print that one and set up for coverage.'

The bell rang again, and suddenly everyone visibly relaxed. The technicians began scurrying around like cockroaches, and the lights over the jail cell scene went off. Angie, clearly awestruck, still had her mouth open wide.

'Well, well, two such lovely ladies visiting on the last day of shooting!' It always amazed me how quickly Patrick could change his voice from Arthur Kirkland's decidedly American accent to his own cultivated British one. What did his voice sound like under real duress? When he'd been shot, he barely mumbled before realizing it wasn't a serious wound.

'You're a lousy flatterer, Patrick,' I told him. 'I'd think you could come up with something more original.'

'That's why they hire writers for me, love,' he said with that eye crinkle. I hadn't learned to avert my eyes from that one yet.

Angie stumbled toward Patrick, who was standing near the 'office' set, and her outfit – a neckline so plunging it was practically a waistline, and a skirt short enough to reduce the entire ensemble to the visual equivalent of a wide sash across her waist – drew stares from some of the crew members. Angie has an impressive body, so the stares were mostly from the male crew members, but not exclusively. 'Mr Mc . . . Patrick,' she said, catching his warning look, 'I was wondering if I might just steal . . .' She glanced toward the set, dark but accessible behind him.

'A souvenir?' Patrick nodded toward the office set. 'So long as you don't take the furniture, it should be all right. Check with me first, before you take anything.'

'Oh, *thank* you!' Angie gushed, and I marveled anew at the change in my closest friend's attitude every time the TV actor was nearby. 'I'll be sure to clear it with you. Maybe the "Mason, Kirkland and

Petrocelli" stationery on the desk?' She'd obviously been scoping it out while the crew had been setting-up the prison set scene.

'Perfect,' Patrick replied. 'I'll autograph it for you, and get some of the others to sign it, so you can sell it on eBay when you get home.'

Angie's face turned more serious than when her twenty-two-year-old cat had died. 'Never, Patrick,' she said. 'Never gonna happen.'

She scurried toward the office set as Rex the bodyguard lumbered toward Patrick. 'Don't forget the shopping bag,' Rex said quietly, but not so quietly I couldn't hear him. 'The party will start right after you finish the coverage on this scene.'

'Oh, excellent point, Rex!' Patrick said. 'It has the gifts for the crew. I'll need that. Please. Would you . . .'

Angie, stationery in hand (they actually made it up with a real letterhead, as if the camera would notice), broke in on them. 'Here you go, Patrick,' she said, noticing Rex – as if it would be possible to miss him, his shaved head and his six-foot-seven bodyguard's frame – but intent on her task. 'Do you mind?'

'Not at all,' said Patrick, who could probably sign an autograph in his sleep. But he made it look like he was paying special attention to this one, even if he wasn't. He did not scribble. Angie was thrilled. 'Now, you leave it with me, and I'll get a few of the others to add their signatures.'

'Mr McNabb? The shopping bag?' Rex would not be deterred.

'Ah, yes. I believe it's in my trailer. Do you mind, Rex?' He held out a key. 'It's in a locked cabinet under the iPod dock.'

'Yes, sir.' Rex nodded and turned. But Patrick, a touch of mischief in his eye, broke in.

'Perhaps Angela would like to go with you to see what the trailer looks like. After all, Rex, you might need a bodyguard of your own, bringing back that bag.' Angie's eyes lit up as she hooked herself to Rex's arm and led him out of the soundstage before the poor man knew what hit him. Rex stole a couple of glances back toward Patrick and me, but his fate was obviously sealed, and he knew it.

'So, what is this urgent business of yours, Sandy? Not that I mind a visit, and I hope you'll stay for the wrap party.'

'It's important, Patrick, and confidential. Is there a place we can talk privately?'

He looked impressed. 'Certainly,' he said. 'There's a wardrobe room just over there.' Patrick pointed across the floor to a door and led me toward it.

We walked inside, and he closed the door behind us. The walls were covered all the way up to the fifty-foot ceiling with racks of clothing, some contemporary, some period: women's, men's, formal, and casual. I swear I recognized a dress from an Ingrid Bergman film of 1956.

'Angie would have a stroke in here,' I said. Patrick chuckled.

'You see? I'm not the only one who likes to collect things from old movies,' he said. 'Now, what's the trouble?'

'You can't trust Junius Bach,' I said, cutting right to the chase. 'He's working against us on this case, and might even be giving information to the district attorney. Don't tell him anything, and don't look for me in the firm's offices any more. I'll be working from home for the duration.'

Patrick looked like he was doing a very bad impression of a very drunk man. His eyebrows shot up and his eyes lost their focus. He shook his head.

'Junius? I can't believe it.'

'Believe it. He did everything but admit it to me less than two hours ago.' I wanted to impress Patrick with my dedication to his case. It suddenly meant a great deal to me that he remain loyal to me, and not to Junius Bach. Besides, I had just as wide a vindictive streak as the next girl, assuming the next girl was Lucretia Borgia.

'But, why? It doesn't make sense. Junius doesn't gain anything by sabotaging my case.' Patrick began to idly fondle the fringes of a 1920s flapper dress (red, of course) hanging just at his head.

'He wants *me* to fail, and he wants to fire me,' I said. 'This is personal, and it has nothing to do with you.'

'You're sounding just a bit paranoid, Sandy,' he said. 'Perhaps you're misinterpreting . . .'

The door opened, and two men I hadn't seen before, dressed like the technicians outside, walked in. They wore baseball caps pressed low on their heads, and were looking down just slightly, so it was hard to see their faces in this light. Atlanta Braves baseball hats, I noticed.

'Do you mind?' Patrick said. 'We're having a private conversation here.'

'I'll bet it's *real* private,' said the taller man, and if there is such a thing as a vocal leer, he provided it. 'But we're forced to interrupt this *private* conversation.'

My back immediately tensed. The tension increased when I noticed the shorter man locking the wardrobe room door from the inside.

Patrick's eyes narrowed in genuine confusion. 'Is there a problem, gentlemen?' he asked.

The shorter man tapped the larger one on the biceps and chortled. 'You hear that? He thinks we're gentlemen.'

The taller one ignored him. 'We're here because you didn't take the hint in the car, or at UCLA,' he said to Patrick, his voice hoarse but even. 'You didn't die when you were supposed to.'

Shit, I thought, inhaling sharply. 'Get behind me, Patrick,' I said, and tried to step in front of him.

'Don't be silly, Sandy.' Patrick pushed me away with his left arm. 'This is just a misunderstanding. Isn't it, gentlemen?'

'No,' the taller one said. 'I think she understands perfectly.' Each of the intruders reached into his jacket pocket and brought out a box cutter.

'OK, I get it,' Patrick said, 'that jokester, Jude Law, has gone too far this time. Tell him we were really scared, OK? But that's enough.'

'Jude Law,' the shorter one said, snickering again. 'He thinks we know Jude Law.'

Keep them talking, I thought. *Talking is better than slashing.* 'I don't understand,' I said. 'Why do you want to kill us? What have we done to you?'

'*You* haven't done nothing,' the shorter one said. 'You're an innocent bystander. It's *him* that's offended people.' The two men began advancing on Patrick, who tried again, unsuccessfully, to push me aside.

'What people?' I pressed. If I was going to get whacked, I at least wanted to know on whose orders.

Patrick moved his right arm this time, pushing me away while his left arm came up behind us and pulled down a free-standing clothing rack. He managed to step through it as he pulled, dropping the rack and the clothing in the intruders' direction.

He pulled me with him as he retreated into the room, but it

wasn't large, and the entrance through which the intruders had come was blocked by, well, them. The two men jumped back to avoid the falling rack, lost a moment, then advanced more quickly, brandishing the box cutters.

Backed into a corner, with Patrick at my left side, I couldn't think straight. Words were coming out of my mouth faster than I could think them.

'Patrick, tell me now – did you kill Patsy?'

He stared at me with a where-did-*that*-come-from expression, and said, 'Maybe this isn't the time.'

'This is exactly the time. I need to know.'

His gaze softened, and he said quietly, 'Of course not.'

Patrick stepped in front of me as the intruders reached us. The taller man raised his box cutter into the air and, reflexively, I gasped, trying desperately to think of something to say or do, but I couldn't focus over the voice in my head screaming *PANIC! PANIC! PANIC! PANIC!* Even screaming out loud seemed impossible. It was like a dream where you know that if you scream, you can wake up, but you can't summon even the slightest sound from your throat.

Luckily, the situation did not depend on my quick thinking. The door to the room burst open, the lock disintegrating and wood from the frame flying, and Rex's huge foot entered. The rest of Rex wasn't far behind, and all of Angie was behind him.

'Mr McNabb?' said Rex, as he and Angie ran into the room.

'Here, Rex!' Patrick yelled, and we instinctively melted to the floor. The look exchanged between the two intruders meant only one thing: 'Uh-oh.'

I wrapped my arms over my head and tucked my face to the floor in some sort of helpless, defensive position. I heard loud footsteps, then Angie yelling, 'Sand? Where are you?' And then, nothing.

When I finally came to and looked up, Rex and Angie were standing over me, Rex looking about fifteen feet tall. Patrick was dusting himself off and standing up, and the two intruders were nowhere in sight.

It took me a moment, but I eventually managed to croak out, 'What happened?'

Angie held her hand out and helped me, on shaking legs, to stand. 'I was going to ask you that exact same question,' she

said. 'What were you two' – and she got a glint in her eye –
'*doing* in here?'

I looked around the room where, aside from the fallen clothing,
there was no sign of a struggle. 'What do you mean, what were
we doing?' I asked. 'What happened to those two men?'

Rex looked at Angie. Angie looked at Rex. Rex turned to me.
'*What* two men?' he said.

I looked at Patrick. Patrick looked at me. Then he took a long,
careful look around the wardrobe room. 'There must be a back
door,' I said, turning to Patrick. 'Why didn't you know that?'

'I think somebody had better call the police,' Patrick said.

TWENTY-SIX

Lieutenant K.C. Trench was, after all, a twenty-five-year
veteran of the Los Angeles Police Department, so this was
not his first film set, and even if it were, he would not have
been in awe. Actually, I didn't think Trench would be in awe if
whatever deity he worshipped descended from the heavens and
called him by name.

'So two men in Atlanta Braves baseball caps threatened you
with box cutters, and never mentioned why they might be doing
so? Is that right?' Trench asked us. He was looking up into the
catwalks and lights above our heads. Still, I knew he was watching
for facial expressions, in case either of us betrayed anything. The
man's peripheral vision was amazing.

'That's about right, Lieutenant,' I answered, with an effort to
sound as natural as possible. *Sure. Two men with razor blades
wanted to slit our throats. Yup. Happens every day. Why do you
ask?*

'Mr McNabb, do you have any idea why someone might want
to have you killed? If I'm counting correctly, this is now the fourth
attempt – the drive-by shooting, the sniper attack, the exploding
Ferrari, and this. That makes four, doesn't it?'

Patrick, obviously intrigued by the presence of a real policeman
(another possible research subject), widened his eyes and nodded.

'Yes, Lieutenant. I'm starting to feel just a little picked on.' There was a chuckle, but Trench didn't participate in it.

'Why,' he asked quietly, 'would someone want you dead?'

Patrick's smile faded. 'I really have no idea, Lieutenant.'

'One of the men said he had "offended people,"' I piped up, and Trench's eyebrow raised just a little.

'Offended people?' he asked. 'What people might those be?'

'He didn't say,' I said, but I knew Trench understood as well as I did that there were probably hundreds of people Patrick had managed to offend over the years.

'I wasn't asking you,' Trench said dismissively. 'Mr McNabb?'

Patrick made a show of thinking, which was mostly believable. He shook his head. 'I can't think of anyone, Lieutenant. I truly can't. It could be . . . no, I really don't believe they'd take it so seriously.'

'Who?' said Trench, his voice barely registering interest.

'There's a group of people who might be blaming me for what happened to Patsy, and they've been known to be a little . . . extreme in their devotion to her. Some of them would actually set up camp outside our house.'

'What is this group called, Mr McNabb?' Slight irritation was the only emotion evident in his voice.

'They call themselves PIOUS,' he said.

I felt dizzy all of a sudden. 'PIOUS?' I managed to utter. 'PIOUS is an acronym?'

'What do you know about this group, Ms Moss?' Trench's eyes were now on the group of technicians, actors, and producers gathered around the set as uniformed officers continued to search the wardrobe room behind us.

'Until two seconds ago, I didn't know it *was* a group,' I told him. I was sitting in the director's chair with 'Guest Star' written across the back and wishing Trench would look at me when I spoke to him. Patrick had draped his suit jacket over my shoulders, as if being threatened with a razor blade would naturally make me cold. 'It was written on a . . .' I kept talking, but my voice trailed off at Trench's inattention.

'A what?' Trench barked.

'A BARBIE DOLL,' I answered, more loudly than I'd intended.

'Someone nailed a Barbie doll to my front door, and wrote "PIOUS" on it. I didn't know what it meant.'

Patrick furrowed his brow and said, 'It stands for Patsy's International Order of United Servants. We used to joke about it, Patsy and me. Whenever she'd leave her underwear on the floor or something, I'd say she should get one of her United Servants to pick it up. They'd camp out beyond the gate, and sleep in sleeping bags. It was kind of spooky.'

Finally, Trench's laser stare focused on me. 'And why did you not mention this the last time we spoke?' he asked.

'It happened after the last time we spoke. Somebody nailed a doll to my door, Lieutenant. I'm not sure that really merits a call to nine-one-one.'

'Perhaps not under normal circumstances, but when one's life has been threatened – *more than once* – I would think it would prompt a call to your friendly detective lieutenant. Don't you? Particularly in a murder investigation.'

'I promise to call you the very next time it happens,' I said as sarcastically as possible – as if this guy had been much help to me, anyway.

'Thank you.' Not a glimmer, not the slightest upturn of a lip. Damn, he was good!

'Does your classifying this as a murder investigation mean you're reopening the case, Lieutenant? Does that mean you're not convinced Patrick is guilty even if the D.A. thinks so?' I was now convinced my client was not guilty, and wanted Trench on my side.

This time, the slightest hint of a smile showed for a split second. 'That, Ms Moss, is not my department,' he said.

Patrick, citing his professionalism, insisted on doing the final scenes as soon as Trench and the police vacated the soundstage, but that would probably take an hour or more. So the wrap party was rescheduled for the next night.

This, of course, deflated Angie, who informed me she'd have to find a second party-worthy outfit, and thus intended to spend the rest of the day shopping, preferably on Rodeo Drive. I didn't bother to mention that she'd probably have to sell an entire Dairy Queen franchise to afford one outfit from any establishment bearing that address. Let the girl have her fun. Besides, I had some serious work to get done.

Angie, in her new capacity as my chauffeur using her rental car, dropped me at my apartment, where I started to set up my working home office while avoiding Bach and, presumably, securing a post-trial lawyer's job. The forthcoming job search was something of a disheartening prospect, because all the people I knew in Southern California worked at Seaton, Taylor, Evans and Bach.

I hadn't been at home ten minutes when the doorbell rang. Wary of additional PIOUS deliveries, I checked through the keyhole, then let in a frantic-looking Evan.

'What's going on?' he demanded, practically flying inside and checking every room for intruders. *Thanks*, I thought. *If you weren't here, I never would have looked in the other rooms.* 'Your office is empty, and I heard something about an attack at the studio . . .'

'Calm down,' I said, realizing just how pointless that particular phrase is. (Has anyone ever calmed down when you told them to?) I explained why I'd cleaned all the files out of my office.

'You can't be serious,' Evan said finally.

'Which part?'

He sat down heavily on the sofa, dislodging an accordion folder I'd placed on the other cushion. 'You think Junius Bach is deliberately sabotaging a case belonging to his own firm? That'd be criminal!'

'I told you someone was giving information to the D.A. Bach all but admitted it,' I said. 'But that's the problem. There's no proof, and if he denies it, I can't report him, because who are they going to believe? But *I* know it, and I have to act on it until this trial is over.'

'You can't be right,' Evan said, shaken. 'You must have misunderstood.'

'There's nothing to misunderstand. He just about told me he's doing it.'

'*Just about?* You might have misinterpreted . . .' Evan's head flopped into his hands, but after a brief recitation of my conversation with Bach, I heard him say, 'No, it was clear enough, wasn't it?'

'Yes. It was clear enough. Now, are you going to help me?'

Evan's head snapped up like it was on a spring. 'Of course I'm going to help you. What made you think I wouldn't?'

'You need your job, don't you?'

He sputtered, a sound that came very close to a Bronx cheer. 'This *is* my job. Junius Bach himself told me to help you, and that's what I'm going to do until he tells me otherwise.' Evan stood and walked over to me. He kissed me lightly on the lips, then put his arms around my waist. 'In any way I possibly can,' he added with a mischievous look in his eyes.

I allowed myself to enjoy the thought, but, after a moment, extricated myself from the embrace. 'That's nice, but we have work that needs to get done. Did you file for that continuance?'

'Yes. I stayed until the judge got in, and he denied it immediately.'

I collapsed into a chair and bit on the pen I had in my hand. 'Wow. Something's got to be pushing him. I wonder if Bach knows the judge well.'

'Bach knows every judge in the lower half of the state well, but you can't blame him for everything that happens to us. The judge read the motion and denied it, without comment. We have to move on.'

I exhaled heavily. 'That means we have three weeks until the trial starts. Three weeks!'

'It could be worse,' Evan offered.

'How?'

He paused, apparently considering the thought for a long time. 'It could be one week.'

TWENTY-SEVEN

Robin J. Flynn was, by any measure, an interesting woman. At the age of twenty-eight, she'd already been an Olympic athlete, a Rhodes scholar, a municipal official, and a swim-suit model. The fact that she worked as a corporate executive for a sporting goods manufacturer and drove a Porsche didn't impress me one bit.

The swimsuit model thing was a tad annoying, though.

'Ms Flynn, you were an Olympic archer, and you've actually written a book on archery. Is that right?' I was preparing Robin for her expert testimony, and trying very hard not to notice Evan, who sat across the room trying to avoid ogling various parts of Robin's anatomy, all of which were eminently ogle-able.

'That's right,' Flynn said confidently. 'It's called *Aim to be a Champion.*'

'Did you write the book yourself? No ghostwriter?'

Robin looked shocked, and glanced at Evan, who had to look away so quickly, I thought he'd sprain a neck muscle. Good. 'Oh, no. I wouldn't put my name on a book that someone else wrote. The book's all mine.'

'That's good,' I said, 'but if I ask you at trial, just answer yes, that you wrote it yourself. Keep your answers direct.'

'Sure. I mean, yes.'

'Now, Robin, have you gotten a chance to look over the police report on the death of Patsy DeNunzio?'

Flynn's eyes widened a little. 'Yes,' she said. 'It was awful, wasn't it?'

'Let's stick with "yes," OK?' I turned my back on Robin and looked with just a little desperation at Evan, who appeared to force himself to meet my eyes. He gave a miniscule shrug, as if to say, '*Who did you expect me to get? William Tell?*'

I turned back to Robin. 'Did you see anything in that report that would indicate to you that Patrick McNabb was not responsible for the death of his wife?'

Robin was very quiet, and obviously thinking very hard. She picked up the copy of the police report I'd given her, glanced at it again, then put it down and looked me in the eye.

'No.'

My eyebrows involuntarily shot up so high, I was sure they were hovering near the apartment's ceiling. 'No?' I asked, my voice rising a little more than I'd intended. 'Just "no?"'

'I thought I was supposed to keep my answers short and direct.'

This was like pulling teeth – without Novocain. 'Well, that's true, but I'm a little disappointed you didn't find anything that can help our case.'

'It's very difficult,' Robin answered. 'The type of arrow used would certainly have penetrated through bone and muscle very efficiently at the proper distance, and the bow was strong, had been recently restrung, and was extremely well cared-for. There's no reason to think it was done with any other weapon.'

I thought hard. 'How about strength? Would it have taken an unusually strong man to launch the arrow that hard?'

Robin shook her head sadly. 'I'm sorry, no. Given that bow's condition and the type of arrow being used, it wouldn't have to be an especially strong man, just one who'd used a bow before and knew something about archery.'

'Could it have been an accident?'

Flynn looked up, as if peering into her right frontal lobe. 'I really don't think so,' she said. 'The arrow had to hit her at just the proper angle to penetrate her heart, and that's exactly what it did. Someone aimed very carefully, I'd say.'

Swell. If I sign up any more expert witnesses like this, I can collect double pay and work as the executioner, too.

'Thanks, Robin. I appreciate your coming by today.'

Flynn stood, and went out of her way to bend over to pick up her purse, so Evan could see angles he hadn't gotten before. 'Do you know when you'll be calling me as a witness?' she asked, directing the question toward Evan.

'I don't know if we will be calling you, Robin.' I made sure to answer quickly. 'But if we do, one of us will call you a few days ahead of time.'

'OK,' she said, standing and smoothing out her incredibly tight dress. 'I'll look forward to hearing from you,' she added, staring into Evan's eyes. She wiggled her way past him and out the door of my apartment.

I flopped onto the sofa and made a noise that came out sounding a lot like a person trying to ignore an ulcer. 'Well, *she* was a ton of help.'

'What did you want?' Evan asked. 'For her to lie?'

'Not lie so much as help. Would it have killed her to find some angle that wasn't damning to Patrick?' *Or at least to have been less sexy?*

'You know, you have to confront the idea that he may be guilty. Only a few days ago, you were telling me yourself he probably did it. Now, you're convinced he's as innocent as the driven snow. Make up your mind, Sandy.' Evan walked over and sat down next to me, putting his head back on the couch and closing his eyes.

'Snow isn't innocent,' I corrected him. 'Snow is pure.'

'It's a metaphor.'

'We've got to find somebody who can cast at least a little doubt on the D.A.'s case. Who else knew Patrick had the bow and arrow?' I rubbed my puffy eyes.

'Anyone who'd been to his house. It was prominently displayed, and not in one of the cases he has now. It was right out on the wall. Anybody could have seen it.'

'That's good,' I said. 'We can establish that Patrick wasn't the only one who knew the weapon was handy.'

'But no one else was in the house that night,' Evan said, eyes still closed. 'Even the butler had the night off.'

'Come on. At least it's something.' I heard the cell phone ring, and reached for it.

'We've got a lead *and* a problem,' Garrigan said before I could even say hello. 'I found Silvio, the boyfriend, but he's in Ensenada, Mexico.'

'That's not a problem,' I said. 'We can drive there in a couple of hours, right?' One good thing about relocating to southern California – I was only a hop, skip, and a jump from some fabulous beaches in Mexico.

'That's not the problem,' said Garrigan. 'The problem is, your friend McNabb is there with him.'

'No he's not,' I said, feeling my stomach flip-flop. 'Patrick can't be in Mexico. If Patrick leaves the state, let alone the country, I'll be responsible for . . .'

'He's there,' Garrigan said.

'We're on our way.'

TWENTY-EIGHT

Ensenada, Mexico is like any other oceanfront city, as long as you're staying at a resort like El Oceano Hermoso, a five-star hotel with three swimming pools, four dining rooms, a casino, and hourly parasailing lessons, all on a mile-long private beach. Following Garrigan's directions, which consisted mostly of 'keep the ocean on your right,' had proved simple and effective. After the three-hour drive to Ensenada (I insisted on driving Evan's car, so we'd actually get there the same day), I was in no mood for small talk. But the talk couldn't have gotten any smaller if printed on the dialogue balloon of a Bazooka Joe cartoon inside a gum wrapper.

'Did you have any trouble finding the resort?' Patrick asked, ever the good host. In his bathing trunks and cabana jacket, he was so relaxed I had to fight back an urge to strangle him.

'Do . . . you . . . have . . . *any* . . . idea . . . how much trouble you've gotten into? Gotten *me* into? Were you *listening* to the judge at your arraignment, Patrick? If you're seen down here, I can be disbarred and fined so much money I'll be paying off *your* trip to Mexico for the rest of my life!'

Patrick responded by doing the most infuriating thing possible: he smiled. 'Relax, Sandy,' he said. 'No one knows I'm here, and I'll be back in Los Angeles before anyone knows I'm gone. The important thing is we found Silvio Cadenza! He's right here in the hotel, and we have him cornered.'

I stole a glance at Nate Garrigan, who was leaning against the door in case Patrick decided to bolt. Garrigan shrugged. 'I have no idea how he found out I'd traced Cadenza down here, but when I arrived, he greeted me in the lobby,' Garrigan said. All eyes turned to Patrick.

'It's quite simple,' he said with great amiability. 'I had you followed.'

Garrigan blinked twice, which, for him was the equivalent of a conniption. 'You did what?'

'I hired a private investigator. Sandy said you couldn't find the person who'd offered me all the money for Jimmy's shoes, so I hired an investigator of my own. He followed you while you were looking for Silvio, because I suspected he was the one who offered me the money.'

Garrigan might very well have considered stretching Patrick's neck to three times its normal length, but he made no move. 'And when I located Cadenza, your P.I. knew it, and called you.'

'Yes. Luckily, I was already a little south of you, and I have a somewhat faster car than you do. Not your fault, Mr Garrigan.'

I stood up and surveyed Patrick's lavish hotel suite, which no doubt he'd paid for in cash. In one room, there was a grand piano, which I was relatively sure no one in the suite could play. A wet bar and a home theater were in another area. I couldn't see the bedrooms, but I'm willing to bet that Patrick, who was planning on staying here by himself, had at least three.

'Why, exactly, do you suspect Cadenza was offering two and a half million dollars for Cagney's shoes?' I decided to ask.

'Why don't we go and ask him?' Patrick suggested.

Silvio Cadenza turned out to be a short, balding man, about five-foot-six, who could have passed for ten years younger than forty-five, his actual age. And his suite, while quite attractive, was not half as lavish as Patrick's. No piano. A big-screen TV, but no home theater. Probably only two bedrooms. A hovel, by comparison.

He didn't seem the least bit surprised when Patrick led us into the living room. He nodded a few times, and rarely took his eyes off Patrick.

'Silvio,' Patrick said without the crinkling eyes.

'McNabb.'

Patrick introduced the rest of us to Cadenza, and Evan made a point of standing next to me, either to protect me if violence broke out, or to establish himself with me while Patrick was in the room. I supposed it was better than singing a chorus of 'Bess, You Is My Woman Now.'

'We've had a difficult time finding you, Silvio,' Patrick continued. 'Have you been hiding?'

'If I was hiding,' Cadenza suggested, 'you wouldn't have found me. Now, what do you want? I'm on vacation.'

'From what? I don't remember you ever doing a day's work.' This was a side of Patrick I hadn't seen a lot of before – one without any of the usual charm he used to get his way.

'I don't need to get into a pissing contest with you, McNabb. The way you see it, I stole your wife. The way I see it, she was already gone, and I happened to be there when she left. She was in love with me, and I was in love with her. I don't think you could say the same thing.'

Patrick didn't even bother to snort – he ignored the statement. 'Why did you call me and offer me millions for Jimmy's shoes, Silvio? You must have thought Patsy would get them in the divorce.'

'Shoes? What shoes? Now I'm a cobbler?' Cadenza thought he was amusing. He certainly was amusing himself.

Patrick didn't have the chance to respond when Garrigan stepped forward. 'Mr Cadenza, we're here to investigate the death of Patsy DeNunzio.'

'What's to investigate?' Cadenza said, staring directly into Patrick's eyes. 'I think we all know who killed her.'

'I didn't do it, Silvio,' Patrick said, suddenly softening his voice in what I assumed was some sort of actor's trick.

'Right. And I didn't steal your wife. It's all how you look at it.' Cadenza, taking on a disgusted look, spoke to Garrigan without making eye contact with anyone but Patrick. 'What do you want to know?'

'Well, for one thing, where were you on the night Patsy was killed?' Garrigan asked, inserting a little gravel into his voice.

'I was at home, alone. I watched *The Bachelorette*. What else do you want to know?'

'Any way you can prove you were alone? Or that you were at home?'

'You know,' Cadenza said, still staring at Patrick, 'if I'd known I needed an alibi, I probably would have arranged it better. You should have thought of that, too, McNabb. Sloppy, being found there like that.'

Garrigan broke the invisible line between Patrick and Cadenza by standing between them and commanding Cadenza's attention. 'You were the father of Patsy's baby. Weren't you, Silvio?'

Cadenza shrugged. 'Probably. You want DNA? I'll pull out a hair.'

'Hair doesn't have DNA unless you pull it out the right way,' Garrigan said. 'You're taking it awfully well for a guy who was in love with the deceased.' I saw he was trying to irritate Cadenza, but I couldn't think why.

'I've had some time to collect my thoughts. Is there anything else you need to know?'

'Did *you* know that someone else had sex with Patsy the night she was murdered?' Garrigan asked with a wicked leer.

'What do you mean, someone else?' Cadenza's face was no longer impassive. This was news to him. I started to understand Garrigan's ploy.

'He means me,' Patrick said, stepping out from behind Garrigan. 'Patsy and I made love before I found her out on the floor of the dining room.'

Cadenza's eyes flashed, but then he sat back and sighed. 'Well, you were her husband, after all. Makes me wonder why you shot her with an arrow. Maybe you couldn't get anything else into her, huh?'

Patrick clenched his teeth, but Garrigan, smiling an evil smile and looking right at Cadenza, stepped in Patrick's way again before the smaller man could move. 'It might also make you wonder why he would kill her,' Garrigan said. 'Maybe someone else did it out of jealousy, huh, Cadenza?'

'I just found out about it five seconds ago,' Cadenza said, a small bead of sweat starting on his forehead. 'When did I have time to be jealous?'

'That's your story,' said Garrigan.

'And I'm sticking to it.'

Garrigan nodded, and turned toward the door. Patrick grabbed him by the shoulder, reaching up. 'What, aren't you going to ask him about the shoes?' he said.

I walked over to Patrick and took him by the arm. 'Let it go with the shoes, Patrick. You don't have any evidence at all.'

'I have instinct, and phone records.' Patrick stood firm. 'He called me and tried to offer me two and a half million dollars for Jimmy's shoes.' He walked to Cadenza and stared into his face, only a few inches away. 'Why?'

Cadenza spoke very slowly. 'I don't know what you're talking about,' he said.

Garrigan grabbed Patrick by the shoulder again and led him toward the door. Patrick tried to shake him off, but the investigator was too big to budge. The rest of us followed them to the door.

'I'm gonna prove it,' Patrick said, his voice turning more cockney by the second. 'I'm gonna prove you've got Jimmy's shoes!' Garrigan then pushed him out into the hallway.

I stayed in the room long enough to hear Cadenza's brief comment: 'Shoes.'

TWENTY-NINE

Much to Evan's chagrin, I rode home in Patrick's Lexus. This had the dual effect of allowing me to see that Patrick actually returned to the United States as quickly as possible (thus reducing the probability that I would end up in jail and without a lawyer's license) and cutting down on the traveling time, because Patrick drove approximately seventeen times faster than Evan would.

It also gave me time to berate him again for leaving California to begin with.

'Patrick, you have responsibilities,' I began. 'If you don't care about not going to jail yourself, the least you can do is take into account the fact that I *do* care about not going to jail. I'd prefer to stay out of prison, if that's OK with you.'

'Don't be melodramatic,' he told me. 'You're not going to jail.'

I took a few deep breaths to calm myself. 'Patrick,' I said, 'I hope you were listening to what the judge said at your arraignment. If you leave the state, let alone the *country*, I'll be held responsible. He'll consider me in contempt of court, and I'll be put in jail. So don't tell me I'm getting melodramatic.'

'Well, we are on our way back, so you don't have to worry any longer, love,' he said with no tension whatsoever. 'It'll all work out. I have every confidence in you.'

'You're impossible.' We were silent for a few moments, until I could stand it no longer. 'OK. Tell me about the shoes.'

'What about them?' He seemed sincerely puzzled by my question.

'I don't get what the big deal is. Sure, you're a collector and they're a rare item. Yes, someone you don't know supposedly offered you two and a half million dollars for them. But for someone like you, that's not really even life-changing money. I don't get why you seem so obsessed with finding these shoes.'

Patrick stared at the road for such a long time I wondered

whether he'd heard me. I stayed silent, though, and waited, and eventually, he spoke without turning his head or moving his eyes. He continued to stare at the road, and I stared at the speedometer, which was pointing at a number that appeared to be over ninety miles per hour.

'I think there's a note in one of the shoes,' he said. 'Patsy used to laugh at me because I was so taken with them, and I would hold them and take them out of their case and measure my feet against them. She thought it was funny.

'But there was a tear in the lining of the left shoe, just under the tongue. Perhaps an inch and a half, and I worried about it. If I left it untended, it could get larger, and damage the shoe. But to repair the lining would be to alter the condition of the shoe as it had come down through the years. It was a dilemma, and Patsy thought that was funny, too. We had something of . . . a row about it.'

I desperately wanted to ask what this had to do with a note, but I held my tongue. Patrick was trying to keep some emotion or another in check, and I didn't want to find out which one it might be. The man was, after all, charged with murder.

'I couldn't decide what to do, and the next day, while I was examining the tear, I noticed the corner of a piece of paper sticking out, and I was sure I'd never seen it before. The paper wasn't yellowed or aged in any way, so I knew it hadn't been there on my previous examination. I got a pair of tweezers, and took the folded paper out very carefully.

'Once I did, it was obvious the paper was new. It was a sheet of Patsy's personal note paper. And when I unfolded it, there was a handwritten note from Patsy. It said, 'Get over it, Patrick. It's just a shoe. Leave it alone.' And I laughed for the longest time, and never had the shoe repaired.'

'So you put the note back in, and you think it's still there?' I didn't understand why that note would hold so much value.

'No,' said Patrick, still stone-faced and watching the road. 'It became an inside joke of sorts. After we had a fight, Patsy would leave me a note in the shoe. Sometimes she'd apologize, and sometimes she would call on me to apologize. But there was always a note. In her notes, she said the things she just couldn't say to my face.' He stopped for a moment, and I thought he might have sniffled a bit. 'And the last night, when I was there, well, I didn't really have . . . time . . . to check the shoe for a note.' He was silent, and I chose not to look at him.

'So you think there might be a new one there.'

A long pause. 'Yes,' came the reply. 'And it'll contain the last words I'll ever get from Patsy. So I want that shoe very badly.'

We sat and watched the road for the rest of the trip – or, at least, the portion of the trip before the bright flashing lights behind us indicated that Patrick was being pulled over for speeding. Then, I turned to him and spoke.

'Please tell me,' I said, 'that we've crossed back over the border into California.'

THIRTY

The interesting thing about holding cells, I've decided, is they give you a lot of time for thinking. Of course, 'cell' might be too harsh a word for the windowless room in which Patrick and I were being detained – it was more an institutional waiting area, much like the Division of Motor Vehicles or a private waiting room in an emergency ward at a suburban hospital.

The police in La Joya, Mexico (roughly a seven-mile drive to the California border) were polite, and spoke excellent English, but Patrick insisted on talking to them in Spanish, which I could only assume was unaccented, or sounded like cockney-Spanish. They were terribly sorry to have to detain the television star, they said, but rules are rules, and when a man is accused of murder in the States, well, there were certain procedures that had to be observed. They said all this in English, so the 'young lady' could understand.

While we waited in a pair of plastic chairs, we said nothing to each other. I was ready to strangle him, and therefore was better off not getting into a discussion with my intended victim that might draw police attention. Patrick, for his part, stared directly into space, with a facial expression that can only be described as serene.

After being told the Mexican police would 'check with the Los Angeles court,' we were left in the cell with the door closed but, as far as I knew, not locked. Why bother? There was nowhere for us to go.

What bugged me more than anything else was the knowledge that now Evan would probably get home before me, even driving at ten miles under the speed limit the whole way up I-5. Sorry. 'The Five.'

As I simmered, I came to the conclusion that there was no point in castigating Patrick. It would make me feel better, but he was incorrigible. He'd simply grin at me and tell me how 'brilliant' I was, and that would lead only to certain violence. Still, the silence was starting to get to me.

'Patrick,' I said finally, 'who else knew you had the bow and arrow?' What the hell – I'd been meaning to ask him all day.

'Everyone knew.' Patrick seemed to wake up when I spoke to him. His head perked up and his face became animated. 'I'd only had it a month, six weeks maybe. And we'd had a party right after I got it, so I could show it off.'

'Tell me who "everyone" is,' I pressed, keeping him on topic. 'Everyone you showed it to at that party, as best you can remember.'

Patrick sat back and closed his eyes. For a moment, I thought he was going to sleep. But then he started reciting names, and I had to reach for a pad and pen that were in my purse, which the police – for some reason – had not confiscated.

'Well, Patsy's sister, Melanie, of course. My producers, Lizz and Manny.' (These later turned out to be Elizibith Warnell and Emmanuel B. Richler.) 'Some of the cast from *Legality*. Patsy's manager.'

'DuPrez?'

'Yes. And her bass player, Erubiel Santanaya. Maybe one or two other musicians.'

'Was Silvio Cadenza there?' I wanted to have a clear picture of possible suspects. I couldn't hang the crime on one of them in court, but if I could arouse suspicion, that might be enough to constitute reasonable doubt in the minds of some of the jurors.

'Yes,' Patrick's lip snarled a bit. 'That was when I began to suspect there was something between them. He kept coming over and touching her on the arm.'

'I thought you didn't mind by then – that you and Patsy were on the outs already.'

'No man likes it when another man blatantly moves in on his wife,' Patrick said without opening his eyes. 'No matter how bad your marriage, you don't like it.'

'How much didn't you like it?' I asked.

Patrick opened his eyes and turned to me, grinning just a bit. 'There's no trust with you, is there? I've repeatedly told you I didn't kill Patsy.'

'You'll forgive me if I can't accept that on faith. In court, I have to prove things. I can't tell the jury, "You have to believe me because me client told me very sincerely that he didn't do it."'

'I suppose not,' he exhaled. 'Look. There's a long way between not liking someone and being moved to deadly violence against them. I'm not saying I would have invited Silvio Cadenza to my next birthday bash, but if I were going to kill someone, it probably wouldn't have been Patsy.'

'Even when you found out she was pregnant?'

'I found out when you told me,' he said. 'I don't know if Patsy herself was aware yet. Besides, this is Hollywood. There are five women in a twenty-mile radius who have children by their actual, current husbands, and three of the husbands are in their eighties.'

I reminded myself I wasn't questioning Patrick for the prosecution, and got back on the path I'd started. 'Who else there might have seen the bow and arrow?'

'There were fifty people there that night – it was a small party,' he said. 'But there might have been another hundred who'd seen it in the house on other days. I don't keep a list of visitors. Perhaps Meadows would know better.'

'Anyone you can think of who had a grudge against Patsy?'

Patrick closed his eyes again and yawned. 'When she was on top, sure,' he said. 'But in this town, once your star fades, nobody cares about you enough to hate you any more.'

The door opened, and an officer – the one who had pulled over Patrick's car – walked in with a clipboard in his hand. Patrick stood up and immediately began talking to him in Spanish. I held up a hand.

'I'm Mr McNabb's attorney,' I said. 'You two really need to

speak English, so I can understand the charges against him.' I stood up and faced the officer.

'The charge against him is speeding,' the officer said with just the hint of an accent. 'I'm giving him a ticket.'

'And your inquiry with the California authorities?' I asked.

'You are free to go,' the officer said. 'But the judge – he is not so happy with you.'

THIRTY-ONE

After a day of developing strategy and interviewing expert witnesses on film memorabilia, the *Legality* wrap party was not exactly what I needed. I would have preferred about sixteen uninterrupted hours of sleep, but felt it important to meet some of the possible suspects Patrick had mentioned in an informal setting (preferably with alcohol available to loosen some tongues). I also wanted to keep an eye on Angie, who'd returned from Rodeo Drive empty-handed, but had managed to find a suitably jaw-dropping outfit at her usual boutique, Target (which she pronounced 'Tar-jay').

Held in a restaurant so exclusive it had no name and no outdoor sign, the party was an event of either unbearable elegance or horrifying excess, depending on one's point of view. Angie came down solidly on the side of elegance, while I leaned toward the contrary position.

The below-ground restaurant, a large rectangular room with no windows, was decorated with the latest in modern design. Seven different shades of beige on the walls were punctuated by splashes of primary color, seemingly lifted straight from a box of Crayolas. I couldn't see much of the walls, however, because the place was jammed with people, tables, and a bandstand, at which a ten-piece classical ensemble was playing Schubert under the direction of the conductor of the Los Angeles Symphony Orchestra.

'Look at this place.' I nudged Angie as we headed for a table with Elliott Gould and Raven-Symoné. 'You half expect to see the ice sculpture of Michelangelo's *David* urinating vodka.'

'*Yeah*,' Angie replied. 'That would have been cool.'

I am not a snob by nature, but this occasion certainly seemed to provide a justifiable exception. 'The amount of money being spent on this one party is obscene,' I tried again.

'Isn't it?' Best to drop the subject, I concluded, even while approaching the station at which a man in a chef's hat and uniform was carving roast beef and handing it to those who walked by. This, and the dinner wasn't even being served yet.

Angie headed for the roast beef as Patrick approached us and put his hand on my shoulder. 'Amazing, isn't he?' he said, indicating the chef. 'That's all soy, you know. Too many vegetarians in the room.'

I stared in disbelief. 'It has gristle,' I pointed out.

'The man's an artist.'

I looked around. 'Where's Rex?'

Patrick gestured toward the door. 'He went out to the car to get that bag again. The one from when we . . .'

'Don't mention it. What's in that bag, anyway?'

'Gifts for the cast and crew. I had gold harmonicas made for each of them.'

I couldn't believe it. 'Harmonicas?'

'It's the one thing you can be sure they don't already have.'

My client is completely out of his mind.

I faced Patrick. 'During the evening, when you see someone here who could have known about the bow and arrow, please point them out to me. Discreetly.'

Patrick clicked his heels and did a small bow. 'Yes, *mein capitan*,' he said in a flawless German accent. 'It shall be done.'

I ignored his act. 'Anyone here now?'

Patrick scanned the room dutifully. 'Well, obviously Patsy's people won't be here tonight. So aside from the ones you already know, there's only a couple of cast members and Lizz and Manny.'

'Show me Lizz and Manny.'

He looked at me a moment, then started darting his eyes to the right every few seconds. *Look, dart. Look, dart.* I seriously considered calling EMT for assistance.

'Patrick,' I asked, 'are you having a seizure?'

'Well, you wanted me to be discreet, didn't you?' He gestured with his head. 'Lizz and Manny are right over there.'

I sucked my lips into my mouth and bit on them, praying for patience, then managed, 'Which ones?'

'The tall blonde woman in black and the short dark man with the eyebrows – also in black.'

It was lucky for me that Emmanuel B. Richler had remarkable eyebrows, because 'the tall blonde woman in black' described forty percent of the people in the room. But the man who appeared to have two black caterpillars crawling across his forehead could not be missed.

'Introduce me,' I said.

Patrick took me by the arm and navigated me toward the two, who appeared to be 'making the rounds' of the room, shaking hands, air kissing and hugging various cast and crew members. They stopped when they saw Patrick approaching.

'Patrick!' Elizibith (no, that's not a misspelling) Warnell nearly launched herself at him as they neared. 'I haven't seen you all evening!' She kissed him heartily, which Patrick seemed to enjoy. Apparently, his boss was just a little bit more tipsy than during the average day on the set.

'You saw me fifteen minutes ago, Lizz darling,' Patrick reminded her, pointing. 'Just over there. By the bar.'

Lizz ignored him, eyeing me in my sensible Attorney Suit. 'And who is your lovely companion?' she said, her voice dropping.

'My attorney. Sandy Moss, this is Lizz Warnell, and that is Manny Richler.' Manny approached, extending a hand, and when I took it, he pulled me toward him and kissed me severely – and sloppily – on the mouth. Patrick was right – the roast beef *was* all soy.

'Why should Lizz have all the fun?' Manny said when he finally broke lip lock with me. They all laughed, some more sincerely than others. I thought I could clear out the room if I just said. 'Hashtag Me Too' loudly enough.

'I didn't realize television production companies were so social,' I said.

'We're a *family*,' Lizz shouted. 'A *family*! I love each and every one of these people like they were related to me. What we've been through together . . .' She stopped to pat a tear from her eye, or to make one appear – it was hard to determine.

'Really?' I said. 'What *have* you been through together?'

Lizz and Manny looked at each other in disbelief. Could I possibly not *know*? 'Oh!' Manny belted. 'We had such a hard time getting this show on the air to begin with! The network fought us all the way.'

'Why?' I didn't really care, but I wanted to see what Manny considered adversity.

'We pushed the envelope with this show,' he said to me in a confidential tone. 'We went farther with legal issues and nudity than anyone ever had. The network was afraid the FCC would be on our backs, and theirs, every week.'

'Really! So how did you manage?' *This town is a giant, hungry ego. Feed it, Sandra, and you shall prevail.*

'We refused to back down,' Lizz told me. 'We told them we wouldn't compromise, and, judging by their reaction, we knew they wanted to be in bed with us. *Us.* So they had to let us do what we wanted.' She smiled sweetly at Manny, who grinned back with equal affection.

'They know who they're dealing with,' he added.

'Amazing,' I let slip.

'Yes, isn't it? But we got the show we wanted on the air, and eventually that made our friend Patrick a star. Didn't it?' Lizz put her arm around Patrick's broad shoulders.

'I couldn't have done it without you,' the star agreed.

'So then you socialize quite a bit when you're not working?' I asked, so innocent I thought I might spontaneously sprout pigtails.

'Oh, not really,' Lizz said. 'When we have a shooting schedule, everyone has to be up so early, and the hours are so long, that we barely have time to see our own families.'

'You have children?' I asked.

'Oh, yes. I adopted two a few years ago. They're amazing, and they're around here somewhere.' Lizz gestured vaguely with the hand holding her martini glass.

'And you, Mr Richler?' I turned the full power of my maximum-kilowatt smile on him.

'Please. *Manny.* And no, no kids. At least, not that I know about.' He waited for a laugh that didn't come. 'But we did see Patrick at that party at his house, what? A couple of months ago?'

Patrick nodded. 'Yes,' he said. 'I believe it was in February.'

'Yeah,' Manny went on. 'You'd just gotten that . . . oops. Sorry, Patrick.'

'Not to worry. I was showing the bow around that night, wasn't I?' Patrick managed to look tortured and elegant at the same time. If there were an award for acting at parties, we would have won in our respective categories. But I couldn't decide if I was in a leading or supporting role.

'Do you know much about that kind of bow, Mr . . . Manny? I need to find an expert witness to explain it on the stand.' I thought I might appeal to Manny's need to be the best at *something*, particularly something Lizz didn't do.

But it was Lizz who answered. 'Oh, no,' she said. 'Manny never so much as picks up a bow. I'm the one who introduced Patrick to the bow club here in town. But I'm no expert. He shoots much better than I do.' By her delivery, she clearly didn't believe the truth of that last sentence.

I regarded Lizz, then Patrick. 'Really? How did he pass you so quickly?'

'Well,' said Lizz through clenched teeth, 'he practices much more than I do.'

Angie rushed over to break up the foursome. 'Sandy!' she shouted. 'I just met Barbara Eden!'

THIRTY-TWO

The Beverly Hills Bow Club sat on a hill overlooking much of Los Angeles, at an elevation high enough for me to wonder if I should've brought an oxygen tank. But for the time being, my breathing appeared to be normal. It was the setting that was surreal.

Under the sweltering California sun and the humidity, hanging like a ceiling about ten feet over our heads, men and (a few) women lined up on the only flat surface the club could manage: an asphalt plane that, but for its proportions, could have been a basketball court. It was much larger in both directions, and I was glad for the extra yardage. I was equally relieved that there was a wire mesh fence all the way around the roof, keeping stray arrows from falling down on unsuspecting tourists hoping to find a good photo op with the HOLLYWOOD sign.

Divided into compartments not unlike a gun shooting range, but without a roof, the club members were aiming arrows at targets from distances of five to ninety meters, according to the club's manager, Miles Carney, a surprisingly rumpled man (for Beverly Hills) of about forty.

The club was not actually in Beverly Hills, Carney explained, but 'The Encino Bow Club' didn't have the same ring to it, and the owners (who were anonymous) felt they were close enough. So far, no one had argued the point.

'Some of the more competitive archers will actually try to simulate an individual competition, meaning they'll shoot a hundred and forty-four arrows at a variety of distances and pay very close attention to their scores,' Carney was explaining. 'Others just come for the fun of it, and they'll get themselves a quiver and feel happy if they manage to hit the target at all.'

'Which kind of archer is Patrick McNabb?' I asked. Patrick had told me that a number of the *Legality* crew were members here – including his boss, Lizz.

'He definitely fell more into the competitive category, but he didn't care if his scores weren't as good as anyone else's. Pat competes with himself.' Carney wasn't looking at me – he was watching the archers, some of whom seemed to be more interested in speed than accuracy.

'Who was more competitive with the others?' I asked.

Carney smiled but didn't make eye contact. 'Oh, Lizz, for sure. I saw her stomp off and drive away more than once when Pat's score was better than hers.'

'Interesting.'

Carney nodded. 'You know, Pat brought his wife here once – showed her how to use the bow, and she was a natural. Could have been an Olympian, with some training. She was tearing up the targets, at all distances. Never saw anything like it.'

I raised an eyebrow. 'Really. How long before she died?'

'A week or two. No more than that.'

This was sounding better and better. 'Who else was here that day?'

Carney looked as if he knew where I was going, but didn't want to acknowledge it. 'Pat; his wife; Juliet – you know, the one who plays Ozzie on the show – one of the writers, Bill Orcada; and Lizz.' He saved that name for last, clearly wanting to gauge my reaction.

I didn't disappoint. 'Even more interesting. Did Patsy's score beat Lizz?'

Carney nodded. 'I believe that was one of her stomping and driving off days.'

I gave him the smile he wanted. 'Interesting,' I said again.

The next ten days were filled with interviews and research, all done from my apartment. A mere four residents of the Hollywood 'community' proved willing to stand up for Patrick, a man accused of murdering his wife: 1. his agent; 2. his manager; 3. his publicist and 4. his personal assistant. Co-stars, newly on hiatus from the series *Legality*, were mysteriously tied up on other projects, none of which could be named for fear of queering the deal. Patrick himself said none of his fellow actors had mentioned prior commitments while working on the series, but allowed that 'something might have come up at the last minute.' I considered his evaluation to be generous to a fault, not out of character for a man who gave away Ferraris to people he knew less than a week.

Because the producers and Meadows, the butler, were to be witnesses in other areas of the case (and in Meadows' case, for the prosecution), they weren't the best candidates for character references. I had to concentrate more on punching holes in the district attorney's case, which, from what I could tell, would focus on the divorce proceedings and the forensic evidence involving the bow and arrow.

Evan came by my apartment every day, though he worried, he told me, that Bach might fire him for not coming into the office. According to Evan, Bach ordered him off Patrick's case, making a comment about 'letting that little bitch twist in the wind.' But I decided to consider that hearsay.

Angie was somewhat more colorful in her description of Bach, suggesting not only that his parents hadn't married, but also that he had a particularly severe Oedipus complex.

She rarely left my side, which was starting to become irritating.

But the series of death threats and attempts on me and Patrick had convinced Angie there was no safe place or time for her best friend, and she would not be moved. (In my heart of hearts, I suppose, having her around made me a little less afraid. But hey, nobody had tried to kill me in over a week, and that was something of a record since my move to L.A.)

Angie was also adapting to the Southern California lifestyle and climate, mostly by wearing as little as possible, even in air conditioned places. It was lucky, I thought, that she rarely left the apartment, because her skimpy attire would more than likely cause an unfortunate number of minor car crashes in the streets of Los Angeles. That is, if anyone could maneuver through the traffic at a high enough speed to actually incur damage.

The one thing Angie refused to do in order to go L.A. was bleach her hair, which was a blessing. A Greek-Italian blonde from Jersey who stood nearly six feet tall and wore remarkably little clothing probably would have been a little much even for the Angelinos to handle. Besides, Angie didn't have any tattoos or body piercings, and likely wouldn't have fit in on that front, either.

We spent much of the first week interviewing experts on movie memorabilia, knowing that Cates was clearly going to at least *mention* Cagney's shoes as part of his case. Each expert valued the shoes at roughly the same price I'd seen online, and therefore would not make a difference in the life of a man making hundreds of thousands of dollars a week, pretending to be a lawyer on television. I found it interesting that the fake lawyers were making more than the real ones I knew, but that was a topic for another day.

Two days before the trial was to begin, I was preparing my opening statement and feeling the caffeine rush of abject terror I always had before going to court. *I'm not ready! They're going to massacre me! My client's going to die!* The usual, only from the other side of the courtroom, this time. So that last part was a novelty.

Prosecuting a case is a more emotionally secure position, almost to the point of smugness. There is such a high probability that the defendant is guilty in most cases, you can sleep quite comfortably at night. The defense, I was finding out, could have a more nerve-racking effect, particularly in the rare example of a case in which I found myself: one in which the lawyer actually believes the defendant is not guilty.

Angie was making the third pot of coffee for the day, and it was only ten in the morning. Sleep deprivation was wearing on me, but Angie could have attended an uninterrupted showing of all nine *Star Wars* films and stayed awake. Well, maybe not through *The Phantom Menace*, but a nap there wouldn't be due to fatigue. Since moving to Hollywood, I was realizing that maybe I wasn't as highbrow a moviegoer as I'd previously thought.

Evan, however, was asleep in the armchair, having missed out on his usual ten hours of sleep the night before because he'd been tracking down a rare shoe collector in Yorba Linda – until the 'ungodly hour' of nine p.m.

'I don't have enough,' I said out loud to no one in particular.

'Yes, you do,' Angie recited. 'You do this every time.'

'I really don't,' I told her. 'This time, the case is thin. I wish I were as thin as this case.'

'You look fine. Shut up.'

'You know what I mean. All I've got is that Patrick didn't kill Patsy for the shoes. What about the divorce settlement? Weren't there millions at stake there? Wouldn't a lot of men have killed for that?'

'A lot of men, yes. Patrick McNabb, no.' Angie turned the coffeemaker on and walked over to me. 'The man gave you a two-hundred-thousand-dollar Ferrari after he knew you for three days. Does that sound like a man worried about his income?'

'I guess not,' I conceded. 'But I can't prove anything.'

Evan didn't even move when the phone rang. Down for the count until noon, he seemed more mannequin than man. Angie picked up the phone and handed it to me.

'Garrigan.'

'Hi, Nate,' I said, trying to sound cheerful. 'What's up?'

'I've got something for you,' Garrigan sounded positively giddy. 'You're gonna like it.'

I sat up straight. 'I could use something like that,' I said. 'What is it?'

'I'm at the police lab. It's been enough weeks now that they got the DNA back from Patsy's body.'

'So?'

'So remember the baby that wasn't Patrick McNabb's? It wasn't Silvio Cadenza's, either.'

I shook my head vigorously to rouse myself. '*What?*'

'You heard me. But here's the best part. Want to know whose baby it *is*?'

'Tell me, Nate. Don't keep me in suspense.'

'Henderson T. Meadows. The butler did it.'

THIRTY-THREE

'Ow!'

'What?'

'I stubbed my toe.'

'It's three o'clock in the morning. You want me to turn on the light?'

'NO!'

'Ooooookaaaay . . .'

'Ang?'

'Yeah.'

'You awake?'

'No. This has been a recording of me. You know I don't sleep much. What is it, Sand?'

'I'm not ready.'

'You got yourself out of bed and came in here to tell me this? Yes, you're ready. You're always ready.'

'Not this time. This time, he's going to die if I'm not ready, and I'm not. I didn't have enough time. If only I could have gotten that continuance.'

'But you didn't, and you've been working your butt off for weeks, and you're *ready*, Sandra. You are. I've seen this before.'

'This is different.'

'No, it's not.'

'Yes, it is.'

'OK. *How* is it different?'

'Angie, I've never done a criminal defense before. I've always been on the other side.'

'So you know what the other side is going to do, don't you?'

'Well . . . yeah. I guess I do. I know what I'd do if I were prosecuting.'

'So you know how to counter what he's going to do, don't you, Sand?'

'Not really. I think he's got a pretty good case.'

'No, you don't. You wouldn't be this worried about Patrick if you thought he'd really killed his wife.'

'And that's why this is different. Before, I was always sure they'd done it, and it didn't bother me if they went to jail. They *belonged* in jail – most of them.'

'And this time he doesn't. So that means you're on the right side, aren't you?'

'Maybe I'm on the side that's right, but it's not the right side for me. Maybe I don't know how to do this.'

'Sandra, you should see the look I'm giving you.'

'I kind of can. My pupils are dilating.'

'You're a good lawyer. You care. And you're very thorough at what you do. There's no reason to think you're going to do anything but a wonderful job. Now shut up and go back to bed.'

'Thanks, Ang. You know what?'

'What?'

'I think I'm ready.'

THIRTY-FOUR

My mother called the morning the trial started, to remind me to dress nicely and not do anything embarrassing, because 'everybody's going to be watching on *TruTV*.' She didn't offer encouragement or reassurance. I thought that might help explain why I'd moved three thousand miles away.

Angie drove me to the courthouse an hour before the trial was to start. Evan had offered to do it, and seemed a bit miffed at my refusal, but it was important to show up on time, and Evan's driving didn't necessarily guarantee that. Patrick had threatened to 'have a car sent round' the day before, but I gave him a quick look that dissuaded him.

The Clara Shortridge Foltz Criminal Justice Center is not a gorgeous, stylish, trendy building, as one might expect in a city so devoted to image. It is, rather, a fairly nondescript tower with the usual offices and hallways where attorneys make deals and try to avoid courtrooms whenever possible.

Even today, as Angie (who had been warned to wear something conservative – in fact, my exact words were to 'dress like Lois Lane') and I entered the building, the throng of reporters behind us was asking if I expected the case to go to trial at all. And sure enough, when I approached the courtroom door, Bertram Cates, the assistant district attorney assigned to the prosecution, approached.

Cates was a tall, thin man whose neck was designed to be adorned by a bow tie. He had not disappointed today, although the traditional country bumpkin red was shunned in favor of something in teal, to offset Cates' dark black suit. If he'd been wearing suspenders, he could've stepped directly into 1925.

'Ms Moss,' Cates said as we closed the gap between us. 'I can offer you Man Two, and keep your client away from the needle.'

'Manslaughter, second degree?' I chuckled. 'For a man who didn't kill his wife? I don't think so, Mr Cates. But thanks for letting me know exactly how uncertain of your case you clearly are.'

'This should be a pleasure,' he said, and I could tell he considered tipping his hat, despite the fact he wasn't wearing one. He nodded his head instead.

'Where's Patrick?' Angie asked as Cates entered the courtroom. She looked around the lobby. 'I don't see him.'

'Don't worry,' I told her. 'Patrick's just waiting for the right time to make . . .'

A noticeable squeal was heard from the direction of the front doors, and Patrick McNabb, looking for all the world like a man playing a falsely accused defendant, walked into the lobby. Women, held back by police and velvet ropes, shouted to him. Some wanted to sleep with him. Others, chiefly those carrying signs that included the word 'PIOUS,' seemed to have convicted him before the trial began. The two opinions converged in the center of the room, and created a sound like a cheetah attacking a lioness in heat.

'. . . an entrance,' I finished.

Patrick waved grimly to his admirers and ignored the detractors, staring intently at me as he approached. The metal detectors at the entrances slowed down the process of gathering this morning, but Patrick had managed to conserve enough time to answer a few questions from the reporters as he trudged through the lobby to Courtroom #4.

'. . . to be completely exonerated by the time this trial is over,' he was saying when he reached earshot. I frowned severely at him, and he actually stopped, thanked the reporters, and moved on.

'I told you the answer to every question was "no comment,"' I said when he was near enough I didn't have to shout. 'You give no interviews, you make no predictions, you offer absolutely no evidence. Which part of that was hard to understand?'

'They're just trying to do their job.'

'So am I,' I reminded him, and turned to open the courtroom door.

Evan was already waiting at the defense table, which shocked both Angie and me – he must've left his house at four in the morning. Angie sat in the front row of the gallery as Patrick and I took our seats at the counsel's table. Noting the capacity crowd, I was glad I'd reserved a place for Angie to sit. I'd barely gotten my files onto the defense table when the bailiff entered and announced the judge.

I had studied up on the Honorable Walter Franklin, and learned that he was a fastidious man, to the point of obsession. He would not allow anything out of place in his courtroom. He was also a militant anti-smoking activist, which didn't really matter in court – the building was considered smoke-free, as was much of Los Angeles itself. And above all, he cherished speedy, efficient trials. He was exactly the wrong man for this case.

'Be seated,' he grumbled, already in a sour mood, and we hadn't even started. This was not a good sign.

The bailiff read the case number and the charges, which were murder in the first degree, aggravated assault and battery, obstructing a criminal investigation (they love that one), and attempted murder. The logic here is that if you committed murder, you must also have attempted murder. As logic goes, it's not bad.

Patrick McNabb, through his attorney (me), pleaded not guilty to all charges. That was the easy part.

Next came jury selection. Having studied the jury pool ahead of time, I knew the candidates I definitely wanted to include, the ones I'd prostitute myself to avoid, and the vast majority, who were acceptable but not necessarily desirable.

There wasn't much argument from Cates on the jury. He used one of his challenges for a woman wearing a 'Free Arthur Kirkland!' T-shirt (I couldn't blame him for that) and another for a man who said he thought television actors really did deserve more of a break in life because they brought so much joy to so many 'regular people.' Hard to argue with that one, either.

I objected to a potential juror who admitted to having seen a photo of Patsy with the arrow sticking out of her chest in a tabloid newspaper (outside the police files, there was no such photo; it had been concocted in the tabloid's computer system). I sought to strike one potential juror who said she owned all of Patsy's recordings and 'considered her part of the family.' And I was equally unfond of a would-be juror whose brother-in-law was a Los Angeles police officer, because cops, much like prosecutors, always think everyone's guilty.

Once the panel was in place, Franklin called for the prosecutor to make his opening statement to the jury.

Bertram T. Cates, looking very much like a scarecrow in an expensive suit, stood to deliver his opening, and it was a doozy. By the time Cates was finished, *I* was ready to convict Patrick. He hadn't just murdered his wife, he'd probably stolen all her possessions, alienated her family and, in Cates' estimation, caused the last three earthquakes to hit the greater Los Angeles area.

I took notes during Cates' remarks, making sure to remind myself later which areas were most important to refute – like the whole 'not-killing-Patsy' thing. I'd definitely have to mention that.

Franklin looked ominously down at me from the bench and said, 'Ms Moss, before you begin, there is the matter of your client's flight to Mexico.'

I couldn't believe what I was hearing. *In front of the jury?* 'Your Honor,' I asked, 'may I approach the bench?' Franklin waved me up.

'Judge, if you wanted to discuss this, wouldn't it have been more appropriate before the jury was present? This is going to prejudice them against my client.'

Franklin stared down through half-glasses. 'I'll decide what is and is not appropriate for my court, Ms Moss. Step back, please.'

I walked back to the defense table and tried to compose myself. 'The incident to which you're referring, Your Honor, was only a matter of a drive that took a few hours in the course of one day, and was undertaken to try to discover some evidence pertinent to our case. My client never tried to escape his responsibilities here.'

'Ms Moss, you are new to this court, and so I will accept that explanation, but I warn you that any further indiscretion on your client's part will result in the forfeiture of his bail bond and my citing you personally for contempt.'

'Yes, Your Honor.'

'Now, please present your opening statement.'

Yeah, and now that you've set me back ten yards, let me just walk up here and kick it straight through the uprights. OK, Judge?

Typically, I like to walk to the jury box and talk directly to the panel, and this case was no exception. I began my statement by smiling warmly, something I was quite good at, and explaining to the jury exactly who I was, and how I expected they would be concerned with how the testimony in this case would sometimes be contradictory.

'After all,' I informed the five men and seven women (gratefully noting to myself that six of the seven women couldn't take their eyes off Patrick), 'the prosecution isn't here because they think they arrested the wrong man. Mr Cates truly believes Patrick McNabb shot an arrow into his wife and killed her. His witnesses, testifying under oath, will believe that everything they say is the absolute truth. No one is trying to trick you.

'The problem is, I believe that Patrick McNabb did *not* fire that arrow. I believe he did *not* kill Esmerelda DeNunzio. And I believe just as strongly as Mr Cates that everything I say, and everything said by the witnesses I call, will be true.'

I leaned on the railing of the box to create a feeling of intimacy with the jury. 'So, how are you to decide? How should you weigh the truth of Mr Cates' witnesses against the truth of my witnesses? If they say contradictory things, how can both be true?

'That, members of the jury, is where we reach the concept of *reasonable doubt*. If anything that anyone says in this courtroom, no matter who, makes you doubt that Patrick McNabb killed Ms DeNunzio, and your doubt is based on the evidence, then you *must* acquit Mr McNabb. That's how the court system works in this country, and you've heard it a thousand times: innocent until *proven* guilty. If the prosecution makes you *think* Patrick McNabb is guilty, but doesn't *prove* it, you can't convict him. If the defense makes you *doubt* he's guilty, you can't convict him. The burden to prove guilt is on the prosecution. The burden on the defense is not to prove innocence, but to assume innocence unless Mr Cates proves the defendant guilty. It's not going to be easy.'

I turned away from the jury box and walked toward the defense table, but stopped in front of the bench. There, I turned back to deliver the terrific closing I'd prepared.

At that moment, a woman of no more than twenty-five, dressed in jeans and a gray T-shirt, leapt from her seat in the gallery and ran toward Patrick. The PIOUS crowd began to cheer, which alerted the police and the bailiff, who ran after her.

'Patsy's blood is on your hands!' the PIOUS member screamed as she approached me, and she pulled what appeared to be a condom – filled with some dark liquid – out of her pocket. She threw the balloon-like object at Patrick, but missed.

Instead, she hit me directly in the chest, and the condom exploded, sending red liquid all over my white blouse and suit jacket. The police grabbed the woman by the arms as I hurried to the table to assess the damage.

'Those aren't my hands,' I told her.

The PIOUS member's eyes widened as she saw what she'd accomplished, and suddenly, she was just a young girl again. 'Omigod,' she said. 'I am *so* sorry.'

I shook my head and looked at the cops. 'I'm not going to press charges,' I told them. 'But I might bill PIOUS for the dry cleaning bills.'

'She's still being charged,' Judge Franklin said. 'We set up a perimeter, and she broke through it. Besides, she made a mess in my courtroom, and I will not tolerate that.'

'Can I get you some club soda for that?' the dangerous assailant asked, pointing at my chest. 'It's just water with red food coloring.'

The police led the woman away, and I looked at Angie, whose face indicated she wouldn't have been as kind as me. 'Well, there goes impressing my mother on *TruTV*,' I muttered.

'Don't worry about it,' Angie whispered back. 'I put one of your other suits in the bag, just in case.'

'You think of everything.'

'Nah. I hated what you had on.'

THIRTY-FIVE

Detective Lieutenant K.C. Trench fit right into Walter Franklin's courtroom – he was the neatest cop I'd ever seen. He sat on the witness stand, perfectly erect, attentive, responding to the prosecutor with impeccable diction. He wore cufflinks. I'd never met a policeman who wore cufflinks.

'I arrived at the scene approximately thirty-five minutes after the emergency call, and thirty minutes after the uniformed officers arrived,' he told Cates in response to a question.

'Was Ms DeNunzio's body still on the floor?' Cates asked.

'No. It had been removed by the EMS workers, but video and still photographs had been taken, the outline was there, and physical evidence remained in the room.'

'Physical evidence like what, Lieutenant?'

'There was a good deal of blood,' Trench told him without so much as a twitch.

'Was Mr McNabb present when you arrived?' Cates asked, looking at the jury to see if the mention of blood had gotten the reaction he'd hoped for – it had.

'Yes.' This was not the first time Trench had testified in court. He knew how to keep his answers short and to-the-point.

'Describe his appearance.'

'He is approximately six feet tall, dark hair, and green eyes . . .'

'In what kind of state was he that night, Lieutenant?' Cates was obviously struggling to remain patient with his somber witness.

'He was covered in a good deal of blood from his shoulders to his feet,' Trench said, never taking his eyes off Cates.

A couple of the jurors cringed.

'His hands were covered in blood?'

'Being between his shoulders and his feet, yes, they were.' Trench didn't at all mind expressing his impatience with his questioner.

Cates chose to ignore the tone of his witness' response. 'What did he say when you questioned him?'

'He said he had been in the bedroom, and discovered the victim on the dining room floor when he came out,' Trench reported, without referring to notes.

'Were there fingerprints found on the murder weapon?'

'Yes,' Trench said. 'The arrow had Mr McNabb's fingerprints and one other person's.'

'Whose would those be?'

'Ms DeNunzio's. Apparently she had tried to pull the arrow out before she died.' A woman in a PIOUS T-shirt in the last row made a grimacing sound and put her head down in her hands.

'Were there any other fingerprints found in the room besides Mr McNabb's and Ms DeNunzio's?'

'No,' Trench answered.

'No further questions.' Cates sat down at his table and consulted with his second chair.

'Ms Moss?' said the judge.

I rose and walked to Trench carrying a legal pad and pen, which were more to hold for comfort than for any legal purpose. I always found it easier to question a witness if I had something in my hands.

'Lieutenant Trench, did Mr McNabb confess to the crime?'

'No, he did not.' Trench's gaze, now that it was focused directly on me, was intimidating, even if he didn't mean it to be. But then, there was no indication he didn't mean it to be.

'Did he ever express any concern over his own well-being?'

'No.' Trench wasn't going to give me anything I didn't ask for specifically.

'What did he say to you besides what you've already told us?' Patrick had given me a very good recounting of the conversation.

'He asked who could have done this, and wanted to know how we would find Ms DeNunzio's killer.'

'How would you describe his emotional state?'

'It's difficult to say,' Trench said. 'He *is* a professional actor.'

'And you are a professional detective. What was your impression?'

'He was distraught.' Perfect.

'As for the fingerprints found on the arrow, where on the arrow were they located?'

'They were in more than one location,' Trench answered.

I nodded to Evan, who walked to the bailiff. Evan produced an arrow from a leather case kept behind the bailiff's station, and brought it to me.

'Your Honor, with the court's permission, I'd like to enter into evidence this arrow, which is the same make and model as the one used in the crime.'

'Objection, Mr Cates?' the judge asked.

'None, Judge.'

Franklin nodded. I took the arrow from Evan and showed it to Trench. 'Can you show me, on this arrow, where the fingerprints were found, Lieutenant?'

Trench took the arrow from my hands, and held it in his left hand. With his right, he indicated a spot on the shaft, less than halfway from the tip. 'Here,' he said, then moved his hand to a spot about three inches closer to the fletching (or feathers), away from the tip. 'And here,' Trench added.

'So, on this part of the arrow, there were no fingerprints belonging to Mr McNabb?' I indicated the far end, or nock, where an archer would hold an arrow before releasing it.

'No.'

'What color were the fingerprints in the spots you indicated, Lieutenant?'

'Red,' Trench said.

'So, in your opinion, Mr McNabb had come in contact with the blood before touching the arrow?'

Cates stood. 'Objection. She's asking the witness to speculate.'

'I'm asking for his professional opinion as a homicide detective, Your Honor,' I said.

'I'll allow it,' Franklin said. 'Proceed, Ms Moss.'

Trench answered without being prompted or reminded. 'It would appear his hands already had the blood on them when he touched the arrow, yes.'

'Would that indicate that Mr McNabb was trying to remove the arrow from Ms DeNunzio's body?'

'Objection,' Cates said before getting to his feet. 'She's doing it again, Your Honor.'

'This time, I'll sustain it. Lieutenant Trench can't decide how fingerprints got onto the weapon, Ms Moss.'

I nodded. 'Lieutenant Trench,' I said. 'Did you find any fingerprints on the bow that were also found on the arrow?'

'Yes,' said Trench.

'Whose fingerprints were those?'

'Mr McNabb's.' Trench might just as easily have been describing how to program a Blu-ray player.

'What color were they?'

He actually blinked, the Trench equivalent of a double-take. 'What color?' he asked.

'Were they red, like the ones on the arrow?'

'No, they were not,' Trench said. 'There was no blood found on the bow.'

'Is there any way of knowing from a fingerprint how long it's been on an object?'

'Not really,' said Trench. 'A fingerprint generally stays on an object until cleaned.'

'So, Mr McNabb's prints on the bow might have been from days, or even weeks, before the murder?'

'I would have no way of knowing,' Trench said before Cates could object.

'Thank you, Lieutenant,' I said, returning to my seat.

Evan beamed at me as I sat. 'Nice work,' he said.

'You're . . . very, very good,' Patrick whispered to me.

'Redirect, Mr Cates?' said the judge.

'Yes, Your Honor.' I expected as much. Cates stood and turned his attention once again to Trench. 'Lieutenant,' Cates began, 'is there any way of knowing in what order fingerprints are left on an object?'

'In what order?' Trench asked. He might as well have been talking to an ostrich about nuclear physics.

'Yes. Can you tell by looking at a fingerprint whether the item was touched before or after another object?'

'No.' Trench's voice indicated he *was* talking to an ostrich about nuclear physics.

'So, it is possible that Mr McNabb fired the arrow, then put down the bow and walked to the body. His fingerprints would then be on the bow, but he would not have touched the body, and his fingers would not be bloody yet. Is that right?'

'Objection, Your Honor.' I jumped to my feet.

'Overruled. If he can speculate for you, he can speculate for Mr Cates.'

'It is possible,' Trench said.

'And it's also possible that he wiped his prints off the part of the arrow he held when he was aiming, and then touched it with the blood on his hands, to make himself seem more sympathetic and cloud his responsibility. Is that also possible?' Cates was going way over the top here. I couldn't let him continue.

'Objection!'

'Sustained. The Lieutenant wasn't there when the crime was being committed, Mr Cates. And he can't speak to Mr McNabb's motives.'

'Very well, then,' said Cates. 'No further questions.'

Trench didn't so much as glance at me or Patrick as he left the courtroom. Patrick leaned over as Cates prepared to call his next witness.

'Well, you're good, anyway,' he said.

THIRTY-SIX

The next three days were taken up with testimony by the uniformed officers who'd arrested Patrick, and by the medical examiner, who revealed little of note (but I reserved the right to call him as a defense witness, noting that the paternity of Patsy's child was not questioned by Cates).

Then came a parade of forensic experts, all of whom added little to what Trench had said, which I considered to be a commentary on both their efficiency and the lieutenant's. Bloody footprints were added to the fingerprints, and their direction was debated at length until the jury was probably ready to fire arrows at both attorneys and the judge.

On the fifth complete day of testimony, Cates apparently decided he needed to do something to shake up the jury a little, so he called Juliet Rodriguez, the undeniably gorgeous actress who played 'Ozzie' Estrada on *Legality*. The faces of the jury, particularly the male members, perked up as Rodriguez walked by, her unbearably tight skirt rivaled only by her equally tight blouse. The air conditioning in the courtroom, set by an automatic thermostat, turned itself on.

'I knew from what Patrick had told me that the marriage was not going well,' she said after being sworn in. 'You could tell from his mood.'

Cates, enjoying the jury's sudden attention, raised an eyebrow. This was probably one of the only times he could actually hold the attention of a beautiful woman. 'Describe his mood.'

'Well, he'd show up on the set and barely say hello some mornings,' Juliet volunteered. 'You knew they hadn't had a good night the night before, you know?'

Several male jurors became glassy eyed as they envisioned Juliet Rodriguez having a good night. One female juror shared their expression.

'Did Mr McNabb say anything to you about his marriage?'

I was quick to object. 'The D.A. is asking for hearsay,' I told the judge.

'This goes to Mr McNabb's state of mind, Your Honor, and not any factual evidence or physical evidence. We're merely trying to establish that he was upset about his marriage.'

'I'll allow it,' Franklin said. I sat down, biting my lips to keep myself from arguing.

Cates turned back toward Juliet Rodriguez. 'Did Mr McNabb say anything to you about his marriage, Ms Rodriguez?'

'Yes,' she said in a small actressy voice. 'Patrick said he thought Patsy was cheating on him, and the marriage wouldn't last much longer.'

'Did he talk about being depressed?'

'Yes,' Rodriguez said. 'He said he was taking medication.'

I shot out of my chair. 'Now that *is* hearsay,' I insisted.

Franklin nodded. 'I have to agree. Ladies and gentlemen of the jury, just because Ms Rodriguez says Mr McNabb told her something in a conversation does not make it true. You must disregard the testimony about anti-depressant medication, as it has not been established by any facts.'

The jury nodded, but I knew Cates had expected that, and besides, asking a jury to disregard juicy information was like trying to stuff whipped cream back into an aerosol can. Cates nodded, but couldn't contain his grin.

'I'm sorry, Your Honor, but I don't think that's enough,' I said.

Walter Franklin looked up, apparently startled at the impudence of this New Jersey upstart. 'I beg your pardon?' he asked.

'I think Mr Cates has poisoned the water with innuendo that does unmerited damage to my case,' I continued, still on my feet. 'I'd like permission to try to defuse some of that damage.'

Franklin's eyes narrowed to slits. 'What do you have in mind, Ms Moss? You'll be given time to cross-examine this witness.'

'It's not the witness I'd like to question, Your Honor. I'd like to poll the jury on one question unrelated to the facts of this case.'

'This is highly unorthodox, Ms Moss, and I don't believe I'll allow it. I can't let you talk directly to the jury.'

'All right, then, how about the prosecutor? Or the people seated in the gallery?'

Franklin sat back in his chair, seemingly considering the damage done by what he'd allowed and overruled thus far. I was certain he was reflecting on what might be brought up on appeal. 'I'll allow you one minute, Ms Moss, but there will be no questioning of the jury or the witness.'

'Thank you, Your Honor,' I said. Meanwhile, my thoughts raced. *Is this possible? What am I doing to my client?* But finally, the thought, *Hell, this is Hollywood* reassured me the plan would work.

I turned toward the gallery and began. 'None of you is under oath, so I'm going to take you on faith. Who here has ever, in their lives, been treated for depression?' I held my breath.

A torturous moment passed. Then Angie put up her hand. Three people in back rows followed suit. Another few looked around and saw those hands, then put up their own. After giving the question some thought, more and more hands followed. When the wave had passed, only five people in the gallery had their hands in their laps, and they looked a little dubious.

Everyone else had a hand in the air. Two jurors added their own. Others probably would have, but thought they shouldn't.

Patrick McNabb put up his hand last.

I turned back to the judge. 'Thank you, Your Honor.'

Cates did not put his hand in the air (although a little bird told me later he was on medication for Obsessive-Compulsive Disorder, which required him to wash his hands twenty-seven times a day), and he was not pleased by the display around him. He looked back at Juliet Rodriguez, almost as an afterthought.

'No more questions,' he said.

THIRTY-SEVEN

'I haven't given enough thought to what I'm going to do with Junius Bach,' I said, collapsing into the easy chair in my living room. 'He'll be on the stand in the next day or two, and I have to figure out how to handle him.'

Evan sat on the couch and eyed Angie, who was on the floor,

starting to do sit- ups. 'The most damaging thing he's going to testify to is the outburst at the divorce settlement conference, when McNabb told Patsy he wanted to kill her,' he said. 'Isn't that hearsay? Can't you immediately get it stricken from the record?'

'Sure, just like I got Julia Rodriguez's hearsay testimony stricken from the record,' I said. 'The jury still got to hear it.'

'Can't you nullify it the same way you did Rodriguez? That was amazing.' Evan might as well have rolled over on his back so I could scratch his belly.

'What, ask the whole audience how many times they heard Patrick threaten to kill his wife? That doesn't sound helpful,' Angie said as she rolled up into 'bicycle pedal' position and continued exercising.

'I could ask them how many of them have threatened to kill their spouses,' I suggested.

'Yeah, that sounds great,' Angie replied.

'It could work,' Evan said.

'Evan, I was kidding.'

'Oh.'

Evan tried to avert his gaze from Angie, who had her legs in the air as she lay on her back. 'Couldn't you at least put sweat-pants on or something while you do that?' I said. At the moment, Angie's skirt was more a theory than a fact.

She stood and headed for the bedroom to change. 'Some people are so conventional,' she said over her shoulder.

Evan stood and started to pace. 'There must be some way you can neutralize Bach without letting the jury hear his testimony. Can you cite conflict of interest?'

'Bach's been subpoenaed, but he's testifying willingly. The judge isn't going to throw him out based on an objection from Bach's own associate.'

Evan frowned and nodded. That, I realized, was the answer he expected to hear. 'Can you counter him with a rebuttal witness, like one of the stenographers? Or maybe you could put yourself on the stand and let me question you.'

'You're not admitted to the bar yet, Evan, and besides, what would I say on the stand? That Patrick *didn't* say he would kill Patsy if she took Cagney's shoes? He said it.' I lay back and closed my eyes for a moment.

Angie came out of the bedroom wearing short sweatpants and a T-shirt that read 'Farleigh Dickinson University' that she'd stolen from an old boyfriend. 'This better?' she asked Evan, who stared at her a moment, as if realizing for the first time that this creature was female. He nodded.

I bolted upright, and Evan, startled, held out his hands. 'Are you all right?' he asked.

I felt my face break into a grin. 'I think I've got it.'

Angie grinned along. 'Yeah? Spill.'

'Suppose I call a rebuttal witness. Suppose I call Junius Bach's wife and ask her if he's ever said he would kill *her*?'

It took a moment to sink in, then Angie started to laugh. 'I *like* it!' she said. 'I like it a *lot*!'

'It could be something,' Evan said, seemingly relieved I wasn't having a heart attack or something else he couldn't cure. 'But suppose he's never told his wife he would kill her.'

'I used to be married,' Angie told Evan. 'Every married person has said that to a spouse at least once.'

'Just because anyone who's been married to *you* would threaten violence doesn't mean everyone would,' Evan countered. 'It's a common expression, but Bach is a very controlled man at work. He might be the same way at home.'

'What do you suggest?' I asked. 'We can't follow him home and have his wife wear a wire.'

'Let me pre-interview her,' Evan said. 'I can work that question in with a few others – tell her the office is working on a surprise roast of her husband and we want to have lots of good material.'

Suddenly, I saw Evan in a better light than I had before. 'You're sneakier than you look.'

He stared. 'What do you mean?'

I chuckled. 'OK. Maybe you're not. But it's still a good idea. While he's at the office, call Bach's wife and see if you can set up an interview.'

Evan went to the kitchen with his iPhone and started dialing. Angie shook her head. 'You're adorable with him, you know,' she told me. 'Such a proud mom.'

'He's not *that* much younger than me.'

'Still, it's cute,' she said. 'You look like you want to cup his little chin in your hand and kiss his forehead when he gets a good idea.'

'Say, *I* have a good idea,' I said. 'Shut up.'

THIRTY-EIGHT

Cameron Menzies was a bookish-looking sort of fellow, a man who, in another age, would have been called 'tweedy,' but was now better described as a 'nerd.' What once would have been considered merely 'weird behavior' would now probably place Menzies on the high-functioning end of the autism spectrum, because he was totally and obsessively devoted to one thing, and one thing only – motion picture collectibles.

These traits, of course, made him the perfect witness, and I was sorry Cates had gotten to Menzies before I could. Pity to lose a one-track mind like that.

He was, at the moment, explaining to the court why certain collectibles carry a higher resale value than others.

'You have to understand that most film props and other collectibles are not one-of-a-kind items,' Menzies said. 'If an actor's going to wear a jacket in a scene, for example, there will be multiple jackets ready, in case one is soiled or torn. James Dean's jacket in *Rebel Without A Cause* is a perfect example. There were actually four jackets, and that was not a very high-budget film for its time. And of course, Dean died not long after that, and the value always increases when the artist dies, because collectors know there won't be any more.'

'So then, the shoes Mr McNabb owned from *Yankee Doodle Dandy* are not the only ones James Cagney wore in the movie?' asked Cates, doing everything but fingering his lapels with pride.

'Oh, no. But they're a valuable pair, because Cagney actually did wear them during the filming of the dance number *Yankee Doodle Dandy*. Still, there were at least two other pairs ready when he needed them, and it's unlikely he wore only one pair of tap shoes during filming. Indeed, he went on to play George

M. Cohan a second time, in the Bob Hope film *The Seven Little Foys*, and he wore different shoes in that film.'

Menzies probably would have gone on for thirty or forty minutes, but Cates had another question. 'How much are these shoes actually worth, if Mr McNabb were to sell them privately or at auction?' Cates then turned to watch the jury – he already knew the answer to the question he'd asked, and wanted to gauge their reaction.

'I'd be surprised if they'd bring more than twenty-five thousand dollars privately, and maybe a bit more at auction – maybe thirty thousand or so,' Menzies said, frowning. 'They're not in mint condition, and as I said, not unique items. Such things are sometimes undervalued, although they are extremely valuable to film historians and enthusiasts.'

'But that group rarely has a great deal of money, and could still pick up these shoes for a relatively reasonable sum. Isn't that right, Mr Menzies?'

Menzies' frown grew deeper. He clearly felt it was a crime that film buffs didn't, as a class, have more money to spend on preserving the fake things they held dear. 'That is probably correct,' he allowed.

'No further questions.' Cates sat down, pleased with himself.

I smiled as I approached the little man. 'Mr Menzies, how much would *you* pay for the shoes?'

'Me?' Menzies seemed confused, as if I were trying to sell Cagney's shoes to him and we were negotiating price.

'If you had the money. How much would they be worth to *you*?'

Menzies smiled, and his eyes left the courtroom for another, better place. 'Millions,' he said.

'Are they worth that much on the market?'

'No,' he said.

'Thank you, Mr Menzies.' I sat down.

There was no question that Henderson T. Meadows had to be uncomfortable on the witness stand (a good butler hates to air the family's laundry, and this guy was a candidate for the rinse cycle himself), but you'd never know it by looking at him – excellent posture that didn't look forced, and clothing perfectly pressed. Meadows might have actually been auditioning for the part of a butler in a 1930s movie, except he was wearing a business suit, and not a tuxedo. He looked out of place in the business suit.

Cates wasn't about to let me get the drop on him – he had the same information from the medical examiner as I did. 'So, you were intimate with Ms DeNunzio in a physical way. Is that right, Mr Meadows?'

'It is not for me to determine whether it was right or wrong, but your statement is correct,' Meadows told him. I loved the answer – it not only insulted Cates, but also confused the jury.

But Cates wasn't letting go. 'So you slept with her?' Sensing that Meadows might correct his usage again, he added, 'You had sexual relations with her?'

Meadows might have been asked if he'd played tennis that morning. 'I did,' he said simply. 'Once.'

'Can you describe the circumstances surrounding that encounter?'

Meadows didn't bite his lip or twitch or do any of the things witnesses do on TV. He looked dispassionately at Cates and answered, 'It was one of the nights when Mr McNabb and Ms DeNunzio were apart. He was filming late that night, and she had argued with him on the phone. They weren't getting along well.'

'Had that been going on for some time?' Cates asked.

'Yes.' Meadows didn't nod – it would have been beneath him. 'They argued often.'

'Do you know what they were arguing about?'

Meadows widened his eyes in an expression that could only be described as appalled. 'A good servant does not eavesdrop, Mr Cates,' he said.

No, but he shtups the lady of the house the first chance he gets, I thought.

'Please go on,' Cates managed.

'Ms DeNunzio was upset, and she came to my quarters after I had retired for the evening. She expressed a desire to be . . . held, and I tried to resist, but I confess, I had always found her quite attractive. Eventually, my better judgment escaped me.'

'You had sex with her.' Cates practically spat the words out, trying so hard to get Meadows to say it himself.

'Yes,' was all the reply that came.

'Were you aware she was pregnant when she was murdered?' Cates asked.

'No. I had not been in contact with Ms DeNunzio at all, in any way, since Mr McNabb moved out of the house. I had gone with Mr McNabb.' *Follow the money.*

'Were you aware you were the father of her child?' Cates dropped the bombshell so he could control it. The jurors still demonstrated surprise, leaning forward to hear Meadows' calm, controlled, but quiet answer. A feather dropped on a pillow would have seemed like a cannon blast in the silent courtroom.

'Until you told me about the police report, I had no idea,' Meadows said. 'As I said, there had been no contact between us at all.'

'Before the night you spent with Ms DeNunzio,' Cates said, ably changing the subject, 'had you witnessed any arguments between her and Mr McNabb?'

'Yes.' Meadows was clearly more comfortable discussing domestic strife than his own sex life, but not much. 'They argued frequently in the months before the divorce.'

'I know you didn't eavesdrop,' Cates allowed, 'but surely you couldn't help hearing some of what they were fighting about.'

'I'm aware that Mr McNabb suspected his wife was unfaithful to him,' Meadows said.

And you're living proof she was, I thought.

'Did you ever hear him threaten her physically?'

'I don't recall hearing any threats of violence, but he did say he would stop paying her debts. He said that more than once, but I know he was at least paying off some of them.' Meadows was clearly forced against his will to tell this detail of his employer's life. I braced myself. Cates must have something up his sleeve, or he wouldn't have asked a question he knew would be answered that way. He'd have preferred a threat of violence.

'Did you ever *see* Mr McNabb threaten Ms DeNunzio?' *Uh-oh.*

'Yes,' Meadows answered immediately. 'He raised his hand to strike her once when she said she'd liquidate his collection of . . . memorabilia.'

'Thank you, Mr Meadows,' Cates said, and sat himself down. Meadows turned a cold eye toward me as I approached.

'Mr Meadows, when Mr McNabb raised his hand, did he actually strike Ms DeNunzio?' I was breaking a rule – I didn't know for a fact that Patrick hadn't hit Patsy – but I thought Cates would have emphasized it if Meadows had told him otherwise.

Sure enough, 'no' was the answer from the butler. 'He stopped himself before he made contact, and then he apologized.'

'Now then, Mr Meadows, about this affair you had with Mr McNabb's wife . . .' Meadows didn't exactly cringe, but his eyelids did flicker. I continued, 'What happened after you two were intimate?'

'I don't understand,' Meadows said. 'What do you mean, what happened?'

'You said it only happened once. Why only once?'

'It was a mistake, an accident,' Meadows said, for the first time appearing flustered. 'It shouldn't have happened once. It certainly wasn't going to happen again.'

'Was that your opinion, or Ms DeNunzio's?' I asked. 'Did you want to continue the contact?'

'No. Ms DeNunzio was very clear it was a one-time event, and I agreed with her.' Meadows looked briefly at Cates, hoping there would be an objection. There wasn't.

'So Patsy told you the next morning, or later that night, that that was the only time you'd make love to her, and you accepted that.'

'Yes,' Meadows said. 'I accepted it.'

'If she'd said it could continue, would you have accepted that?'

Now, Cates did stand. 'Objection. She's asking the witness to speculate on a situation that never presented itself.'

'I'm talking about the witness' feelings, Your Honor,' I said. 'This is calculated to produce relevant testimony.'

Franklin thought for a moment. 'I'll allow it, but don't go too far, Ms Moss.' Cates sat.

'Thank you, Your Honor. Mr Meadows, if Patsy had said you could continue the affair, would you have done so?'

Meadows had taken the break to compose himself, and now was the complete butler again. 'I would have liked that,' he said. 'But I knew it was impossible, and I accepted it.'

'So you weren't jealous of other men Patsy slept with? You didn't get just a little bit angry when Patrick came home and you knew they were making love to get over the argument?' I knew I was pushing it, and I knew the next word I'd hear shouted.

'*Objection!*'

I turned and walked back to the defense table. 'Withdrawn, Your Honor. No more questions,' I said, and sat down next to Patrick, who was shaking his head.

'What?' I said to him.

Patrick watched Meadows walk by, fully erect and pressed, as he left the courtroom. 'Poor bugger,' he said. 'She broke his heart.'

THIRTY-NINE

'I got her!' Evan was like an eight-year-old who'd just managed an autograph from his favorite baseball player. 'Mrs Bach! She said it! Now you can get a subpoena.'

He sat down at the table in the conference room where Angie, Patrick, and I were having lunch, which had been 'brought round' by *Dolce Enoteca* at Patrick's insistence (and expense). Evan eyed my risotto hungrily. I allowed him a forkful, but no more. A girl's got to have priorities.

'That's great, Evan. Did she buy the office roast story?' I was grateful, but this was expensive food.

'Hook, line, and sinker. She offered up a few choice tidbits to anyone who might want to roast Bach a little more well-done. Like, he brushes his teeth with five-dollar-a-bottle imported water.'

Angie and I chuckled and, after a moment, Patrick joined in. He was probably wondering what was funny about that – didn't *everyone*?

'This is huge,' I said with my mouth full, making glances at Angie's calamari. 'I have to put on a real show about being outraged at Bach's testimony, then bring on Mrs Bach to undermine it. If I play it properly, it'll work. Evan, can you request the subpoena?'

'Depends,' he said, looking a little hurt.

I understood immediately. 'Oh, all right.' I passed him the rest of the risotto.

'Be happy to,' Evan said with a smile.

By all accounts, Melanie DeNunzio was the dullest witness to appear in the trial so far. CNN actually cut away from the trial after twenty minutes of her testimony to show the arraignment of a man accused of stealing his neighbor's washing machine. When told about it afterward, I said I considered it a good programming decision – if only because a viewer then could find out how someone steals a washing machine.

Cates tried to make Melanie seem interesting, playing up her closeness to her sister and the fact that she, Melanie, had been at the party the night Patrick McNabb had showed off his bow and arrow acquisition from *The Searchers*. But in the end, the jury, as did the rest of the courtroom, saw Melanie as a rather ordinary woman whose sister had treated her like a rather ordinary woman.

The one moment that made the courtroom perk up was when Cates asked Melanie if she knew about the arguments between Patsy and McNabb. 'I know they were upset,' Melanie told him. 'Obviously, things weren't going well.'

'How was it obvious?' Cates said, clearly salivating at the thought of an insider revelation.

'Well, they were getting a divorce, you know,' Melanie told him. He quickly dismissed her and handed me the reins.

'Did Patrick McNabb ever hit your sister, to the best of your knowledge?' I asked Melanie.

'Oh, no.'

'Did he ever act violently, or in any way threaten her?'

'Well, there was one time he said he was going to cut up her credit cards,' Melanie said after some thought.

'Thank you, Ms DeNunzio.'

The week's main event was clearly going to be Junius Bach's testimony. But, because most of the jury had no idea who Bach was, there was not the anticipated gasp of recognition when his name was called as a prosecution witness. This probably irritated Bach, but he was far too professional to let it show. He did refuse to look at me as he walked by my table on the way to the witness stand.

'Mr Bach, you are the managing partner of the law firm Seaton, Taylor, Evans and Bach, are you not?' Cates began with the obvious.

'I am,' Bach said definitively.

'And that is a very prestigious law firm devoted to family law, including divorce proceedings, child custody matters, and things of that nature, isn't it?' Cates asked the question with little inflection, but Bach treated it as somewhat condescending.

'Yes,' was all he said.

'Lawyers at your firm represent many prominent celebrities, do they not?'

If he continues to question the man this slowly, we may be here until the next Olympics.

'That's correct,' Bach said, agreeing with everything so far.

'Among those people is the defendant, Patrick McNabb. Isn't that right?' Cates was watching the jurors, and it took a few moments for that information to sink in with them. Luckily, Bach was a practiced attorney as well, and he waited until the jurors' eyes told him to speak.

'That's correct. We were representing Mr McNabb in the divorce proceedings.'

'And the attorney handling Mr McNabb's defense in this case, Ms Moss, is a member of your firm, isn't she?'

The jury took longer to digest that, and again, Bach waited, but this time, his gaze was aimed at me. 'Yes, she is *an associate* at the firm,' he said, but he didn't seem happy about it.

'Isn't it rather unusual for the managing partner of a law firm to appear as a witness against his own client with one of his own attorneys on the other side of the case?' Cates asked, as if it had never occurred to him before.

'It's extremely unusual,' Bach answered. 'I don't believe I've ever heard of it happening before.'

'So why are you appearing here today?' *Um, because you called him as a witness. Was I the only one paying attention here?*

I couldn't take any more. I stood up. 'Your Honor, I don't see how this witness' testimony can be seen as anything but a conflict of interest, and I request that you disallow it.'

'Please approach the bench, both of you.'

Cates and I walked to the bench, and the judge put his hand over the microphone to keep the conversation from being recorded or heard in the courtroom. 'The witness is appearing voluntarily, Ms Moss, and as far as I know, your only basis for asking me to throw him out is that he's going to say things you don't like. Now, do you have another reason?'

'Your Honor, Mr Bach is playing office politics, and his appearance here is merely an indication of how badly he wants me to fail.' Miraculously, I managed to spit the accusation out while looking the judge right in the eye, and I didn't vomit. That was the extent to which I was succeeding.

'Ms Moss, Junius Bach is the managing partner of the firm you work for. If he doesn't like you so much, why doesn't he just fire you?' It was a good question.

I shifted my weight, which had increased with the risotto, from one foot to the other. I felt like I'd been called in front of my second grade class. 'Because,' I said, 'Mr McNabb is a wealthy client, and Mr McNabb doesn't want me fired, Your Honor.'

Cates barely concealed his laughter. 'Doesn't this sound just a little bit paranoid, Your Honor? Everyone's out to get poor little Ms Moss, aren't they?'

'Your Honor, I would not be surprised if Mr Bach and the district attorney discussed this matter at length during witness prep, and for that reason alone, I think Mr Bach's testimony should not be allowed.'

'Ms Moss, that *is* paranoid. Step back, both of you.'

I wasn't surprised at Franklin's decision, but protocol required me to go through the motions of his rejection.

'I'm going to allow Mr Bach's testimony. Your motion is denied, Ms Moss.'

I nodded, chiefly because bursting into tears would have seemed unprofessional.

Cates continued his questioning. 'So, Mr Bach, why are you appearing here today, testifying as a witness hostile to your own client?'

'I was present at a meeting before Ms DeNunzio was murdered that might have some relevance to the case.'

'That was the divorce settlement conference, correct?' Cates asked.

'Yes. It was the meeting at which a settlement of the distribution of assets to the marriage was to be devised.' Bach was as emotionally inscrutable as a beach ball – and at least a beach ball has interesting colors.

'There was no settlement agreed to, was there?' Cates asked, as if he didn't know the answer.

'No. The conference did not go well, and there was a considerable argument between Mr McNabb and Ms DeNunzio, which I did my best to mediate.' *Yeah, by throwing gasoline on it*, I thought.

'What was the argument about?'

'As far as I could tell, it was about who would own a pair of tap dancing shoes owned by James Cagney. Ms DeNunzio told Mr McNabb he couldn't have them, and he became very agitated.'

'Agitated? In what way?' Cates asked. *How many ways are there to become agitated?*

'He told Ms DeNunzio he'd kill her before he saw the shoes end up in her hands.' A couple of the jurors, both women, gasped. They all looked at Patrick. He responded by looking as guilty as a man could look. I closed my eyes and tried to picture myself on a beach in Bimini. Alone. Or maybe with Evan.

'Those were his exact words?' Cates was relishing the moment.

'Objection, Your Honor. Asked and answered,' I said.

But the judge wasn't buying. 'We need to know if there was any possibility that Mr McNabb was misunderstood. I'm allowing it, Ms Moss.'

'His exact words were, "You touch so much as a shoelace, you cheap whore, and I will personally see to it that it's the last thing you touch. I'll see you dead before I let you have those shoes. You understand, Patsy? I'll kill you."' Bach might have been reading his tax return for all the emotion he was showing. Actually, he might have shown more emotion reading his tax return.

'How do you remember the exact words?' Cates asked. I thought of objecting strictly by citing on the 'oh, please' statute, but savored the thought of my moment to come.

'I had my assistant make a transcript of the meeting. I always do,' Bach seemed quite pleased that he could do such a thing.

'Do you think Mr McNabb meant his words literally when he said them, that he really would kill Ms DeNunzio?'

'Objection!' was out of my mouth so fast I had to check to make sure it *was* my mouth, and not some stranger's that had opened. 'Asking the witness to speak to Mr McNabb's thoughts now?'

'Sustained,' Franklin said.

'No further questions,' said Cates, and Bach turned his emotionless, shark-like stare toward me as I stood.

'Mr Bach, have you ever said you were going to kill someone?'

He stared at me. 'No.'

'Never? Even as an expression? "I'm gonna kill you?" That sort of thing?'

'Never,' Bach said.

'Never said it to your wife, for example? People say that when they don't really mean it, if they get mad at someone close to them. You never told your wife you'd kill her?'

'Never,' Bach said with a touch more emphasis.

I made my best 'OK, then . . .' face, and said, 'No further questions, Your Honor.'

Bach was dismissed, and on his way out, he managed to look at me even less than the not-at-all he had on the way in. I tried not to take it personally.

FORTY

'I *told* you that you were ready,' Angie said as we ate dinner that night in my cramped kitchen. Taking a break from preparation, research, and Evan, we were wearing T-shirts and shorts, and eating large bowls of pasta with Paul Newman's sauce, the only kind I would buy (*he gives the money to charity*) and the only supermarket sauce Angie would deign to eat ('it's almost like real sauce if you don't taste too hard').

'Don't get cocky,' I replied. 'We've had some good days and some not-so-good days.'

'But no bad days,' Angie reminded me. 'Even when Cates has made a point, you've managed to punch holes in it. And he doesn't know what's on its way.'

I took a long drink of Diet Sprite, which Angie considered to be absolute sacrilege in the same room, let alone the same meal, as ziti. 'Neither do we,' I reminded her. 'Keep *that* in mind.'

'Who does he have left on his list?'

'Nobody too exciting. Still no expert on archery to explain how Patrick managed to shoot the arrow without getting his fingerprints on it. All he's really got left is Lucien DuPrez.' I wiped sauce off Angie's chin.

'Patsy's business manager?'

I nodded. 'I'm guessing he's going to talk about how bad Patsy's career was going and why she needed the money from the divorce. Make her seem more sympathetic, and show how greedy Patrick is that he wouldn't just settle and let her have it.'

'So greedy he gave you a Ferrari, and didn't care when it blew up.' Angie took a sip of red wine.

'Everybody has a different definition of greedy,' I said.

'How badly can DuPrez hurt your case?'

I tilted her head. 'Not much, I don't think, unless Cates knows something I don't, like Patrick told DuPrez he was going to shoot Patsy with an arrow. And even that would be hearsay.'

'Sounds like it's gonna be an easy day, then.'

'That's what worries me.'

Lucien DuPrez, as it turned out, couldn't hurt us very much. He did indeed testify that Patsy's career had hit the skids, that her net worth was about half what it had been only a year before, and that she was about to have to live like a semi-regular person, giving her reason to want to gouge Patrick for every dime she could in the divorce.

'Were you aware of any financial pressure Mr McNabb was placing on Ms DeNunzio before she died?' Cates asked him.

'I know she was coming to me every two days asking for more spending money,' DuPrez answered. 'I know she was asking him first, and getting nowhere. And I know she wanted to sell off some of their joint possessions to raise cash, but he wouldn't agree to it.'

'Things like the Cagney tap shoes,' Cates said, which, to me, didn't seem like a question. It must have been, though, because DuPrez answered it.

'Yes. She mentioned that an anonymous buyer had offered more than two million dollars for the shoes.' There was a murmur in the gallery.

'That much?' Cates asked. 'We've heard testimony they weren't worth more than, perhaps, twenty thousand.'

'Yes, Patsy was surprised, too. But she knew the offer had come in, and Patrick McNabb was not considering it.'

'He was not.'

'No. Patsy said Patrick wouldn't let her have a dime of his money, and, to maintain her lifestyle, he wouldn't sell the shoes they both legally owned.' DuPrez licked his lips, probably thinking of the money. 'I knew, of course, that her income was decreasing, and she could have used the help.'

'Do you know who made the offer for the shoes?' Cates said. As he asked, the doors to the courtroom actually burst open (I'd never seen that in a real courtroom before, but I was starting to expect such things: Hey, this *was* Hollywood) and one of Cates' associates all but ran in, made it to the table, and whispered to the second chair, D'ontell Liebowitz, an African-American woman who'd clearly not kept her maiden name, and who had not said a word so far in the trial.

'Patsy didn't know, and she didn't tell me, so I had no way of knowing,' DuPrez replied, but virtually no one in the courtroom heard it. D'ontell's eyes had gotten so wide at what the associate had told her that they threatened to engulf her entire face. She tugged on Cates' sleeve so hard I half expected it to come off, like in a Three Stooges movie.

Instead, Cates leaned over with an irritated expression that changed to one of amazement as he heard what she had to say. He straightened quickly. 'Thank you, Mr DuPrez. No further questions,' Cates said, and was back in his seat before DuPrez's mouth finished dropping open.

I was so curious that Evan had to pat my hand and gesture for me to begin questioning. *Oh, yeah.*

I stood and approached DuPrez, trying hard not to look behind me at what Cates was doing, but hearing the courtroom doors open and close again. 'Mr DuPrez, you said Ms DeNunzio was desperately in need of cash at the time of her death?'

'That's right.' DuPrez, anxious to get the spotlight back, straightened up in his chair and let his many gold necklaces dangle for the jury to see. 'Her income had dropped precipitously in the previous year.'

'And she had no projects that could have brought in money?'

'A couple of little gigs here and there,' DuPrez said. 'She'd recorded an album that didn't sell. Her income had dropped like a stone.'

'Dropped to what?' I asked.

'I'm sorry?'

'How far had Ms DeNunzio's income dropped? How much money did she make in the year before she died?' I'd managed to regain focus and was intent on DuPrez now.

'She made about two million dollars,' DuPrez said. Members of the jury leaned forward, thinking they'd obviously misheard him.

'So Patsy DeNunzio made two million dollars the year before she died, and she was still almost broke?' I asked, my voice as incredulous as I could believably make it. 'How is that possible?'

'When a person makes a lot of money like that, on paper, it seems like a lot, but after taxes and fees, you know . . .' DuPrez seemed to realize, suddenly, that the jury didn't love him, and was confused.

'What? It drops to only a million?'

'Objection,' came a woman's voice. I turned toward the unfamiliar voice to see D'ontell Liebowitz standing where Cates normally stood. Cates was nowhere to be seen.

'Sustained. Let's keep the sarcastic comments to a minimum, Ms Moss.'

'Yes, Your Honor. My apologies. Mr DuPrez, does that mean Ms DeNunzio, at the time of her death, was in debt from her spending, and needed money to pay her debts?'

'Yes,' DuPrez said. 'She was in debt, and was selling off what she could to pay her creditors.'

'To whom was she in debt?'

'A good number of people,' said DuPrez. 'No one in particular.'

'Were you one of them?'

'I'm sorry?' That had caught DuPrez off-guard, which was surprising. Surely he'd known, as her financial manager, if she owed him money.

'You said she was coming to you for spending money. Did Patsy DeNunzio owe you money at the time of her death?' I tried to sound calm and reasonable, the best tone for a lawyer savaging someone on the witness stand.

'Yes, she did,' DuPrez said. 'Me and a large number of others.'

'How much?'

'How much what?' Now he was just buying time.

'How much money did she owe you?'

'Well, I don't have the figures in front of me, so I can't be precise . . .' That was as much time as he could afford.

'Feel free to estimate,' I encouraged him sternly.

'About a million dollars.'

'Could you speak up, Mr DuPrez? I don't think the jury heard you.'

'A million dollars,' he repeated. 'But that's not as much as you think it is.'

'I don't know, Mr DuPrez,' I said, looking at the jury. 'I think it's a pretty large sum.'

'Objection,' said Cates, who apparently had returned.

'Withdrawn. No further questions, Your Honor.'

The judge looked down at Cates and regarded all the commotion, but didn't comment. 'Redirect, Mr Cates?'

'No, thank you, Your Honor.'

The judge dismissed DuPrez, who looked like someone who – despite his recent discomfort – would have stayed in the witness chair until someone removed him physically. Cates could barely contain his grin, which some might describe as eating something other than Cheerios.

'Your Honor, the people would like to recall Melanie DeNunzio.'

'Very well.' The crowd could barely mask its disappointment. Melanie DeNunzio had been the least interesting witness to date, and that included a day and a half of testimony by the coroner.

Melanie walked in looking a little taller than she had before, as she'd forsaken her trademark slump for a prouder, more erect stance. She strode to the witness stand and sat down. The judge reminded her she was still under oath.

Cates, who, on this day, was actually wearing suspenders, seemed to subdue the urge to snap them self-righteously as he approached Melanie. 'Ms DeNunzio, I have only a few new questions. Can you tell me if you know who killed your sister?'

I narrowed her eyes. *How the hell would Melanie know who killed Patsy?* What was going on here? I stole a glance at Angie, who'd rounded her mouth into a tight 'o' shape.

'Yes, I do,' Melanie answered. She'd been coached well – and in a hurry.

'Who was it?' No good could come from this answer.

'It was Patrick McNabb,' Melanie said. There actually was a gasp around the courtroom, and Patrick, more than anyone else, looked astonished.

'How do you know?' Cates asked.

'I was there,' Melanie said. 'I saw him do it.'

FORTY-ONE

I looked at Patrick. He sat stock-still in his chair, staring at Melanie with a look I'd never seen in his eyes before.

Hatred.

'Why were you in the house that night?' Cates asked Melanie.

'I drove over to return some clothes Patsy had loaned me. I had a key, so I let myself in. The lights in the front part of the house were out, so I thought no one was home, or Patsy was asleep. I went in through the side, through the kitchen, like I always did. When I got there, I heard voices in the dining room, so I went to see who it was.'

'Whose voices were they?'

Melanie took a moment to dab at her eyes, which didn't appear to need dabbing. 'It was Patsy and Patrick,' she said. 'They were arguing.'

Patrick slowly reached for the pen and pad in front of him

and wrote, in clear, neat, block letters, 'SHE'S LYING.' He pushed the pad in front of me.

'Did you walk into the dining room?' Cates asked, his voice as smooth as anything the Skippy company ever produced.

'No. I looked through the pass-through from the kitchen, where they used to place food during parties and whatever. And I saw them. Patrick was holding the bow, you know, just fiddling with it, but they were yelling at each other about Jimmy's shoes. The tap shoes, you know.'

I know, I thought, *I know. Stop telling me that I know what I know!*

'What happened then?' Cates asked.

'I don't know. It was freaky. They were arguing, but not really getting that mad, and suddenly, calm as anything, Patrick picks an arrow out of the, you know, arrow thing next to the bow and shoots it right at Patsy. Just like that. Calm.' Melanie was looking up, as if trying to remember the name of her first boyfriend. 'I almost screamed, but I was afraid he'd hear me, and then he'd fire one at me, too.'

'What did he do then?' Cates was having the time of his life.

'He walked over, calm as anything, and wiped off the part of the arrow sticking out of her. Then he reached into his pocket and pulled out his cell phone, and called nine-one-one. Next thing I know, he's pretending to be all upset, and yelling, "Somebody shot my wife!" and all like that.'

'And what did you do?'

'I ran. I didn't want to be there when the cops got there. I figured they'd think I was in on it.'

This is fishier than a Friday night during Lent, and I'm not even Catholic.

'But you saw it happen.' Cates wanted that to be clear.

So did Melanie. 'Oh, yeah, I saw it, all right.'

'Your witness, Ms Moss.'

What? Already? Melanie actually looked afraid as I approached her.

'Ms DeNunzio, why didn't you tell the police what you saw?' It seemed a logical question.

'I told you – because I thought they'd think I was in on it.' Melanie was reciting now, saying what someone had told her to say. The district attorney? Call me naïve, but I just couldn't believe that.

'Why didn't you tell them afterward? Why didn't you tell the D.A. before? In short, Ms DeNunzio, why are you telling your story, such as it is, now?'

I'd deliberately tried to make my voice a little louder and sterner than before – I thought Melanie might crack under the pressure. But Melanie seemed to derive some strength from the browbeating, and sat back in the witness chair, relaxed.

'She was my sister,' she said simply.

'How did that *happen?*' I was too agitated to sit. Instead, I just stood and watched Patrick, Angie, and Evan situate themselves around the table in the conference room. We only had an hour for lunch, and I couldn't even think of food.

'Somebody got to her,' Angie said with no hint of doubt. 'Maybe they know something about her, or they made her think she'll get Patsy's money, or . . .'

'But she *will* get Patsy's money,' Patrick said. 'Well, no. I misspoke. She'll get some of Patsy's memorabilia. She would have gotten money, but Patsy was in so much debt there wasn't much left except her business interests, rights to old albums and the hip hop record, if anyone wants it. I paid some of the debts but once it became clear we were divorcing I stopped. Still, there wasn't much for Melanie to inherit. It's in Patsy's will. DuPrez gets everything she owned professionally.'

'Then, what do *you* get?' Angie asked.

'Nothing. I didn't ask for anything. I get only things I owned, the things I brought to the marriage, like Jimmy's shoes. No money, no business considerations. I didn't see any point. I have enough money.'

I paced and thought. *OK, maybe just a little food.* 'Should we order out?'

'I'll have something brought round.' How did I know he'd say that? Patrick produced a cell phone and touched a button.

'Sit down, Sandy,' Evan said. 'You're making me nervous.' So I sat next to him and put my head down on the table. Just a short nap until the food arrived . . . where was it already? I was hungrier than I'd thought.

'Patrick, did you see anyone there that night? Hear a car? Anything? Could there have been someone else there?' I figured if I couldn't eat yet, I might as well gather additional information.

Patrick shook his head. 'No. No one. I'd have known if someone was there, and besides, I never did *any* of those things she said that night. Patsy and I weren't arguing, we were . . . well, you know. It was one of the nicest nights we ever spent together.'

I began to rub my temples with my forefingers. The clues were there, but I couldn't recognize them. Something was shouting at me, but I was too far away to hear . . . But there was a way to find out! 'You know . . .' I began.

Evan, ever hopeful, seemed to note my encouraging tone. 'What?' he asked eagerly.

A court officer stuck her head into the room. 'Your food's here,' she said.

'Finally!' I said. 'I could eat a horse!'

Knowing when to hold 'em and when to fold 'em, Cates rested his case when we returned from lunch.

Once he was seated, I faced Franklin in my best TV lawyer mode.

'Your Honor, the defense would like to call a rebuttal witness.'

Franklin frowned. 'A witness not on your list, Ms Moss? Does this go directly to testimony already presented?'

'The prosecution opened the door, Your Honor.'

The judge produced a sound like a whoopee cushion being sat upon. 'All right, then. Call your witness, Ms Moss.'

'The defense calls Martha Bach.'

The concept of a 'surprise witness' is something invented for television and movies. In reality, all witnesses are listed long before the trial, but when an attorney decides a witness should be brought in to contradict testimony the other side has presented, it's possible to bring in a rebuttal witness, and as such, Martha Bach should have been a surprise to the prosecution.

The problem was, no one at the prosecutor's table so much as blinked when she proceeded to the stand from her seat in the last row of the gallery. *Had she told her husband she'd be testifying today? Had he told Cates?* Why didn't anybody care about my dramatic opening?

Mrs Bach was sworn in and sat in the witness chair. But for the regal presence she exuded, she looked for all the world like she was mounting the throne of England. *Perfect*, I thought, *let her send waves of authority out into the room and seem even more impressive than she already is.*

'Mrs Bach, you are the wife of Junius Bach, who testified here previously, are you not?' I wanted to let the jury make the connection without repeating what Bach had said on the stand.

'I am,' Martha said proudly. *Who wouldn't be proud of marrying one of the great back-stabbing attorneys in Los Angeles?*

'Although I know you weren't here when your husband testified, Mrs Bach, he did say something that pertained to you.'

'Really?' Martha seemed perplexed at such a thing. Talking about her in public? How awful!

'Yes. He was asked about the expression, "I could kill you," and whether he'd ever said that to anyone. He said he's never said such a thing to anyone in his life.'

Mrs Bach looked at me as if I were speaking fluent Apache. 'Yes?'

I savored the moment. 'Mrs Bach, has your husband ever said he was going to kill you?'

Martha Bach digested the question and seemed to give it serious thought. 'No,' she said.

Huh?

'I'm sorry, Mrs Bach, but perhaps you didn't understand the question. I'm not asking if your husband ever physically threatened you, or even made a serious verbal threat. I'm asking if he's ever used the phrase, "I'll kill you," or something similar to that, in a conversation with you.'

'No,' Martha repeated. 'Never.'

I shot what I hoped was a threatening look at Evan, whose eyes were the size of baseballs. I looked back at Mrs Bach, then to the judge. In all this frantic looking, something at the rear of the courtroom caught my eye. It was the most fleeting glimpse of Junius Bach. I turned my head to confirm it – there he was, smiling broadly.

Son of a bitch!

'Ms Moss?' Franklin admonished me.

'Your Honor, may I approach the bench?' The judge waved

me forward, and I tried to search his eyes for compassion. What I got was confusion.

'Your Honor,' I said, 'what this witness is saying completely contradicts what she told us before she testified. I can only assume she was lying to us then, or is perjuring herself now.'

'Ms Moss, I know this is your first trial in my court, but I'm going to assume you've been in a courtroom before.'

'Yes, Your Honor.'

'Then why do you think this is my problem? Your witness hasn't given you the answer you wanted, and that, I can only assume, is due to poor preparation on your part.'

The weeks of sleep deprivation, worry, and sexual abstinence finally took their toll, and I had to restrain myself from shouting in the courtroom. 'To be *fair*, Your Honor, given the short time I had to prepare for this trial, it's a miracle I was able to prepare this well.'

Franklin took off his glasses and frowned at me. 'This is hardly the time to complain about that, Ms Moss,' he said. 'If you had a problem with the short court date, you should have filed for a continuance.'

I wanted to speak. Really, I did. But the part of my brain that normally communicated with my vocal chords wasn't linked to my mouth at that moment. Finally, I managed, 'I *did* file for a continuance, Judge. You denied it.'

'I assure you, I never saw any such motion,' he said. 'I would have given you more time. I thought this court date was a disgrace, considering the charges, but I never saw anything from you.'

My brain reeled. Everything I'd relied upon was crumbling around me. The surprise witness had surprised me, and the continuance I'd been cruelly denied had never been . . .

Plus, someone had leaked information to Bach and the D.A. about his wife. Someone had given away my plans. Someone had countered my every move and frustrated my best strategies.

I spun as the obvious finally came into focus. I faced my table – *my* own *table!* – where the only person who could possibly be responsible was sitting, looking at me with the most innocent, trusting eyes in the room.

Evan.

Son of a bitch!

FORTY-TWO

'Son of a *bitch*!' I screamed at Evan. After requesting, and being granted, a recess until the next day, I managed to hold it together on the drive home (in Angie's car, but with Evan in the back seat, so I couldn't say anything). I invited Evan up to the apartment 'to talk about the case,' but hadn't said much else. I'd felt like I would burst with anger, but I couldn't show it until we were alone. I looked for signs I was wrong, and found none. Angie and Evan probably thought I was being sullen because of the beating I'd taken at the hands of Melanie and Mrs Bach.

The difference was, one of them was happy about it.

Angie, clearly astonished by my outburst, held me back from Evan, who was standing in front of the sofa. I could have launched myself at him – I wanted to – but if he'd ducked, I would have gone through the living room window and into the Los Angeles night below.

'What the hell are you talking about?' I don't think Angie had ever seen me this angry before. She spun and faced Evan. 'Did she just find out you're married?'

'No,' Evan said. 'Of course not.'

'Then, what?'

I could barely talk through my clenched teeth. 'He knows. Go ahead. Tell her. But if you think *I'm* upset . . .'

'Tell me what?'

Evan's face relaxed into what I now understood it must have looked like when he wasn't lying, if that was ever a possibility. He seemed to age three years, his eyebrows dropped two inches, and his mouth, whose innocence I'd so admired, pursed into a hardened cynicism I'd have thought impossible the day before.

'Sandy's going to tell you I've been working for Junius Bach the whole time, that I've done everything I can to sabotage this case, and that I am, in her opinion, the lowest form of life on the planet.' He turned to me. 'How am I doing so far?'

'At least you have the good taste not to deny it.'

Angie, however, was not handling the news well. I watched as her hands took on a claw-like appearance, her eyes widened, and her forearms tensed to the point you could count the veins. Luckily, I'd moved past the violent stage, and was trying my best to catch my friend's eye.

'Ang. Ang, forget it. He's not worth it.'

'Yes, he is! He's worth every minute of it! Even if I end up doing time, he'll be worth it!' Now it was my turn to do the restraining.

'But I couldn't finish the case without you,' I said.

'Finish the case?' Evan gloated. 'The case is finished. Oh, you were clever, weren't you, bringing in Bach's wife? And for what? So she could be the last nail in Patrick McNabb's coffin!'

Angie's voice dropped to a growl. 'Are you *sure* he's not worth it?'

'Positive.'

I addressed Evan. 'You did it all. You pretended to file for a continuance, which the judge told me he would have granted, and then you told me it had been denied. You gave every last piece of strategy to Bach, and he passed it on to the D.A. And then you pretended to have a romantic interest in me . . . so you could get better information.'

'It sure as hell wasn't for the sex,' Evan said.

'*What* sex?'

'Exactly.'

Angie's eyes never left Evan. 'I'm really thinking he's worth it, Sand.'

'In another minute, I might agree.' I looked at Evan again. 'You were willing to . . . to sleep with me in order to report back to Junius Bach? What kind of paralegal are you?'

'My God, you're dense,' Evan sneered. 'I'm a lawyer. I've been a lawyer for four years. Bach thought it would be a good idea for me to pretend you were my mentor, but I thought I could be more effective as a lover.'

'Not after I get through with you,' Angie snarled. Evan might have blanched a bit at that.

'OK. OK. I have to think.' I sat down. Evan wasn't Evan. At least, not the Evan I thought he was. And I'd told him everything about the case . . . Wait a second. Not *everything*. I looked at him, eyes as cold as I could make them. 'I want you to leave now,' I said. 'I want you to never come back.'

'Suits me fine. I have someone waiting for me, anyway.'

'Oh my God,' Angie said. 'You *are* married, aren't you?'

'No,' Evan said. 'But I'm living with Robin Flynn, the bathing suit model.'

Too fast, I thought. *It's happening too fast. Next I'll find out he drives stock cars for a hobby on the weekends.*

'I'd really like to kill him,' Angie said.

'Go ahead,' I replied.

Evan laughed coldly. 'Don't be absurd.'

'They never did find that guy you used to date from Keasbey, did they?' I asked.

'Not *all* of him, no,' answered Angie.

Evan was out the door without a response.

'Well, that was a mistake,' I finally admitted.

'You can't blame yourself,' Angie answered. 'There was no way you could have known.'

'No, that's not what I meant,' I said. 'It was *their* mistake. Now they've made me mad.'

FORTY-THREE

Patrick had not gloated, as I thought he might, when told of Evan's treachery. He merely nodded, said something about 'young D'Artagnan' having 'left the service of the queen for the evil Cardinal Richelieu,' and asked what was next.

Lizz Warnell was next, and I began by asking her, on the witness stand, if Patrick's behavior on the set of *Legality* had ever been affected by his marital problems.

'No,' Lizz answered. 'I don't recall him ever being anything but delightful on the set. Patrick didn't let his personal life intrude on his work.'

'You also knew him on a social basis, didn't you?' I asked.

'Those were only rumors,' Lizz said. 'We were both married at the time.'

'I meant, you saw Patrick *and his wife* socially away from work, didn't you?' I had to be careful not to let Lizz's somewhat delusional comments taint the jury's perception of Patrick.

'Oh, yes. We on *Legality* are a family,' said Lizz, who evidenced her desire to get with the program. 'We saw each other quite often. I was shocked when I heard Patrick and Patsy were splitting up. They seemed so happy.'

'I'm sure it was quite surprising. Now, Ms Warnell, you heard testimony from some cast members and crew that Mr McNabb was a regular at the Beverly Hills Bow Club, where he practiced his archery. Did you belong to that club as well?'

'I did, and I do,' Lizz answered. 'I find it exhilarating.'

'Do you, the cast members, and the crew ever compete while you're at the club?' I asked wide-eyed.

'Oh, yes. We make little side wagers on who'll score the highest, or get the most arrows on the inner circle – things like that.' Lizz, always ready to play with – and beat – the boys, was pleased to discuss her hobby.

'So, who's the best?'

Lizz looked a little startled. 'I'm sorry?'

Cates stood up, making a show of his impatience. 'Objection, Your Honor. What relevance does this have?'

'What relevance?' I said to Judge Franklin. 'The victim in this case is shot through the heart with a bow and arrow – one arrow, a miracle of a shot – and the district attorney doesn't understand the relevance of the defendant's prowess in archery?'

'If Ms Moss wishes to make the point that her client is very good with a bow and arrow, I have no problem, Your Honor,' said Cates, 'but asking Ms Warnell for her opinion, and not presenting her as an expert witness, appears to make no point at all.' I realized that Cates wanted to suggest to the jury that Patrick was an expert archer without running the risk that Lizz would say someone else shot better than he did.

'Ms Warnell is not an expert, but she *can* have an opinion,' I countered. 'She shot arrows with Mr McNabb and the others on a regular basis, and was present when they competed. If you were at the final game, you don't have to be the Commissioner of Baseball to know who won the World Series.'

'Overruled,' Franklin said with just a touch of admiration in his voice. Coming from a woman, the baseball analogy must have hit a home run with him. He didn't know I had three brothers and hit better than all of them.

'Ms Warnell, who, of the cast and crew, is the best at archery, in your opinion?'

During my exchange with Cates, Lizz's eyes had been darting back and forth, betraying no preference for either of our arguments. Her dilemma – one I'd planned – was exquisite: should she boast about her own prowess, and thereby implicate herself in the minds of the jury, or concede that Patrick was the better shot, and publicly admit she wasn't the best at some activity? If there was one thing I'd learned in my short time in Hollywood, it was that ego would always prevail.

'I'd have to say I'm the best,' Lizz said.

'But there was a visitor once who was better. Isn't that true?' I knew Lizz hadn't seen this one coming – I hadn't prepared her for the question.

'I'm not sure I know what you mean.'

'Didn't Patsy DeNunzio visit with her husband once, not long before they separated? And didn't she show a remarkable talent for archery?'

'Objection!' Cates barely made it out of his chair. 'Is Ms Moss actually suggesting that Ms DeNunzio shot *herself* with the arrow?'

'Of course not, Your Honor,' I answered with a condescending laugh. 'I'm trying to establish the nature of the competition that goes on at the club.'

'Overruled.'

I turned back in Lizz's direction. 'Ms Warnell, did Patsy show herself to be a remarkable archer during her one visit to the club?'

Lizz gritted her teeth so severely, I wasn't sure she'd be able to open her mouth, but she managed. 'Yes,' was all she said.

'Would you say she was better than you?'

The transformation in Lizz's face was astounding: her skin took on a much darker, redder hue; her eyes widened and took on a bloodshot quality; her hair appeared to absorb humidity and puff out on either side of her head. She was trying as hard as she could to keep it together, but the pressure from inside her head must have been tremendous. Any physician watching from the last row would have leapt up and administered blood pressure medication intravenously.

'Better? Than I am?'

'Yes. In your opinion, was Ms DeNunzio, without any lessons, training, or practice, a better shot than you? Was she, in fact, better than anyone in the cast and crew of *Legality*?' I kept my voice light, conversational. You'd never have known from my tone that I was forcing a woman to dissolve in public.

Lizz mumbled something very short, but it was unintelligible.

'I'm sorry,' I said sweetly. 'We couldn't hear you.'

'YES!' Lizz bellowed. 'She was better! The little brat came right off the street and shot a record score! Just like that!'

I raised my eyebrows in innocent surprise. 'Really? How did that make the regulars, like you, feel?'

'Pissed off!' Lizz shouted. 'How would you feel if the janitor walked up here and started trying this case better than you are?'

'Relieved,' I admitted. 'No further questions.'

Cates' cross-examination, which lasted only ten minutes, was uneventful, after which the judge called a lunch break and Patrick, Angie, and I walked into the hallway's usual crush of reporters, fans, and celebrity stalkers. Angie and Patrick turned toward the conference room, where we'd made a habit of having lunch, but I didn't follow.

'Sand,' Angie said, 'where you going?'

'I'm going to skip lunch today,' I told her. 'You two go. I have someone I need to go see.'

'Is it Evan?' Angie asked. 'Because I'd like to go along as an armed guard.'

'It's not Evan,' I chuckled. 'I have a meeting scheduled here in the courthouse. Tell you about it later.'

I walked away, ignoring the reporters, fans, celebrity stalkers, and Angie and Patrick's puzzled expressions.

Evelyn Draper wasn't a great beauty, but in prison fatigues, courthouse lighting, and no makeup, Scarlett Johansson wouldn't have launched a thousand ships, either. When Evelyn sat down across the table from me, her eyes began to moisten. Having been a prosecutor for years, I was used to prisoners getting emotional after some time in prison, but I'll admit it – I hadn't expected this.

'I'm so sorry about your shirt!' Evelyn wailed. 'I didn't mean to get that stuff on you – it was supposed to hit Patrick McNabb.'

'I know,' I said. 'It washed right out.' (Actually, I'd thrown the blouse away, after trying three times to wash it myself, and one dry cleaning fiasco. Food coloring is not terribly forgiving.) 'I don't understand why you're still here.'

'I couldn't make the bail: they wanted *ten thousand dollars*! And I don't have that kind of money.' Evelyn stared at her hands for a moment.

'Couldn't you get a bail bondsman to put up that much?' To a bondsman, it wasn't a lot of money in the grand scheme of things.

'They charge a fee,' Evelyn said. 'I'm not exactly living large at the moment.'

'How about PIOUS? They wouldn't spring for you?' I knew the answers to these questions, but I wanted to drive them home for Evelyn, to make her a little more receptive to what I was about to propose.

'It's not like there's a PIOUS headquarters in town, or a central office, or anything,' Evelyn answered. 'It's just a bunch of people, mostly girls, who really liked Patsy's music.'

'Well, I guess they'll be happy when the new album is released,' I said.

Beat, two, three . . .

'*New album?*' Evelyn's face lit up, and suddenly she was Scarlett Johansson for a moment. 'There's going to be a new Patsy album? How's that possible?'

'Tracks she recorded before she died. Patrick owns the rights to them, and he's instructed me to sell them to the highest bidder. I haven't had time to contact the record companies yet, but . . .'

'Oh, you've *got* to,' Evelyn gushed. 'You can't imagine what it'll mean to the fans!'

'Well, I'll get to it, I'm sure. I came here because I wanted to talk about your situation. You know I'm not pressing charges. You're being held on the authority of the court.'

'Yes, I know.' Evelyn stared at her hands again as reality set back in.

'I think I can help,' I told her. 'Suppose I see to it that your bail money is put up today? And at trial, I'll defend you pro bono. Do you know what that means?'

'That's free, right?' Evelyn's voice was small – she was wondering whether to believe Patrick McNabb's attorney.

'Yes, that's right. You won't have to pay me to represent you in court. It'll be free.' I waited and watched. Evelyn had to guess there'd be a catch, and slowly, she looked up and met my gaze. Her voice was a little less reedy, a little more wary.

'What do I have to do?'

'Nothing. I'll defend you either way. But I do have a favor to ask. If you say no, I'll still help you out, and it'll still be free. But as a friend, you might want to do this thing for me.'

A friend? OK, maybe that was pushing it. Evelyn's face registered a trace of cynicism. I knew the PIOUS people must have told her not to trust Patrick or anyone around him, that he was the killer who took Patsy away from them and ruined their lives. But prison always gave people time to think, and Evelyn had clearly not forgiven herself for the 'blood' throwing incident. I was just a sweet young woman – a lot like her – offering to help her when none of those PIOUS people had come to her aid. Besides, I'd made myself the vulnerable one, offering to represent her for free, no strings attached. I couldn't have made the decision any easier for her.

'What do you want me to do?' she asked again.

I couldn't help but smile. I had her. 'I know that Patrick McNabb didn't kill Patsy, but I can't prove it. I think you can help me do that.'

Evelyn's eyes shifted back and forth a moment. 'How?'

'You can get PIOUS to help.'

FORTY-FOUR

Miles Carney did not look comfortable in a tie. This, of course, was because he *wasn't* comfortable in a tie. But in a town where everyone appeared more able to pretend than most, Carney did not fit the mold. He pulled at his collar as if it were a boa constrictor.

Sitting in the witness chair, Carney explained his position at the Beverly Hills Bow Club (of Encino) and, after some resistance by Cates, was allowed by the judge to be admitted as an expert witness on the subject of archery.

He gave his background: an Olympic archer in 1996, a consultant on the Russell Crowe version of *Robin Hood* as well as *The Avengers* (teaching programmers how to make Jeremy Renner look like a master archer, even if the arrows were computer-generated), and now, manager of the club where stars came to sharpen their hand–eye coordination and fire arrows at a target that wouldn't sue or prompt PETA protests.

'Mr Carney, you've examined the police photographs taken at the scene of the murder. Is that correct?'

'Yes.'

'And based on those photographs, what can you tell us about the person who shot Patsy DeNunzio?'

'Well, it's someone who really knows their archery. That was a very straight shot and, assuming that whoever it was meant to hit her in the heart, remarkably accurate.'

Having questioned Carney before, I knew exactly what to ask. 'Based on the photos, what, if anything, can you tell us about the distance from which the arrow was shot?'

'I'd have to say it was shot from some distance, maybe twenty or twenty-five meters,' Carney said.

'And a meter, for those of us who are Americans, is how many feet?' I got a light chuckle from the jury, which was exactly what I was going for.

'Twenty-five meters would be a little over eighty feet,' Carney said.

I put on my puzzled face. 'How can you tell that from the photos, Mr Carney?'

'Well, it's based on the angle of the arrow,' he said. 'Based on the way the arrow fell into her chest, and how deeply it was imbedded, you can tell it hit her from above. That means it didn't come straight at her, from a short distance, but on an arc. Either someone fired from a good distance away, or shot her from the ceiling. I think the first possibility is more likely.'

'Indeed. So, could Patrick McNabb have fired that arrow from inside the same room as Patsy? Would he have had room?'

I was watching the jury. One woman nodded her head. That was good.

'Well, it was a very large room, and the ceiling was high enough to manage it, but no. The distance is wrong. The room is sixty by forty-five feet, and that's just not big enough.' Carney had forgotten about his collar now, and was concentrating on the questions.

'Any idea where the arrow might have been shot from?'

'It's hard to know because the body had been moved a little from the point of impact, and she might have spun around or something.'

'From another room? The bedroom, perhaps?' I wanted to beat Cates to the punch, but leave him enough room to hang himself.

'No, no way,' Carney said. 'The doors wouldn't have allowed that kind of altitude. Maybe from outside the house, from a window or an outside door, if there was one attached to the dining room.'

'So, in your opinion, Patrick McNabb could not have fired that arrow?' *Sell it, Sandy, sell it.*

'I don't think so,' Carney said. *OK, not definitive, but pretty good.*

'The arrow couldn't have been shot from only a few feet away, as Ms DeNunzio's sister suggested?'

'No chance. It's not physically possible.' *Better.*

'Your witness, Mr Cates.'

If Cates was at all rattled by the testimony, he didn't show it. 'Mr Carney, let me see if I have this right. You say the angle of the arrow sticking out of Patsy's body indicates it was shot from too far away to have come from the same room. Is that right?'

'Yes.'

'But you also said you couldn't be sure what direction the arrow had come from, because Patsy might have moved around after being shot, or the body might have been moved after she fell. Given all that possible motion, how can you know what angle the arrow was shot from?'

Thank you, Mr District Attorney.

'Because the arrow was imbedded much too deep in her chest to have moved. The police said Mr McNabb was trying to remove it, and could not move the arrow at all.' The arrow, in fact, hadn't been removed until the autopsy.

Cates didn't flinch. 'You also said the arrow might have been shot from a window or door. There are French doors to the dining room, and a number of windows. Do you think those might be the most likely places to shoot from?'

'Probably, but I haven't been to the house, so I can't say for sure,' Carney answered.

'Ah, you haven't been to the house.' Cates was trying to raise doubts in the jury, but it wasn't much to build on. 'So how do you know Mr McNabb didn't fire the arrow from the door or window?'

'Mr McNabb said he was in the bedroom and then the dining room. He didn't leave the house,' Carney said.

'Well, that is, as you said, based on his own statement. How do we know he didn't lie about that, and that he went outside to fire the arrow to deflect suspicion?'

'Objection!'

'Overruled. Witness is being asked for his opinion.'

Cates leaned on the railing and asked again. 'How do we know it wasn't Patrick McNabb, Mr Carney?'

'We don't *know*,' Carney said, 'but in my opinion, Patrick isn't a good enough archer to hit a moving target that small, from that distance, with that force. He's good, but he's not *that* good.'

'But you don't know, do you?' Cates was grasping for a straw.

'No,' Carney said, 'I don't know. I wasn't there.'

FORTY-FIVE

'Your Honor, I'd like to call a rebuttal witness.'

My head shot up. I'd barely made it into the courtroom on time that morning, and before I could begin, Cates was grandstanding.

Judge Franklin was no less irritated. 'This had better go to guilt, Mr Cates.'

'It does, Your Honor. It goes directly to the testimony of Mr Carney yesterday.'

'Objection, Ms Moss?'

I stood. 'The prosecution had no expert witness on archery on his list, Your Honor. This seems like sour grapes.'

'It's not, Judge,' Cates said. 'This is relevant.'

Franklin, his dream of a short trial long since gone, refrained from moaning. 'All right, but be quick, Mr Cates.'

'Yes, Your Honor. The People call Robin Flynn.'

So, Evan strikes again. Flynn worked her way to the witness stand. Angie and I both had to fight the urge to trip her.

She gave her highly impressive credentials to establish her expert status, and then the judge again warned Cates to get to his point quickly.

'Ms Flynn, you read the testimony from Mr Carney, who testified yesterday?'

'Yes, I did.'

'Do you agree with it?'

'No,' Flynn said, unsurprisingly. 'Having looked at the same photographs, I can't agree there was that high an angle on this arrow. A truly expert archer probably could have shot it straight from a shorter distance.'

'And how, then, would you account for the angle of the arrow?' Cates asked.

'Any number of ways. It could have been moved after the fact by a man with very strong hands. And perhaps Ms DeNunzio was bending over when it was fired.'

'Do you think there's any way to know for sure if that arrow was fired from within the room?'

'I'd have to say no,' Flynn said.

'Your witness,' Cates said to me, a smug look on his face.

I stood and approached my former expert slowly. 'Ms Flynn, how expert an archer would a person have to be to make the kind of shot you've described?'

'How expert?' Flynn wanted something she could quantify.

'Yes. Would someone, for example, have to be of Olympic caliber? Someone who could qualify in most tournaments? Something like that?'

Robin Flynn considered the question. 'Probably, but not definitely. If . . .'

'That's the only answer I needed. Thank you, Ms Flynn. Do you know Patrick McNabb?'

'No,' Flynn said. 'I've seen him on television, but that's all.'

'So you've never seen him shoot an arrow?'

'No.'

A sudden, frantic thought occurred to me. 'Ms Flynn, do you belong to the Beverly Hills Bow Club?'

'No,' Flynn said.

I breathed an internal sigh of relief. 'Where do you practice, then?'

'At the Nottingham Club in San Clemente. I live about an hour outside of town.' *No wonder Evan was always late to work – it wasn't his driving! It was the distance! Wasn't he using that apartment where he cooked me dinner? Did he borrow it for the night from a friend – or the law firm?*

'But that's only about an hour from Los Angeles?'

'Depending on the traffic, yes.'

Cates was about to ask about the relevance of my questioning, but I cut him off at the pass. 'Thank you, Ms Flynn. No further questions.'

I all but ran back to the defense table and motioned Angie to lean over the railing so I could whisper to her. 'There's another archery club in the area,' I said. 'Get Garrigan on the phone and tell him we need a membership list *right now*.'

Angie nodded, and was gone.

Walter Franklin, eyebrows raised in an arc, looked down at me. 'If you're finished with your conference, Ms Moss . . .'

'Sorry, Your Honor.'

'Would you like to call another witness?'

'Yes, Your Honor. The defense calls Patrick McNabb.'

FORTY-SIX

'Things hadn't been good for quite some time,' Patrick was saying. 'A month, maybe a month and a half. Patsy, I knew, was seeing other men.'

'Were you angry?' I watched the jury from the corner of my eye. The women were enthralled, the men a little wary.

'Well, no man *likes* to have his wife cheat on him,' he answered. 'But I understood we'd gotten married too soon, before we really knew each other, and I think we both fell out of love at the same time. I loved Patsy, but I wasn't in love with her any more. I think she felt the same about me.'

'Did you do anything about the infidelities?'

'I moved out.'

'There were also some pretty dramatic arguments, weren't there, Patrick?' I used only his first name when addressing him, to make him more human to those who'd only seen him on television, or sitting silently in the courtroom.

'Well, when you have two performers in the room, the arguments are going to be pretty dramatic,' Patrick said, smiling sadly. 'I'm afraid we did shout a bit.'

'One of those arguments came at the divorce settlement conference.'

'Yes.' Patrick seemed to want to set the record straight. 'The famous conference where Patsy threatened to destroy Jimmy's shoes, and I told her I'd kill her first.'

'So, you admit saying that?' I was letting Patrick play his part, and he was doing so beautifully. We were becoming a pretty good team.

'Yes. Yes, I did. I wish I hadn't.' Patrick took a moment to close his eyes, and I couldn't tell if it was to stop tears from flowing, or to start them.

'Did you mean those words literally?'

Patrick stared at me as if I'd grown a third ear in the center of my forehead. 'Good lord, of *course* not!' he said. 'It's an expression, like "just shoot me," or "I could just strangle him." You don't *mean* it when you say it. It's merely a way of saying, "I'm angry."'

I chose my next words very carefully. 'Why were you at your former house the night Patsy was murdered?'

'I was actually going to apologize about that argument,' he answered. 'And, to be honest, to see if I could get Patsy to change her mind about the shoes. Plus, I had one other motive for going, but . . .'

'I'm sorry, Patrick, but you'll have to say it.' I hadn't rehearsed this with him, but he was doing beautifully just the same.

'Well, I knew that, after we had a *really* loud fight, we'd always . . . that is, we used to . . .'

'You would make love?'

'Yes,' Patrick said, actually blushing – *damn*, he was good! 'That's how we made up.'

'So, at the moment Patsy was killed, just after you'd made love, you were not angry with her?'

'Not at all. I think we'd come to a good place in our relationship, where we could let each other go and still have some affection for each other. We'd agreed that night to a fifty-fifty split in the divorce, which would have allowed her to pay off her debts and start over, and I would keep the movie souvenirs I like to collect. And now, I'm so glad I went there that night, even if I'm convicted of doing something I didn't do, because at least I know we were friends when she died.' Patrick covered his eyes with his hand and his head shook a little. It was either a magnificent performance, or the genuine article. Even I couldn't tell.

'Patrick.' He didn't look up. 'Patrick?' This time he did. 'One last question. Did you kill your wife, Esmerelda DeNunzio?'

Patrick's answer was a sob, but it was a discernible sob. 'No,' he said. 'I did not.'

'No further questions, Your Honor.'

The judge nodded at Cates, who stood. He walked to the witness box, and slowly began to clap his hands. Slowly, and with great sarcasm, he applauded.

'That was quite a performance, Mr McNabb.'

I'd barely taken my seat and immediately rose. 'Objection. Is there a question there?'

'Sustained. Keep your opinions to yourself, Mr Cates.'

'Certainly, Your Honor. Mr McNabb, you say you always had sex with your wife after a heated argument?'

'That's right.'

'Were these special moments for you?' Cates seemed to be fishing for something, but I couldn't tell what.

'Yes, they were. They were very tender moments, and difficult to discuss with others.'

'You seem to be able to do so quite nicely.'

I wanted to kill Cates. No, sorry – I felt angry toward him. 'Objection.'

'Sustained. I won't warn you again, Mr Cates.'

'I understand, Judge. Mr McNabb, how did you feel when you found out your wife was sleeping with your butler?'

Patrick looked at Cates with as much cool as James Dean in *Rebel Without A Cause*. 'Until my attorney informed me of that during this trial, I wasn't aware of it,' he said.

'How about when you found out your wife was carrying another man's baby?'

'I don't like the way you're portraying my wife, Mr Cates,' Patrick said. 'Our marriage was just about over by then, and I understood she was seeing other men.'

'But you were angry, weren't you?'

'Objection,' I protested. 'Asked and answered.'

'Sustained. Get to a point, Mr Cates.'

'Yes, Your Honor. Mr McNabb, about the shoes, the James Cagney tap shoes – did you steal them from Patsy DeNunzio's house after she was murdered?'

Patrick's eyes flashed fury. So *that* was what Cates was up to – trying to get Patrick to blow up on the stand and show his anger – and it was working!

'No.'

'But you did intend to steal them, didn't you?'

'I don't consider it stealing,' Patrick said, 'because I owned the shoes to begin with. But I don't have them now.'

'Because someone beat you to it.'

'*Your Honor!*' Maybe I could get the heat off Patrick.

'I'm allowing it, Ms Moss.' I sat down.

'You didn't answer the question, Mr McNabb. Did you intend to take the shoes from Patsy's house?'

'All right, yes. I did intend to take them. I didn't see where they were doing anyone any good there. But it didn't matter because they were already gone when I arrived.' Patrick was controlling himself, but just barely.

'Do you think your wife gave them to one of her other lovers?' Cates goaded.

Judge Franklin remained silent. *Damn him!*

'No.' Patrick was hanging in there.

'You don't think so? As a memento for an especially good night? A "special moment?" No?'

'Stop it!' Patrick shouted. 'Stop talking about her that way, or . . .'

He stopped, but it was too late. 'Or you'll what, Mr McNabb? *Kill* me?' Cates walked away. 'No further questions.'

FORTY-SEVEN

The judge struck Cates' final remark from the record, but the damage had been done. I sat in my easy chair, trying to watch television to get my mind off the trial. It wasn't working – news of Patrick's testimony, with clips taken from *TruTV*'s live broadcast, dominated every station's news teasers. You couldn't watch a *Bachelorette* dump somebody without hearing about Patrick McNabb's outburst on the stand.

Angie walked in with the pizza we'd decided to buy, and said nothing as she set it down on the coffee table. I turned off the TV, and picked up a slice with onions and peppers.

'Would you believe it?' said Angie. 'I actually had to talk them out of putting pineapples on the pizza. Honestly, the people out here . . .'

'Can you give it a rest, already – the California-bashing?' I asked, exasperated. 'It's different, OK, but I came here to *be* different, and to have a different life! The people out here are . . . people. You know? They're just people.'

'Sor-*ry*, Sandra. You know, you should signal before you change lanes that fast.'

I shook my head. 'I'm sorry. It's just . . . I don't know which way this case is going.'

'I understand. Eat your pizza.' So we did for a while.

Finally, Angie could stand the silence no longer. 'So what comes next?' she asked.

'Not much, unless my PIOUS contact comes through.'

'Yeah, what the hell was *that* about?'

I shook my head. 'I'm not saying anything unless it pans out. If it doesn't, we haven't lost anything.'

The phone rang, and I got up to answer it. I reached for the phone with one hand and the refrigerator door (to grab a couple beers) with the other. 'Hello?'

'Ms Moss, this is Lieutenant K.C. Trench.' I held out the beers to Angie with a new and different sense of urgency. I felt as if Trench could see the alcohol through the phone lines.

'What can I do for you, Lieutenant?'

'This might seem like a somewhat . . . unusual question, Ms Moss, but, do you have Henderson Meadows there?'

'I'm sorry?'

'I'll assume that means you don't. Well, apparently Mr Meadows has been missing since he left the courtroom on the day of his testimony.'

For his days off, according to Trench, Henderson Meadows kept a small bungalow in Long Beach, about a forty-minute drive from Los Angeles, assuming a neutron bomb had been dropped so there would be no traffic. When I arrived at the address Trench had given me, the lieutenant immediately told me there was no reason for me to be there.

'I know,' I said. 'It just seemed the thing to do.'

'I wouldn't have called you at all, but I know he'd been a witness at your trial. If you were planning on calling him again, there would have been some difficulty.'

'I appreciate it, Lieutenant. You've been nothing but fair the whole time. I can't say that's always the case with police officers and defense counselors.'

'Don't let it go to your head, Ms Moss,' Trench said without the hint of a smile (which is how I knew he was kidding). 'I have a strange obsession with discovering the truth.'

'So you don't think Patrick McNabb killed his wife?'

'I didn't say that,' Trench said.

As he walked away, I looked toward the road and saw Patrick approaching in his car. He looked grim, but his first question was naturally about me.

'How'd you get here?' he asked.

'Angie drove me. She was going to stay, but I told her I'd catch a Lyft back. She was afraid we'd find him . . . not so alive. Angie's a little squeamish.'

'Funny. She doesn't look it. You didn't . . . find him that way, I mean.'

'No,' I said. 'He's not here. Doesn't look like he's been here in some time. When was his last day off?'

'He takes Saturdays, except when we're . . . I'm entertaining, and Tuesdays. So, Tuesday.'

'I take it you didn't report him missing?' I asked.

'No. Apparently he has a sister in the area, and he was supposed to visit her a day or two ago. But he didn't show up. The last time anyone saw him was at the courthouse.' Patrick kicked at some rocks in the driveway. 'I don't understand it.'

'Neither do I.'

We stood there a moment, lost in our thoughts. Finally, Patrick said, 'I don't know why I'm here. I left as soon as Trench called, but now that I'm here, I don't know what to do.'

'Neither do I,' I admitted. 'Why don't you give me a ride home?'

'Love to.'

In the car, we spoke about everything except the trial. I told Patrick about my continuing insecurity about moving from New Jersey, and he laughed.

'What's so funny?' I demanded, my insecurity reaching new levels.

'I came here from England ten years ago without a dime in my pocket and no contacts, no friends, no place to live, no hope of employment. And you're telling me about how hard it is to fit in, at a new place to practice law, when you move from another state? I came from another country!'

'You don't know New Jersey,' I told him. 'It *is* another country.' I smiled.

'My apologies.'

'It must have been awfully hard for you,' I said. 'How did you get started in movies?'

'Well, I'd done some work for the BBC, you know, so I had a reel I could show around. And it had pretty eclectic stuff on it: costume dramas, comedies. I never had a large part, but I did what I could with what I had.'

I smiled playfully, noting I wasn't paying attention to the way Patrick was driving, which meant he was driving the way I would have. 'Did you always believe you were the character, or is that new with Arthur Kirkland?'

Patrick raised one eyebrow and looked at me sideways, keeping his face turned toward the road. 'I don't *really* believe I'm Arthur,' he said. 'But you know, in order to play the part honestly, I have to put myself in his situation.'

'You've certainly done that.'

He nodded as he pulled up to my building. 'All right, then.'

I looked at him. 'Would you like to come up? I could make coffee, if your definition of "make coffee" is going to Starbucks to get some.'

'I'd like to, but I have an early call tomorrow,' Patrick said. 'Something about being in court on time. If I'm not there at the appointed hour, I'm sure Fox News will make it into a major scandal.'

'Come on up. Angie's always glad to see you.'

Patrick smiled with the left side of his mouth. 'I'm always glad to see Angie, so long as she's on my side.'

'She'll always be on your side. She's your biggest fan.'

'But you're not.'

I felt my face get hot. 'I don't watch a lot of television.'

'Let me guess. Just the news and PBS, right? And you go to foreign films, preferably subtitled, not dubbed. You stream Kurosawa, and you read not bestsellers but collections of short stories. You drink white wine and eat salmon. Television is beneath you.'

'Come on up,' I said. 'I think we have some pizza and beer left over.'

'All right, then.'

Patrick parked in a visitor's spot in the underground garage, and we took the elevator up to my apartment. I felt comfortable vibes on the way up, though neither of us said anything. But when Patrick moved casually closer, I didn't move away.

We stopped in front of the door as I fumbled for my keys. Patrick moved a little closer, and when I looked up from my purse, he was a few inches from me, at a distance Angie referred to as 'a lip and a half away.'

'Patrick.'

He didn't lean toward me, but I'm sure it was only because he didn't have time. The door flew open, and Angie, phone in hand, waved us inside. We complied.

'All right. I'll tell her. Yes, I wrote down the number. I swear! OK. Bye.' Angie put down the phone as I closed the apartment door. 'Well, it's about time,' she said.

'About time? I'm probably twenty minutes behind you.' I got two beers out of the fridge and gave one to Patrick. 'Any pizza left?'

'Sandy, I haven't been off the phone since I got back. First, your pal from PIOUS called.'

'Evelyn Draper?' I'd arranged for Evelyn to be released on my recognizance so she could operate freely. 'What did she say?'

Patrick stared at me. 'You're talking to members of PIOUS? Are you mad?'

'No, I'm in a good mood. What'd she say?'

'Just that it had taken some persuading, but she convinced them. That's what she said – "I convinced them." And she got the information you needed.' Angie pointed at the pizza box on the counter, and I looked at Patrick while pointing at the oven and raising my eyebrows. He shook his head as we both took cold slices and paper plates, almost immediately gnawing away.

'Really? That's great,' I said through a mouthful of pizza. Angie was right. They really *didn't* know how to make crust out here. And I don't even want to discuss bagels. 'Did she leave a number?'

'Yeah, but that's not the weird part.'

Patrick sat on a barstool by the kitchen counter, fascinated. 'Do you two always communicate this way?'

'Pretty much,' I said, turning my attention back to Angie. 'What's the weird part?'

'You got three calls from executives at record companies – three separate record companies, all wanting to know how much it would cost to get the rights to a new album by Patsy.'

Patrick nearly fell off his barstool. 'A new *what*?'

I took a swig of beer, enjoying the rapt attention I was getting from both Angie and Patrick. 'Did they ask what kind of album it was?'

'No. What the hell's going on?' Angie said.

'Did they mention figures?'

'One of them said he was authorized to offer an eight-figure deal, but he'd be willing to negotiate if others offered more.'

Patrick's eyes looked like huge hubcaps on a Lexus SUV.

I grinned from ear to ear. 'Better and better,' I said.

FORTY-EIGHT

'Your Honor, I'd like to call a rebuttal witness.'

For Judge Walter Franklin, looking down from the bench, it was all he could do to keep from screaming. 'Ms Moss, there have already been more rebuttal witnesses in this trial than in my last fifteen trials combined. Is this absolutely necessary?'

'It is vital, believe me, Your Honor.'

'Oh, all right. But keep it to the point, please.'

'Yes, Your Honor. The defense calls Marilyn Caswell.'

Caswell, a mousy type with slumped shoulders and a short bob, walked to the stand and was sworn in. She sat, looking gloomy and avoiding eye contact with the jury.

I approached her and spoke in soothing tones. 'Ms Caswell, are you a member of a Patsy DeNunzio fan group called PIOUS?'

'Yeah,' Caswell said. 'Patsy's International Order of United Servants.'

'And you're very dedicated fans of Patsy's music, aren't you?'

'Yeah,' she repeated. 'So?'

'I'm just asking, Ms Caswell. Now, this organization is a very serious undertaking for you, isn't it? I mean, you dedicate a lot of time and effort to your devotion to Patsy.'

'That's right. We want everyone to hear what we hear in the music. Patsy's music has kept me going many times. Once, when I was really down, it kept me from killing myself.' I could have lived without the jury getting *that* revelation, but I pressed on.

'Some of you became a sort of informal security force for Patsy, didn't you? Watching over her home, that sort of thing.'

'Uh-huh,' Marilyn said. 'We called it "keeping vigil." All the big acts have people like that. George Harrison used to call them Apple Scruffs.' She seemed proud of the Beatle comparison. It put Patsy – and PIOUS – into rarefied company.

'Did you ever keep vigil outside Patsy's house?'

'Yeah, plenty of times.'

'Were you keeping vigil the night she died?' I put as much sympathy into my voice as I could, knowing that her devotion as a fan probably made Patsy's murder into a personal affront.

'Yeah,' Marilyn said quietly. 'I was there. I didn't know what was going on inside, or I'd have done something.'

'Oh, I'm sure of that. But you saw Mr McNabb drive up?'

'Oh sure,' said Caswell. 'He'd come by plenty of times. When they were married, he used to bring out snacks for us and make sure we were warm enough – things like that.'

'Did anyone drive up after Mr McNabb?'

'The police, a while later, and then an ambulance.'

I nodded. 'But no one between the two? No one after Mr McNabb and before the police?'

'No.'

'You didn't see a blue 2003 Acura drive up that night?'

'No,' Caswell said, apparently growing a little impatient with this dimwit of a defense attorney. 'Nobody else drove up.'

Cates stood up, showing off his weariness. 'Is this going anywhere, Judge?'

Exactly what I was hoping he'd say. 'Your Honor,' I said before Franklin could answer, 'Melanie DeNunzio testified that she saw Patrick McNabb kill his wife because she'd driven to the house to drop off some clothing she'd borrowed from Patsy. But Ms Caswell has testified she did not see the 2003 Acura, which Defense Exhibit H – the motor vehicle records – will show is Melanie's car. And neither did any of the other PIOUS members who were outside the house that night.'

'I think that's relevant, Mr Cates,' said the judge.

Cates sat down.

'Did you see anything else unusual that night, Ms Caswell?'

'Yeah, and I wish I'd done something about it right away, but it was happening so far away, I couldn't tell what it was. If I'd acted, maybe Patsy might be alive today . . .' Caswell sniffed loudly and blew her nose into a handkerchief she was holding.

'I'm sorry, Ms Caswell. What did you see?'

'I was outside the gate, you know, on the west side of the house, so I was about a hundred yards away, and there are trees and things there, so I didn't see clearly. Honest, I would have found my cell phone . . .'

'It's OK, Marilyn. Please, just tell us what you saw.'

'A man – at least, I *think* it was a man. Outside the dining room window.'

FORTY-NINE

B ertram Cates' cross-examination of Marilyn Caswell did not constitute one of his career highlights. He extracted very little new information, annoyed the witness by once referring to her as a 'groupie' ('I'm *not* a groupie. Groupies *sleep* with the star. I don't sleep with *nobody*.'), and scoffed at her testimony, asking how the mysterious man outside the dining room window might have gotten there, inasmuch as she hadn't seen another car drive up. The witness answered, 'I guess he walked.'

When Cates lit on another idea, and asked if, since she'd seen only McNabb's car drive up, whether Patrick could have been the man outside the dining room window, Caswell said with great certainty that he was not. And when Cates, with great pomposity, asked how she could be so sure from so far away, Marilyn Caswell delivered the crushing blow I'd wanted.

'Because I could see Patrick turn on the light in the bedroom,' she said.

Cates dismissed the witness with no further questions.

Franklin looked down at me through his half-glasses and asked, 'Next witness, Ms Moss?'

I was about to say I was resting my case, but, instead, I was granted a movie moment all my own. Nate Garrigan opened the door to the courtroom and walked toward me purposefully, something close to triumph on his face.

'Your Honor,' I asked, 'may I have a moment?'

'Yes, but just a moment, Ms Moss.'

I rushed to meet Garrigan, who leaned in and gave me the news I'd been waiting for. I'd been expecting *something*, but nothing this good. I shook my head in disbelief, then gave

Garrigan a kiss on the cheek. He looked surprised. I quickly scanned the gallery, noted one specific onlooker, and approached the defense table.

'Your Honor, the defense has one more witness.'

Franklin heaved a sigh. 'It's not a rebuttal witness, is it, Ms Moss?'

'No, Judge. I'd like to re-call a prosecution witness.'

'Someone present in the room?'

'Yes, Your Honor,' I said.

Franklin seemed relieved. 'Good. We won't have to take a break. Go ahead, Counselor.'

'Thank you, Your Honor. The defense calls Lucien DuPrez.'

DuPrez, seated near the rear of the courtroom, looked shocked. His head snapped up, his mouth opened, and his legs actually shot forward in his seat, almost kicking the man in front of him. But he managed to compose himself long enough to stand up and walk to the witness stand.

The judge reminded him of his oath, and I walked to his side. 'Mr DuPrez, thank you for being here,' I said.

'Not at all. I'm interested in the outcome of the trial. I hope to see Patsy's killer brought to justice.'

'So do we all, Mr DuPrez,' I said. Before anyone could object, or throw up, I added, 'But you have an interest in this case that's financial as well as moral, don't you?'

'I'm not sure I understand.'

'Well, let me ask the question another way. Do you stand to profit personally from Patsy DeNunzio's work, now that she's dead?'

'Just as I did when she was alive,' DuPrez said. 'I was Patsy's business manager.'

'You're also her heir,' I reminded him. 'Patsy left you the rights to all her business interests, didn't she?'

DuPrez nodded. 'Yes, she did. But as I explained before, Patsy's work was in decline, and all she had left was a hip hop album I couldn't sell.'

'Yes, you did say that. Has that changed since her death?' I was facing the gallery, not the witness, because I didn't want DuPrez to make eye contact with me and seem sympathetic. I wanted him to search around the courtroom.

'Not really. Patsy didn't put out any new work after that.'

'No, but her market value has risen, hasn't it?'

'Her market value?' DuPrez was being purposely obtuse.

'Yes. Mr Menzies, the expert in memorabilia, said the value of an object goes up when the performer dies, because everyone knows there will be no more. Isn't that true of a recording artist like Patsy DeNunzio?'

'Not really,' DuPrez said. 'If the work had no value before her death, it has no value now. Jennifer Lopez could walk in front of a bus tomorrow, and *Gigli* is still going to be a lousy movie.'

I nodded. 'Interesting. Mr DuPrez, yesterday I very casually circulated a rumor among her fans that I controlled the rights to an album of new material from Patsy. It wasn't true, but by last night, I had received offers from three record companies.'

'It wasn't supposed to be that rap album, was it?' asked DuPrez.

'I never specified, and no one ever asked,' I said. 'The record companies with whom I spoke this morning offered as much as fifteen million dollars for this fictitious album, with no questions about content being asked and not a note of music being heard.'

'Your Honor, is there a question in our future?' Cates asked. 'Ms Moss . . .'

'Certainly, Your Honor. Mr DuPrez, if you're a professional business manager and I'm not, why can I get a fifteen million dollar offer for a fictitious Patsy album, and you can't get an offer for a real one?'

'I didn't say I couldn't get an offer – just that Patsy's career had been in decline.'

'Yes, but I'll ask again. Since her death, hasn't her value made a sharp comeback?'

'I suppose that's possible.'

'Two of the record companies I spoke to asked if this was the same album they were already discussing with you. Have you tried to sell Patsy's last album since her death, Mr DuPrez?'

'Yes, just as I should, as her manager and partner . . .'

'And was the value higher than before?'

'Yes, it was.'

'Thank you for saying so. Mr DuPrez, were you at a party at

Patrick and Patsy's home the night he showed off the bow allegedly used in this crime?'

'I'm sorry to say I was,' DuPrez said. 'I remember admiring the bow.'

'Do you have one like it?'

'I'm sorry?'

'Do you own a similar bow?

'I own a bow, but not one like that.'

'Do you belong to the Nottingham Archery Club in San Clemente?'

DuPrez's eyes widened, then narrowed as he overcompensated. 'Yes,' he mumbled.

'The archery instructor there says you're the most gifted archer in the club. Would you agree with that assessment?' I turned to face DuPrez.

'I think that's a little generous,' DuPrez said. But he ran his hand over his perspiring forehead.

'Do you need a handkerchief, Mr DuPrez?' the judge asked, and DuPrez shook his head no.

'You're being modest,' I went on. 'The instructor at your club, whom I can ask to testify if you like, says you can hit a one-meter target – that is, a target less than three feet square – from more than eighty meters away. Is that true?'

'Oh, I don't think so.'

That was the last straw. I dropped all pretense of pleasantness and said, 'I can bring in the records from the club's recent competition, Mr DuPrez. You consistently hit the one-meter target – which, by the way, is about the size of woman's chest – from almost one hundred meters away.'

'Objection,' said Cates. 'Ms Moss is trying to make a suggestion she has no right to make.'

'Overruled.'

'Mr DuPrez,' I said, 'according to police records, the distance from the outside of the dining room window at Patsy DeNunzio's house to the spot where she stood was approximately fifty feet. That's less than sixteen meters. You would have no trouble hitting a target that size from that distance, would you?'

'Objection!' Cates probably left his shoes when he leapt up.

'Sustained,' said the judge. 'Ask a question about *this* case, Ms Moss.'

'I'll be happy to,' I said. 'Mr DuPrez, were you at Patsy DeNunzio's house the night she died?'

'No,' DuPrez said shakily. 'I was not.'

'Would your answer change if I told you the police found footprints outside the window that match your shoe size?'

'I . . . I . . .'

'Your Honor, who's on trial here?' Cates protested.

'I don't see why I can't pursue this line of questioning, Your Honor,' I said as innocently as possible. 'It certainly seems to be pertinent to my client's guilt or innocence.'

'I'll let you go a bit further, Ms Moss, but just a bit.'

'Thank you. Mr DuPrez, keeping in mind that you are under oath, were you outside Patsy DeNunzio's window the night she was killed?'

'Yes,' DuPrez said. 'But I didn't kill her. I was just looking to see if she was home.'

'And why did you park your car so far from the house? Ms Caswell said no other cars drove up to the mansion that night.'

'I didn't have a key to the gate.' *Yeah, that's it!*

'Couldn't you have called in? Wouldn't Ms DeNunzio have let you in?'

'I don't remember where I parked the car.'

'All right, let's move on. Assuming you knew Patsy's work would increase dramatically in value after her death, and you decided to do something drastic about it, how did you get her sister to lie on the stand? Did you promise her some of the proceeds from Patsy's newly valuable work?'

'OBJECTION!' The room fairly shook.

'That's as far as I'm letting you go, Ms Moss,' said Franklin.

'Question withdrawn. Your witness, Mr Cates.'

'Mr DuPrez, did you kill Patsy DeNunzio?'

'What? Um . . . no.'

'No further questions.' Cates sat down.

'The defense rests,' I said, and sat down, too.

FIFTY

'**Y**ou *are* brilliant!' Patrick said. 'I don't care if you're angry with me for saying it. It's true!'

I sat with Patrick in the deserted courtroom, waiting for the horde of reporters and spectators to dissipate in the hallway. It was a pointless wait, because the reporters and spectators were staying until they got at least a glimpse of the celebrity defendant.

'Not so brilliant,' I said. 'Once Garrigan found DuPrez's name on the Nottingham membership list, and I found out how much a new Patsy album – *any* new Patsy album – would be worth, it made sense – in a sick sort of way.'

'You think DuPrez killed Patsy just to make her album worth more money? Really?' Patrick shook his head. 'It's ridiculous. Patsy was worth more than money.'

'Not to DuPrez. He felt he'd created her from nothing, and now he was getting shortchanged for his trouble. And I'd be surprised if he hadn't come on to her sexually, and been, let's say, rebuffed.'

'Yes,' Patrick said, 'Patsy was a first-class rebuffer when she wanted to be.'

'Did she ever say anything to you about DuPrez?' I asked.

'Just that she was always grateful to him. Imagine, grateful! In her will, she left him everything she was worth, and this is what he did to her. I could kill him.'

'Watch what you say. We've been through enough.'

My cell phone rang, and I picked it up to find Holiday Wentworth on the other end. 'I heard about your day in court,' she said. 'Everyone here's offering their congratulations.'

'Everyone?'

'Well, Junius Bach isn't that thrilled. The other partners found out what he did to you, and why.'

'OK, I'll bite. Why?'

'Well, he hated you since that first day, but that wasn't it. He was actually going to leave the firm and start another, one that specialized in celebrities like McNabb. And he couldn't let this firm look good doing it after he was off the case. So he decided to be *visibly* off the case, testify against you to show how incompetent the firm's lawyers are, and then start his new firm. The partners voted him out of the managing partner slot. Plus, let's just say he's taking a long leave of absence. While the bar association decides whether he can still practice.'

'I'm sure it'll do him good,' I said. 'I bet Evan D'Arbanville isn't that thrilled with me, either.'

'I guess not,' Holly said. 'He got fired by the partners, and I hear his girlfriend, the archer, broke up with him.'

'I hope she broke his arrow. Thanks, Holly.'

'No problem. Just come back to the office when this is done. I'm told I can give you some of the better cases.'

'I'll let you know,' I said. 'I'm not sure family law is for me.'

'I'm sure we can find something for you, Sandy. You're a star.' Holly hung up, and I marveled at what a difference a day can make.

A flash of movement by the door caught my eye. Angie was signaling frantically for us to come out.

She stuck her head through the door. 'Someone here to see you,' she said in a tone suggesting it was a guest I wanted to receive. I nodded.

Evelyn Draper walked in, head still down, manner still timid, but she walked over to me, then turned toward Patrick.

'I'm so sorry I misjudged you, Mr McNabb,' she said.

Patrick held out his hand. 'I understand how you could,' he said. 'Listening to the D.A., *I* thought I was guilty.'

Evelyn chuckled and took his hand.

I caught Evelyn's eye, which wasn't easy. 'I'm afraid I have a confession to make, Evelyn. You helped me so much, finding Marilyn Caswell through PIOUS, and I have to tell you – I made up the new Patsy album. All that's left is the rap album she recorded and I don't think she'd want that released.'

Evelyn nodded. 'I heard,' she said. 'I understand. It's disappointing . . .'

'Perhaps there's something I can do,' Patrick said. 'I was urging Patsy to record standards – you know, sing something with a little more meat to it – and she did a number of tracks in our home recording studio. I'd like for you and some of the other PIOUS members to have copies. I'll make CDs for you. Would you like that?'

'But wouldn't you get more money selling them to a record company?' Evelyn asked.

'This isn't for money. Patsy was singing for the love of the music. It should be heard by the people who loved her.' And he patted her hand.

Angie stuck her head inside again. 'It's not going to get any better out here,' she said.

'OK. Give us a minute.' Angie nodded and closed the door behind her. Evelyn thanked Patrick and walked back out of the room, shaking her head.

I started to pack up my files. 'So what happens now?' Patrick asked.

'Tomorrow, we'll make closing statements, assuming Cates doesn't withdraw the charges entirely, and then the jury will come back with a verdict. I don't think there'll be much question about that. Lieutenant Trench is already making sure DuPrez doesn't leave the city, and I'm sure he's being extremely thorough in his investigation of DuPrez right now. Trench doesn't like to be wrong.'

'How many of us do?' Patrick chuckled.

'I do. I once thought you were guilty.'

Patrick looked sincerely hurt. 'You did? After I'd told you I didn't do it?'

'They all tell you they didn't do it, Patrick.' I slung my brief-case strap over my shoulder. He helped with the files and we headed for the door.

'Yeah, but I'm an actor. I'm so much more believable.'

The hallway was a zoo, of course, but Patrick answered a few questions and signed a good number of autographs before some of the court officers came to usher us to the parking level elevator. Once we managed to get away from the throng, Patrick signed a few autographs for the officers. We thanked them and left the building with Angie, who was driving.

We were almost silent on the way to my apartment, where we automatically headed. Angie dropped us off at the entrance, and headed underground to park the car.

Patrick finally spoke as we approached the elevator. His voice had a more relaxed quality than I'd ever heard before, and I realized, finally, what a strain the trial must have been on him.

'Do you think we'll get to a verdict, or will the D.A. drop the charges?' Patrick asked as I pushed the button to summon the elevator.

'It depends on how much Trench finds out. My guess is he'll be extremely thorough, and we'll be all done by tomorrow.'

'That'll be a relief,' Patrick said as the elevator doors opened and we got in. 'I'm tired of being the most famous defendant in the country.'

The doors stayed open annoyingly long, and two men walked toward the elevator. I was about to hold the door open for them when I noticed they were both walking with their heads down, and wearing . . .

Atlanta Braves baseball caps!

'Patrick!' I yelled, lunging for the 'door close' button. Before Patrick could react, the doors began to close, and I saw the man on the left pull a gun out of his jacket pocket.

I screamed, and immediately after the doors closed, an indentation appeared in the left door, right in front of Patrick. I opened my mouth, but didn't know what to say. Patrick looked absolutely stupefied. Neither of us moved.

And then I realized, in our panic, that we hadn't selected a floor, and the doors would reopen any second.

I sprang to the buttons and pushed the highest number – sixteen. The elevator began to move, and I exhaled.

'Now, what?' I said, looking at Patrick.

He reached for his cell phone. 'I'll call the cops.'

I shook my head. 'You can't get a signal in this elevator. I've tried it fifty times. You'll have to wait until we get out. But where do we get out?'

'I don't know. Anywhere except your floor. They'll be waiting for us there. Who *are* those guys?'

'I can only guess. Wait.' I reached over and pushed the button for the eleventh floor. The doors opened there, and I nudged Patrick out.

'Why are we getting out here?' Patrick asked.

'To confuse them.'

Patrick reached for his cell phone as I led him to the stairs. 'Let's go,' I said. 'Up two floors.'

'To thirteen?' Patrick said as he pushed buttons on the phone.

'Fourteen. There *is* no thirteen. It's bad luck.'

'Wouldn't want that,' Patrick said.

After running up two flights of stairs, I led Patrick back to the elevator. He kept trying his cell phone, but still no service. 'I can't get a signal. Why are we back at the elevator?'

'To *confuse* them.'

'I don't know about them, but it's working on me,' he said. The elevator doors opened, and we got in. I pushed the button for the eighth floor.

'How long can we keep this up?' Patrick asked.

'I don't know. As long as we have to. We'll just keep . . . oh, no!'

'Oh no, what?'

I slumped to the elevator floor. 'Angie.'

'Angie!' said Patrick. 'She won't know, and she'll go to your apartment . . .'

'And they'll be there. What can we do? How can we get her out of there?'

The elevator doors opened at the eighth floor, and Patrick put out a hand for me, helping me up. We headed for the stairs.

'Which way?' Patrick asked.

'Down to five – my floor.' He nodded, and we walked slowly down the stairs. At the landing for the fifth floor, I looked through the stairwell door window toward my apartment.

'I don't see anyone,' I reported.

'What should we do?' Patrick asked. *Isn't the leading man supposed to take charge?* I thought. *How come I'm making all the decisions?*

'I'm going to have to go out there and see if Angie's all right. If she's there, I'll get her out, and if they're there, I can stall them, because they want you.'

Patrick shook his head. 'I'm not letting you get killed,' he said. 'This isn't your fight. I'll go, too.'

'Angie's my best friend,' I said, wondering why I was suddenly insisting on being the one to rush into danger.

'And you're mine,' said Patrick. 'You stay here.'

Before I could argue, he'd reached for the doorknob and turned it slowly, hoping the door wouldn't creak as he opened it. It didn't.

Patrick crept out through the stairwell door into the hallway.

He walked slowly toward the corner, at the end of the hall, where my apartment door stood. I watched as he moved, and every once in a while, he turned back to signal me, with a shrug, that no one was there.

When he got a little more than halfway down the hall, I lost sight of him. I waited, hearing and seeing nothing except an empty hallway. *There's got to be a better way than this*, I thought.

What seemed like hours, but was probably less than a minute, passed, and I couldn't stand it any longer. I reached for the doorknob myself and opened the stairwell door, just to look down the hall to see if Patrick was still approaching the apartment. I slipped through the doorway and into the hall, flinching a bit at the sound of the door closing.

The hallway was stone quiet, and I realized I hadn't been in the building by myself at this time of day since the week I'd moved in, which felt like twenty years ago. Had it really been only a couple of months? Perhaps this wasn't the time to notice how quickly life passes one by.

I was aware of every sound, and I was making all of them – footsteps, breathing, clothes rustling. Suddenly, I felt like a walking brass band. But I could just see my apartment door at the end of the hallway . . . and it was closed. There was no one there.

Should I try the doorknob? I decided I wouldn't use my key. If the door was locked, I'd assume no one was inside, and keep searching. I didn't dare pull out my cell phone now – if my pants legs brushing against each other (*damn you, thighs!*) sounded this loud, my voice would be the equivalent of a ninety-piece orchestra playing in a one-room cabana. I couldn't risk it.

My hand went to the doorknob, and as silently as I could, I grasped it. I was glad not to be wearing a ring, because that would have made a sound against the metal of the knob. I turned the knob so slowly, it felt like it took a full minute for the door to clear and swing open. It creaked. *Damn it!*

As it turned out, it didn't matter. I might just as well have barreled down the hallway in combat boots, screaming at the top of my lungs. No one was in the apartment, but the phone was ringing.

I ran to the kitchen phone, checked the Caller ID, and saw a 'Private Call' description, which meant the caller had blocked the incoming number. Swell. I picked it up.

'Hello?'

'Come on up to the roof,' said a gravelly male voice I recognized from the wardrobe room at the studio. 'Your boyfriend and your pal are up here waiting for you.'

'What if I don't?' I said, because I couldn't think of anything else that sounded brave, and saying 'he's not my boyfriend' seemed a bit inappropriate.

'Then you'll see them flying past your living room window,' said the voice. 'And if you call the cops, we'll know.'

'Who's we? Why are you—'

The caller hung up.

FIFTY-ONE

T he elevator didn't go to the roof, so I took it to the highest floor, then walked up the stairs. I'd considered bringing a kitchen knife or something else to use as a weapon. I'd heard aerosol oven cleaner can blind an attacker for life, but realized I didn't own any. Besides, the caller had said 'we.' I wouldn't be able to handle more than one, and there'd been at least two men after us when we first got into the elevator.

When I opened the door to the roof, I felt a hand behind my head immediately – one that had been expecting me, of course. It guided me to a corner away from the roof entrance.

'Just keep going and do what we say,' said the gravelly voice behind me.

A bizarre scene had been set on the far corner of the roof: a mock living room, with an easy chair, a sofa, an end table, and a floor lamp. On the sofa were Patrick and Angie, hands held behind their heads. Patrick looked downright livid, and Angie, more than anything else, was embarrassed. She probably felt she should have seen this coming. But how could anyone? The case was practically over.

One of the baseball cap men, the one not guiding me to the scene, was standing to one side of the easy chair, holding a gun on Patrick and Angie. With dark glasses over his eyes and his cap pulled down, he might as well have had no face.

In the easy chair was Silvio Cadenza.

'I should have realized it was you,' Patrick was saying when I got close enough to hear. 'You're the only one demented enough to send these two behemoths out to kill me, and inept enough to fail over and over again! You've never gotten one thing right, Silvio.'

'Don't worry,' Cadenza said with a reptilian tone in his voice (or what a reptile might sound like if it *had* a voice). 'You give us enough tries, we'll figure it out.'

The hand forced me down onto the sofa next to Patrick, then the second baseball cap man, standing to Cadenza's other side, leveled his gun at us.

'I don't understand,' I said. 'Why have you been trying to kill us all this time? What did we ever do to you? *You* were the one who stole Patrick's wife.'

'But he stole her from me, forever,' said Cadenza. 'He murdered her for spite.'

'No, I didn't,' Patrick said with disgust. 'If you'd been in court today—'

'I know what you did, and Patsy's going to get justice,' Cadenza said. 'I don't care what legal technicality your little Barbie doll here managed to get you off on.'

Barbie doll?

'Did you nail a doll to my door?' I asked Cadenza.

Cadenza's brows dropped a foot or so, and he looked at the baseball cap men. 'What the hell is she talking about?' He looked at me. 'What the hell are you talking about?'

'Forget it.'

'Anyway, we're assembled here to make sure you don't manage to get away *again*,' Cadenza continued with a shrug. 'You're going to jump off the roof out of guilt,' he told Patrick.

'I don't *have* any guilt, you idiot. I'm trying to tell you—'

'Save it for the guy at the gates to Hell, if they have gates.' Cadenza looked around at the Braves fans again. 'Do they have gates in Hell? They have them in Heaven, which I've never understood. Are people trying to get out?'

'What about the two women?' Patrick asked Cadenza. 'Neither

of them had anything to do with Patsy's death. Even you must be able to understand that.'

'Yeah, well, that's unfortunate,' Cadenza nodded. 'Very unfortunate. The lawyer, though, was helping you get away with it. But the other one – too bad. She chose the wrong guy to hang around with, and it's gonna cost her.'

'Am I going to jump from guilt, too?' Angie asked. 'Because I'm not feeling especially guilty.'

'No, I'm afraid your pal Patrick is going to shoot you. He'll feel even guiltier after that.' Cadenza motioned to the two cap men. 'Make sure you empty the gun before you get his fingerprints on it.'

My mind was racing. There had to be *some* way to at least stall for time. 'The shoes!' I shouted out loud, not even realizing I'd done so.

'Yes,' Patrick agreed. 'The shoes!' He turned toward me. 'What about them?'

'Why did you bid so high on the shoes?' I asked.

'Yeah, why did you call me and bid such a large amount on the shoes?' Patrick asked. He turned to me. 'Good question.'

'Thank you.'

'Patsy needed money,' said Cadenza, 'but she wouldn't take it from me. So I figured that if I bought something really valuable from her, and paid her all kinds of money for it, she'd have the money and I could still keep the valuable thing for her, so she could sell it to somebody else later on when she needed money *again*. Pretty shrewd, huh?'

Yeah, shrewd. You overpay for something to give money to a woman who doesn't own it and can't sell it, so you can keep it for her and she can sell it the next time she overshoots the limit on her credit card on Rodeo Drive. That's a masterstroke, all right. Probably best not to say that out loud.

'So where are the shoes now?' Patrick asked.

'How the hell should I know?' Cadenza told him. 'I never had them.'

I began realizing I wasn't dealing with a very clever man here. Of course, I should've realized this after the third or fourth failed assassination attempt, but my mind was on the case, OK? Anyway, this not-so-clever thug was still going to kill me, and that, somehow, was insulting.

'Listen carefully, Silvio,' I said, my voice as calm and soothing as if someone *weren't* holding a gun on me and threatening to kill me, my best friend, and my client. 'Patrick did *not* kill Patsy. We know who did. It was Lucien DuPrez.'

Cadenza shrugged. 'If he did, we'll deal with him, too. But you've already seen us, and we've shot at you, and tried to blow you up and slash you, so you have a little too much leverage right now. Let's get started.'

'What's with the furniture?' Angie asked, a little too energetically. Keep him talking.

'I have such a back problem, I can't tell you,' Cadenza said. 'I need a nice soft easy chair. And I figured that if we're bringing a nice chair along for me, we might as well haul over the rest for you. You shouldn't have to die uncomfortable. And after you're all dead, we'll clean up.'

Patrick, his face a mask of rage, his arms pulled in to his sides but his hands extended, rose off the couch. 'You'll do nothing!' he shouted. 'You'll leave them alone! Wasn't stealing my wife from me enough?'

'Like you cared,' Cadenza told him calmly. 'You didn't love her. *I* loved her! I loved her so much I'm gonna kill *you* for killing *her*.'

'*I didn't kill her!*' Patrick screamed. He took a step toward Cadenza, whereupon the guns were trained on him. Patrick smiled. 'You can't shoot me,' he said, as if he were realizing it for the first time himself. 'You want it to look like I shot them, then committed suicide. How would it look if I were riddled with bullets?'

'Maybe you shot yourself,' Cadenza replied. 'I didn't look that closely.'

'How did I shoot myself seven times?'

'It'll never stand up in court,' I told him. 'The angle of the bullet . . .'

'That's it! Enough!' Cadenza screamed. 'Shoot 'em!'

As the two men raised their guns, Patrick rushed them. He dove for their legs even as they trained their guns on him.

'Spread out!' I yelled, and Angie and I, no longer held by the two men, leapt up from the sofa and headed toward them from opposite ends of the couch. By the time we arrived, Patrick was at their knees.

We were enough to distract the two Braves fans, though, who didn't know where to look, or whom to shoot. In what seemed like a slow motion instant replay, all three of us – Angie from the right, me from the left, and Patrick low from the center – hit the two men in flying tackles.

The guns went off, each one once. Then, all I could think to do was *punch*, which turned out to be much more effective than my initial strategy: run and hide.

Over and over, I hit the man I'd brought down, letting out all the frustration and fear that had been building in me since arriving in Los Angeles. I was shouting something, but I'm not quite sure what it was, or even if it was coherent. I'd heard of 'speaking in tongues,' but I was relatively sure my new language was Profanity.

One gun went flying, but I heard another shot, and that shocked me. I realized I'd continued to hit a man who was already quite unconscious, and now, from my knees, I rose slowly.

Silvio Cadenza was standing in front of his easy chair, and he was pointing a gun directly at me.

Patrick stood, too, and Cadenza backed up one step, to hold us both in check. He stepped right next to Angie, whose man had also left the conscious world.

The problem was, Angie wasn't moving, either.

She lay on her belly, flat, next to Cadenza, whose gun was still smoking from the 'pay attention' shot he'd fired. *Had that hit Angie?*

'You son of a bitch!' I screamed, and tried to move toward Angie, but Cadenza stopped me with a gesture from his gun hand. I froze, and the tears started to flow.

'What did you *do*?' Patrick snarled at him.

'Don't worry about what I did. Worry about what I'm gonna do,' Silvio said, pointing the gun at Patrick's head.

Before he had a chance to pull the trigger, however, Angie's inert figure moved. In fact, she moved just enough to reach out and bite Cadenza on the right ankle, and he screamed in pain. I tried to reach his gun hand, but he recovered in time.

'Oh, that's enough,' he said. And he raised the gun again.

'You don't want to do that,' came a serene, formal voice from the direction of the roof access door. Lieutenant K.C. Trench walked around the corner, holding his .38 (which, I couldn't help but notice, was impeccably clean and shiny in the sun). Uniformed officers emerged from vantage points behind boxes and chimneys. 'You want to drop the gun and put your hands behind your head,' Trench continued.

Cadenza did so, without speaking, which I considered a blessing.

Angie got up off the cement floor and sneered in Cadenza's direction. 'I hope you get infected,' she told him.

I ran to Angie and hugged her tight. 'I thought you were dead,' I sobbed.

'That's what you were supposed to think,' Angie said with a sardonic lilt. 'Luckily, this guy couldn't hit the broad side of Kentucky.'

'How did you know where we were, Lieutenant?' Patrick asked.

'I didn't,' Trench said as one of the uniforms cuffed Cadenza and read him his Miranda rights. Two others dealt with the supine cap men. One officer was talking into his communications link and requesting an ambulance. 'I came to tell Ms Moss about our search of Lucien DuPrez's apartment, and I ran the plates on Mr Cadenza's car and a truck I assume he used to haul all this furniture here, for a reason I'm sure he'll be happy to explain.'

'You ran the plates without knowing why?' I asked, regaining my composure.

'I'm a cop,' Trench said. 'Consider it my hobby.'

'What did you find at DuPrez's apartment?'

'Enough for me to predict that Mr McNabb will be a free man in every way come tomorrow morning,' said Trench. 'Besides the bow, there were financial records that could implicate him in all sorts of ways, and a pair of very expensive sneakers encrusted with mud that matched the mud outside Ms DeNunzio's dining room window. We also have, after someone explained the definition of the word "perjury," the testimony of Ms Melanie DeNunzio, who will report that DuPrez told her she could have half of what he'd get from Patsy's work in exchange for lying on the stand, and also that DuPrez had given Patsy a good number of archery lessons at the Nottingham club, although she was not a member, because she wanted to impress her husband with how good she was.'

'She did that?' said Patsy's widower.

'Thank you, Lieutenant . . . for saving our lives.' I was starting to sound like a TV actress myself.

'That's my job, Ms Moss. It says so on the car. Oh, and by the way, we found Mr Meadows. He was back in England, apparently fearing for his life. He felt that once Mr Cadenza here found out whose baby Patsy was carrying, he might not be safe on this continent.'

'Why?' asked Cadenza. 'You mean the baby wasn't mine?'

Trench turned toward Cadenza, who was being led away past them. 'You really shouldn't park on the street when you're planning on committing homicide, Silvio,' Trench told him.

'I found such a good space,' Cadenza said with a shrug. 'I couldn't resist.' As they took him, in handcuffs, past me, he said, 'Do you think you might defend me? You're pretty good in court.' I was speechless.

Cadenza was led through the door and down the stairs. In the distance, I could hear the ambulance on its way.

Trench turned back toward me. 'Welcome to Los Angeles,' he said.

EPILOGUE

Trench questioned each of us on the roof for quite some time, then walked away shaking his head but never betraying an emotion. He did take an extra look at me before he left the roof, however.

We walked down the steps to the elevator, and Angie got off on the fifth floor, saying she needed a shower and to brush her teeth. 'I have to get the taste of Cadenza out of my mouth,' she told me, but the look in her eye said something else entirely: 'Go ahead and be alone with him.'

I resisted that idea, and Patrick said he felt he'd like to go home now and rest before going to court to be exonerated the next morning. As I rode the elevator down with him, Patrick asked me to drive him back to the courthouse, where his car was waiting. I wondered, briefly, why he didn't just have another one . . . well, you know. But I was happy to keep him company.

We stood in front of the building, and I told Patrick what Trench had mentioned about the evidence against DuPrez. What I really wanted to do was hold Patrick close and tell him it was all over, but I knew he was still saddened by Patsy's death, no matter how estranged they might have been.

'I don't have a car,' I remembered. 'I'll have to drive Angie's.'

'It's OK,' Patrick said. 'I can call a—'

'No cabs for you. I have keys to Angie's rental. Come on.'

We walked to the garage, Patrick still protesting, and I remembered something Trench had said while we were watching the EMTs take Cadenza's men away. 'You mustn't think you're still in the suburbs, Ms Moss,' he'd said upstairs. 'We found the trunk of your friend's rental car open. Isn't that odd?'

I suspected Trench was playing a joke on me, and sure enough, when I opened the trunk to Angie's rental, there was a shopping bag inside with a note stapled to it: 'Ms Moss: please return this to its rightful owner. We found it at Mr DuPrez's house. Sincerely, Det Lt K.C. Trench.' Typed, no less.

'What do you suppose it is?' Patrick asked.

'I think we both know,' I said. 'Let's grab it and look at it inside the car.'

'No,' Patrick said. 'Come with me.'

Puzzled, I followed Patrick outside to the street, where he pulled out his cell phone, dialed a number, and said simply, 'OK.' Then he put the cell phone back in his jacket pocket.

'Now, I know how you feel about this, Sandy, but you deserve it. I've had a car brought round . . .' *Of* course *he had.*

'Patrick, no. Patrick, I appreciate it, but *no*. No more Ferraris. No Maseratis. No *nothing*, OK?'

'I refuse to take no for an answer,' he said. 'You'll just have to accept it. Here. Look.'

I almost dropped the shopping bag when I saw what was coming. Driving up the street was a brand new Jaguar sports car that must have cost hundreds of thousands of dollars.

And behind it was my Hyundai.

But it wasn't the same Hyundai I'd cried over when it was towed to the body shop. It had been rejuvenated, repaired, and brought back to its original state, as if it had rolled off the assembly line in Seoul yesterday. Gleaming, bullet-free, and with new glass and rubber all around, it was the most beautiful car I'd ever seen. OK, maybe not the *most* beautiful, but it *was* a sight for sore eyes.

'Patrick!' I squealed, dropping the shopping bag. Then I hugged Patrick tightly, and kissed him without thinking. He responded, and we shared a long kiss that expressed a good deal more emotion than I think either of us had intended.

'Oh my God, I can't thank you enough!' I said when we finally separated, breathless. 'You did so much more . . .'

'It also has a new CD changer with an iPhone dock, because I couldn't resist, and a few other improvements.' The driver, Rex, got out of my Hyundai and walked over to us. He handed me a small keypad, bowed just a touch, and walked away without saying a word.

'It will open and lock the doors, and it will start the car so you can warm it up on cold mornings,' Patrick explained. 'I know how much you liked to press that button.'

'This is L.A.,' I reminded him. 'We don't have cold mornings.'

'Well, it'll be handy when you want to see if the car's going to blow up. I also considered bullet-proof glass, but that seemed a bit showy.'

Rex got into the Jaguar, lowering the passenger window. 'Are you coming with us, sir?' he asked Patrick.

'No,' Patrick answered. 'I believe I'll go for a ride with Sandy.'

In the Hyundai, which somehow had been treated to actually *smell* like a new car, I handed Patrick the shopping bag, and as I drove, he opened it.

Inside, of course, was a box that contained Jimmy's shoes. Patrick seemed awed by the reality of them, and he rubbed the leather more than once. He stole a glance at me from the passenger's seat.

'I won't look,' I said. 'Go ahead.'

But I did look – just a little. Patrick felt for a certain spot in the left shoe, and after a little difficulty, managed to extract a small, lavender sheet of paper folded into the tear in the shoe's lining. He breathed just a little more heavily when he saw it.

Patrick closed his eyes, then opened them and unfolded the sheet. He read very carefully what had been written there, and his eyes moistened, and a tear rolled down one cheek. He exhaled, took a moment, and then folded the paper and put it back in the tear in Jimmy's shoe.

'I hope it said what you wanted,' I said quietly.

Patrick nodded. 'I won't bore you with it, but among other things, she said she wanted me to have the shoes, even after the scene at the settlement conference. She knew what they meant to me. And I hope she knew what *she* meant to me.'

'I have no doubt she did, Patrick.'

We drove in silence for a short time, and then Patrick put the shoes back into their box, and the shopping bag onto the back seat of my car.

He reached into his jacket and produced a thin case, extracted an iPhone, and connected it into the Hyundai's new stereo system. 'Let's see how this thing works,' Patrick said.

The music, a lush recording of 'Stormy Weather,' filled the car, and I listened closely. I stole a glance at Patrick, whose face indicated intense concentration. 'Is that . . .'

'It's Patsy, yes,' he nodded. 'These are the recordings I'm going to give the PIOUS people.'

I was shocked. 'She had a lovely voice.'

'Yes, she did,' Patrick said. 'It's such a pity.'

We sat and listened until Patsy began 'Someone to Watch Over Me.' Ella Fitzgerald had nothing to worry about, but Patsy could put the tune across quite well, I thought.

'They fired me from *Legality*, you know,' Patrick said out of the blue.

'What? You're the star of the show!' I couldn't believe it.

'They're calling it "creative differences,"' said Patrick. 'But what really happened was that Lizz didn't like the way you treated her on the witness stand, and decided to punish me for it.'

'Oh, Patrick, I'm so sorry.'

'Don't worry about it. I've already been offered a new series – *Split*. About a private eye with multiple personality disorder.'

'You're kidding.'

'I'm not. And besides, I never kid. It's called "acting."' He struck an 'actorly' pose.

'How will I ever know when you're sincere and when you're just conjuring up emotions to get what you want?' I asked him.

'You'll never know, love,' he said. 'Never.' Then he closed his eyes, and appeared to go to sleep as Patsy sang 'Body and Soul.'

I realized I hadn't asked Patrick for directions once during the drive back to the courthouse and didn't need the Apple Maps on my phone – I concluded I was starting to know my way around L.A. I considered that as I maneuvered my new/old Hyundai toward Beverly Hills at sunset.

It wasn't such a bad thing, I thought.

ACKNOWLEDGMENTS

You'd think after six published mystery series the seventh wouldn't feel like a big deal. You'd be wrong. Sandy Moss has been hanging around in my head for far too long and it's both a pleasure and a relief to get her out there where other people can deal with her. Sincere thanks to the wonderful people at Severn House who read the book and decided it should find more eyes. To a writer that's enormous.

Particularly, thanks to Rachel Slatter and Natasha Bell, who gently tended to the manuscript and turned it into the volume you have in your hands. That's not a small job but when it's done expertly it's often unnoticed, because editors aren't intending to draw a reader's attention to themselves. You can trust me that they've done wonderful work and didn't even step on my jokes, which is a shining achievement in my mind.

Even bigger thanks than usual this time to the phenomenal Josh Getzler, who didn't give up on this book even after I had forgotten about it. When Josh makes a promise he keeps it, and his record remains unblemished. I'm proud he's my agent and my friend.

Similar thanks to the crowd at HG Literary, particularly Jonathan Cobb, who answer my questions and tend to my business when Josh is on the phone or just because they can. It's reassuring to have a professional team behind you.

Otherwise, I remain grateful to each and every reader who decides to pick up a novel because (or despite) the name E.J. Copperman appears on the cover, and to those who just thought the cover art (which is amazing) is attractive or the title sounded interesting. In other words, thanks to everyone who's ever read anything I wrote. That should be pretty comprehensive.

Being a writer isn't just a strange identity to cultivate; it's also a job. Everyone I've named above makes that job easier, which is no small thing. If I've inadvertently left your name off the list, it's bad memory and not ill intent. Consider yourself thanked, then email me and let me know what a jerk I was for not including you in the first place.

Of course, thanks to my spouse and my children (who are adults) for putting up with this goofy lifestyle and even enjoying it. It's frustrating for someone who uses words for a living, but I can't begin to express how much I love them.

E.J. Copperman
Deepest New Jersey
February, 2020